Well Written

Mountain Mastery Series

By
Avery Gale

Chapter One

NATHAN LEDEK STARED at his laptop, disbelief hammering at his brain. Great Goddess, at this rate his head was going to explode. *How? Who? When?* While his mind struggled to decipher the logistics, his body was still lost in the author's descriptions of ménage scenes so hot he'd needed to take more than one break. Where did the Ms. Keme Meadows learn so much about the lifestyle? *Is she a sub? Has she been in a polygamous relationship? Or is this her fantasy?*

Several weeks earlier, Nate had received a strange call from Tobi West. It was a safe bet any call from Tobi would venture outside the norm, but this one had been particularly odd. The feisty woman married to Kyle and Kent West had reluctantly given him a heads-up about the book she'd just finished reading. The call left him scratching his head. Calling to chat about an erotic novel she'd read would have been far enough out on the rim of the bell, but knowing her husbands had initiated the book report was especially baffling.

The West brothers were former Navy SEALs who'd returned to Texas and opened what quickly became one of the most popular and exclusive BDSM clubs in the country. They'd also quietly assembled a team of former Special Forces operatives who now contracted with Uncle Sam and other governments. They were selective about the missions they accepted, only stepping in when the money and cause suited them.

Flipping to the front cover of the book Tobi mentioned, Nate leaned back in his office chair as he scrutinized the images of the two men before shifting his focus to the woman between them. The men were obviously Native American, but the woman's beauty defied being categorized. Everything about her appealed to him. The most exasperating thing was he felt like he knew her on some visceral level. *Not possible. Stick with the facts.*

Most troublesome was the fact the book included a barely disguised recounting of several of Nate's and Taz's missions as Navy Seals. He'd been so shocked the first time he'd read it he was sure he'd missed many of the details. Hell, he was going to have to read the damned thing again and make notes. Who the hell in his inner circle was talking?

He started making a mental spreadsheet, trying to connect the dots, and find the one name who could have known all those details. But he'd gotten so caught up in in the damned scorching BDSM scenes he'd lost track and been forced to start over—fucking twice. Holy hell, he needed to find out who wrote this damned book. Nate pushed back from his desk, looking at the large clock on the wall as he stormed out of the office he shared with Taz. It was still early and his brother would still be sleeping, but Nate wasn't in the mood to wait.

Slapping his palm against the wall of the elevator, Nate paused while the biometric reader identified him and set the car swiftly in motion. He'd blanched when Phoenix Morgan told him what the enhanced system cost. But, since club members often used the elevator, the additional layer of security made it easy to keep unwanted visitors out of the private space he and his brother shared. The top floor of their converted warehouse had been transformed into a luxury apartment they rarely allowed outsiders into.

To the casual observer, the reader looked like a gold-plated seal bearing the club's logo, but the high-tech device could easily be programed to identify any number of people. Right now, they'd only cleared three people to access the top floor—Taz, Nate, and the elderly woman they'd hired as a housekeeper when they first moved in. They'd teased Rosie about her name, the irony hadn't been lost on her. She'd called them George and Elroy for the first year. Rosie spoiled them rotten, and both men dreaded the day she decided to retire.

Before the doors of the elevator slid all the way open, Nate shouldered his way into their spacious apartment and smiled at Rosie. "I don't suppose by some twist of fate my brother's out of bed yet?" It might have sounded like a question, but he knew from her eye-roll she hadn't been particularly impressed with his rhetorical question. He grinned at her and said, "That's what I figured, but thought I'd take a shot. Put on a cup of coffee, please. He's going to be grumpy, and my news isn't going to do anything to help."

TAZ LEDEK ROLLED over in bed, pulling the pillow over his head hoping to block out the pounding in his head. What the hell had he been thinking drinking with the guys from the search and rescue team he and Nate joined a year ago? Fucking hell, most of them were younger—a lot younger—

and their alcohol tolerance levels were evidently far higher than his own. His mind finally cleared enough to realize the racket he heard wasn't limited to the din between his ears. The Great Goddess was punishing him for his stupidity by letting his fool brother beat on the door of his bedroom.

"Fuck off, Nate. I don't have to be at work for hours."

Nate's voice boomed from the other side of the door. "Roll out, Taz. We've got a problem." *Shit.* In Nate's world, nothing was a *problem* unless it was a total cluster fuck. "Office. In twenty. Rosie has coffee for you, and you'd better not smell like some damned college freshman frat rat on Sunday morning either."

Growling under his breath, Taz threw off the covers and stumbled to his feet. God dammit, his brain was throbbing so hard his vision fucking dimmed. Making his way into the connected bathroom, it didn't take him long to settle under the pounding spray of the water. The shower in his bathroom was large enough to host a small party, but it was paltry compared to the one in the master suite. Nate was using the larger suite at the other end of their apartment until they found a woman to share. He'd heard Rosie mutter under her breath more than once about wasting money keeping fresh flowers in a bedroom used by a man. But he and Nate were convinced they'd find *her* soon and abandoning the flowers seemed like giving up.

Letting the warm water pummel the tension out of his muscles, Taz thought back on the night before and wondered again how he'd been so stupid. He hadn't pulled a boner like this since the week after graduating from BUD/s—and let's face it, if *that* didn't merit a good drunk, nothing did. Leaning against the cool marble wall of the shower, Taz opened his mind searching for *her*. Running water was a great energy conduit, so he made it a habit to perform the mental exercise each time he took a shower— no matter how rushed he was by Nate.

Taz had always been incredibly gifted. He could sense the future and feel the emotions of those around him when the circumstances were right. Sometimes he caught words or phrases, but those times were rare because so many people had natural barriers. What he'd learned was that the more open and genuine a person was, the easier they were to read. The biggest challenge he faced with his gift was his inability to control it—opening his mind through meditation helped, but it wasn't foolproof.

The sudden flash of a woman soaking in the enormous garden tub in the master suite made him suck in a hissed breath. As quickly as it had come, the image dissipated, leaving nothing but a lingering sense of longing in its wake. Long black hair, onyx eyes that tilted up ever so slightly, and tanned skin that looked like wet silk. Quickly committing those few details left floating through his mind to memory, Taz finished his shower and made his way to the kitchen. The smell of cinnamon and apples drifted down the hall making his mouth water. Damn, Rosie's breakfast rolls were one of the heaven's favors to the world. Filling a large travel mug with coffee, Taz gave their sweet housekeeper a quick hug and took the plate of rolls she'd pointed to.

"If you weren't already married, Rosie, my brother and I would make you ours in a heartbeat," he said as he walked away.

"Flattery is wasted on me, Tashunka. You should save those sweet words for your woman. I think you are right. She is coming soon." No matter how many times Taz assured Rosie using the shortened version of his name was not disrespectful, she continued to refer to him by his full name. His beloved grandmother always called him by his full name, and he felt an uncertain fondness for the older woman because she reminded him of his nana-son.

Their gifted grandmother had favored the more generic name, nana-son, because it could be used by all the children in the small village where she lived. It was important the villagers, who represented several different tribes, were comfortable with the local healer. People wouldn't make use of her gift if they didn't feel comfortable with her. Taz was grateful he'd inherited a small portion of Onatah Ledek's abilities. He always felt she'd more than earned the name Onatah; she was the daughter of the Earth in every sense of the word.

Tashunka's own name meant 'horse,' something his SEAL teammates had teased him about unmercifully. At six foot five inches, Taz was a big man—in more ways than one. Nate was slightly taller, and together, they often overwhelmed submissives who didn't know them. Each man played separately, but preferred playing together because it was easier to give the sub everything she needed when they worked in tandem. Taz and Nate loved to focus entirely on their submissive's pleasure, ensuring they rarely missed any body language signaling distress, but it was possible to miss the small nuances of pleasure and need.

Stepping into the office, Taz was surprised to see Nate pacing the length of the room and muttering under his breath. *What the hell?* His brother was one of the most unflappable people Taz had ever met. Nate's Zen-like calm, at times, annoyed Taz, and he'd grown up with him. The steady drone of the high-speed printer on the credenza caught Taz's attention, and he raised a brow in question when he saw a thick stack of paper in the tray. "Decide to go into publishing, big brother?"

"Something like that." Nate turned and stalked back to his desk. Turning his laptop, he asked, "Do you remember me telling you about my strange conversation with Tobi West?"

Taz leaned against the mantle of the stone fireplace mantle and nodded. He wasn't sure where the conversation was leading. Nate was already wound up tight, so pushing him to get to the point wasn't going to help the situation.

Leveling his gaze at Taz, Nate growled, "I finally took time to read the book she called about."

"And?" It was unlike Nate to tiptoe around a subject, thank God, because this was damned annoying.

"I'm printing it out for you. Read it and make notes in the margins." *Notes? Why the fuck would I make notes? Didn't he say it was a romance novel? Who makes notes in a damned romance novel?* "That's not much of a poker face, little brother. I can tell by your expression you can't figure out why I'm asking you read it so carefully. It won't take you long to figure it out. Pay particular attention to anything you'd consider too classified to have shared with anyone other than another SEAL. I also want to know about anything you read that pertains to a personal conversation you had with someone. Make sure you note who, when, and where."

Standing up straight, Taz crossed his arms over his chest and said, "What the hell's going on Nate? Classified information? Seriously? How did classified information make its way into a romance novel?"

Chapter Two

TAZ SPENT THE afternoon reading sex scenes so hot he'd finally taken a break. The one question that kept cropping up was how Ms. Keme Meadows learned such intimate details of BDSM play. While Nate had focused on the classified information, Taz's attention was drawn to something entirely different. He'd noted several similarities to scenes the two of them had shared at Mountain Mastery. Taz didn't consider it insignificant that the small details hadn't all come from the same scenes he and his brother had shared. The book's author was either a club member or someone on the inside was feeding her information. Either way, they needed to find out who was so fucking interested in their sex lives.

Looking back over the bits of information he'd jotted down, nothing stood out to him. Several of the things he'd felt were so significant when he'd read them didn't seem to stand out now. Most of the things he'd recognized would likely apply to any number of ménage scenes in countless other clubs in the country. Staring out the office window, Taz wondered if the same words would have caught his attention if he hadn't already been pre-conditioned to look for similarities. He'd long ago learned about the power of suggestion. The human mind was one of the most power-ful healers in the world, and his Native American grandmother had taught him to respect its potential.

Sliding the tablet with his notes into his desk drawer, Taz leaned back in his chair and opened his mind. Images started streaming through so quickly he had to concentrate harder than usual to commit them to memory. A dark-haired water nymph swimming in a mountain lake, a small tent at the water's edge, followed by a sense of bone-chilling cold. Before he could pull any more from the flickering slide show in his head, Taz's phone vibrated in his pocket. The interruption was enough to send the mental pictures skittering away. *Fuck.*

"Yeah." Taz didn't make any attempt to keep the annoyance out of his voice, even though he was more frustrated with himself than his brother. Why the hell hadn't he turned off his damned phone? Didn't matter that it was muted, the vibration alone was enough to break his concentration.

"Kip and Caila are here. Everything is set up, are you still in?"

Taz had forgotten he'd promised to help Kip this evening, but it would be a welcome distraction.

Almost a year ago, Caila had finally given up on her lifelong dream of becoming Kip's wife and fled Pine Creek, Montana—the small mountain town an hour north of Mountain Mastery that was home to all five Morgan brothers, although Colt wasn't there much anymore. After marrying pop sensation Josephine Alta, the former professional bull rider was usually busy overseeing the security detail for his wife's tour. All five brothers were charter members of the kink club Nate and Taz owned. But three of the couples had recently become parents, so they hadn't attended a club night for a while.

Taz considered Kip one of the luckiest son of a bitches

he'd ever met. The younger man had screwed up with Caila in almost every way possible, but still managed to win her after finally coming to his senses and seeing what a treasure she was. Dr. Caila Cooper was everything Taz and Nate wanted for themselves, but she wasn't *theirs*. After they'd found Caila sleeping in her freezing car, Nate wanted to explore the possibility of sharing her. Taz had declined, because he'd known she wasn't *the one* the Universe was sending them—but that didn't mean he wasn't willing to help Kip fulfill one of his new wife's fantasies this evening.

Kip hadn't shared scenes with his brothers since before they were married, so wasn't comfortable asking them to participate in what he'd planned for tonight. Taz hadn't hesitated to agree to join in the fun this evening. He'd known it would be a lot more difficult for Nate to walk away without losing a piece of his heart. *I swear if men can hear the tick-tock of their biological clock, my brother's is fucking Big Ben.*

"On my way. Is everything set up?" Nate's insistence he read the book immediately meant Taz turned over the preparations to his brother.

"Yes. The little vet looks nervous, but it appears to be the good kind. Be sure you watch her carefully." Taz almost laughed out loud. Everyone always said he was the one who was overly protective, but he always shook his head at the misconception. Nate could be every bit as militant about protecting submissives—especially those he considered friends. And it was an even larger issue when he'd seen them at their most vulnerable.

"Will do." Disconnecting the call, Taz took the stairs down to the main room of the club. Kip was rechecking the equipment on the small stage while Caila knelt off to the side. Taz stopped and took several deep breaths to refocus himself on the scene he'd helped Kip plan. Caila's life had been anything but easy this past year, and she'd more than earned tonight's distraction.

Tonight was about giving the pretty little sub an emotional and physical break. Months of wedding planning, dealing with her father's hospitalization and recovery, and working to rebuild his crumbling veterinary practice had taken a toll on the petite, blonde bundle of trouble. The Morgan brothers had nicknamed her Calamity for good reason—the woman was an accident looking for a place to happen. Her tendency to get hurt was probably why Taz had just watched Kip recheck the tilting mechanism on the table for the third time in five minutes.

Taz could have saved him the trouble. If Nate set up the equipment, nothing was going to go wrong—the man was meticulous to a fault. Stepping onto the stage, Taz moved until he was standing in front of Caila. They'd planned the scene down to the smallest detail, and it was time to get started. Stepping in front of her, Taz spoke softly. "Look at me, little vet." When she lifted her gaze to his, her eyes were wide with anticipation. Relieved he didn't detect any hint of fear, he gave her a small smile. "Such a good little sub. Has your Master explained what he's planned for you this evening?"

"Yes, sir." No hesitation. Clear voice. Perfect.

"And you've agreed to let me join the two of you?" He already knew ménage was something she'd expressed an interest in, but it was important for him to know the two of them had already negotiated the scene. It wasn't that he didn't trust Kip, but the rules of BDSM play were clear. Their club had strict protocols for safe, sane, and *consensual*—Taz wanted to hear for himself that this was something *she* wanted.

She swallowed and then started to nod her head before remembering it wouldn't be enough. "Yes, Sir. And...umm, well, thank you for checking, Sir." Damn she was a sweet little thing. Her gratitude touched him in a way he hadn't expected. Kip needed to thank his lucky stars she'd forgiven him for acting like such a douche. Callously walking away from her one night at the club after they'd shared a particularly intense scene had broken her fragile heart. Taz was pleased to see the sparkle back in her pretty blue eyes.

"Up you go, little vet." She didn't hesitate to place her small hand in his much larger one, making him smile at the contrast. Damn, she was a little slip of a woman. They needed to remember to be extra careful tonight—there was no reason for her to carry any marks. After all, the Morgan's play party was only a couple of days away. Taz didn't want to put the skids on whatever Kip had planned.

Taz was also looking forward to visiting with Phoenix Morgan and Micah Drake about the book he'd started reading. Both men had top secret clearance because of their work for Uncle Sam, and tracking down Miss Meadows shouldn't be a security challenge. Nate had already enlisted their help, and Taz hoped they'd have information to share by the time they met in person.

Caila rose to her feet gracefully, and Taz couldn't hold back his smile at the small shiver he saw rattle her petite frame. "Strip, little vet. It's time to play."

Her pupils dilated, and he watched as her quick mind scrambled to process his words through the thick fog of her growing arousal. Glancing at Kip, Taz saw the younger man's eyes flare with barely leashed lust as his wife began loosening the corset she'd been carefully laced into. Taz stood with his arms crossed over his chest, watching as she exposed smooth ivory skin in excruciatingly small increments.

Inch by agonizing inch, her silky skin came into view. *Fuck me, I'm going to have a stroke if she doesn't hurry up.* The damned anticipation layered on top of the view sent all his blood to his cock. The book he'd been reading upstairs hadn't helped, either. Its scenes were so vividly written he'd felt like he was there—again. *I'll probably have a damned zipper tattoo for a month.*

"Be careful, baby. You're pushing two Doms, not just one. Master Taz might not be as understanding of your little game of seduction." Kip's words may have been a warning, but even Taz could hear the underlying note of amusement. He was much more dedicated to the lifestyle than Kip had ever been, and he suspected Caila had gotten used to teasing her Master with her delectable body.

"I'm here to add to your experience tonight, little vet. But rest assured I'll take you in hand if you start topping from the bottom." He heard her sharp intake of breath and suppressed his smile. He and Kip had agreed they would go to great lengths to avoid punishing her—that wasn't what this evening was about. Kip wanted to give this experience to Caila as a delayed wedding gift and to help her vent some of the stress she'd been under for far too long.

When he didn't say anything else for several long seconds, Taz watched uncertainty cloud her clear blue eyes. Perfect. "Close your eyes, little vet." When she complied, he let out a silent sigh of relief. Damn, it was hard to be hardline with her. *What the hell is the matter with me?* Damn. He'd ruthlessly teased his fellow former Special Service teammates when they went all mushy with their women. And here he was—doing the same thing with Caila, and she wasn't even *his*.

Without warning, Taz was staggered by the feeling *she* was near—that their *one* was close. The feeling was so strong Taz found himself casting a quick look around the room. Hell, what did he expect? A spotlight shining down on her and celestial music playing above the din of the club? When it came to spiritual gifts, Taz knew the words *near* and *soon* were relative, and usually their meanings were far more arbitrary that what most people would assume. The Universe has a much broader view of time.

Shaking off the distracting thought, Taz looked at Kip, who was watching him with concern in his eyes. Mouthing the word *later*, he held out his hand for the blindfold in the other man's hand. Securing the length of silk over her eyes, he leaned forward and pressed a soft kiss against the top of her shoulder and whispered, "You're doing beautifully, sweetie. We're going to make you fly now."

Kip threaded his fingers in Caila's long blonde hair and pushed the soft strands over her shoulders before kissing her. Taz pulled the silky mass into his hands and quickly braided it, securing the end with an elastic tie. The table they planned to use had a lot of moving parts, and they didn't want to risk her becoming entangled in the mechanics of the equipment.

Watching Kip and Caila's passionate kiss had been hot as hell, and his cock pressed urgently against his leathers, begging to come out and play. Vowing to make sure this experience was a memory Caila would hold dear forever, Taz skimmed his hands over her shoulders and down her arms to shackle her wrists. He didn't tighten his grip, but even that small hint of bondage was enough to send goosebumps racing up her arms.

Taz smiled at Kip when Caila swayed on her feet after

their kiss. The younger man had a slightly dazed look as well. If Taz didn't get him back on track, Kip would probably scoop her up and make a mad dash for one of the club's private rooms. If that happened, she'd get the orgasm her body was already chasing, but she wouldn't get ménage she'd fantasized about.

During the all his years as a Dom, when he'd talked to subs about their needs, Taz had noticed very few of them denied wanting to experience sex with more than one man. Oh, there'd been a few over the years who'd been too shy to admit it, but he'd seen the look of hunger in their eyes.

Taz helped Kip secure his sweet sub to the table. Between the two of them, it was accomplished with quick efficiency. Again, a picture flashed through his mind; this image was even more vivid than those he'd had earlier. A small scar on a woman's shoulder in the shape of a crescent moon—clear and then gone so quickly he had to make a special effort to commit the image to memory. Something about the picture seemed vaguely familiar, but now wasn't the time to try to figure out what had triggered the feeling.

Kip didn't waste any time moving between Caila's spread legs. The rolling stool, much like the ones used by doctors, had already been adjusted to accommodate his height. Kip teased his sweet sub by lapping her slick pussy like an excited puppy. Taz smiled and shook his head. If Kip didn't pace himself, he was going to send her over before Taz could get the nipple clamps in place. Chuckling to himself, Taz decided it was probably time to kick himself into a higher gear. He didn't usually like to make changes to a scene on the fly, but since he wasn't the Dom calling the shots this evening, he'd follow Kip's lead. As he finished latching a secondary strap around Caila's torso, Taz leaned down to circled her pale pink nipple with the tip of his tongue.

He was satisfied when she strained to arch her back against the restraints, emitting a low groan of frustration when the wide straps didn't allow her to lift herself closer to his touch. Taz loved bondage—any submissive he and Nate claimed would have to enjoy all manner of restraint or it would never work. Taking away Caila's ability to see forced her to focus on her other senses. Removing her ability to move would hopefully go a long way to keep the little trouble magnet safe.

None of them had forgotten what happened the last time Caila was at the club. When her feet had become entangled in an area rug, she'd taken a header before Kip could intercede. Caila's forehead cracked against the wooden front of a sofa, resulting in a gash requiring twenty-two stitches to close. She'd also gotten a concussion out of the deal. Taz refused to call her Calamity, despite the fact he believed she'd more than earned the nickname. His refusal was based on the hurt he'd seen flash in her eyes when anyone other than one of the five Morgan brothers used the moniker.

Once her pretty, pink nipples were tight peaks, Taz pulled the small clamps from his vest pocket. Leaning close, he spoke softly and pitched his voice low enough she wouldn't mistake the difference. His Dom voice would erase any question about how things had changed between them. "Your nipples are tight little rosebuds and the most delectable shade of deep pink. They are going to look even more spectacular in the pretty diamond clamps. These are my gift to you, little vet. A memento of our time together this evening."

He didn't give her a chance to protest before putting the first clamp in place. Jerking against her bonds, she gasped and trembled. "Breathe through the discomfort, sweetness. We'll take it slow. Your Master wants you to skate on that fine line between pleasure and pain." Taz was sure, he'd swear he heard her growl something that sounded a lot like "discomfort, my ass." He just looked at Kip and smiled.

Kip hit the remote for the small plug he'd slipped into her nicely rounded ass, giving Taz a huge grin. The small bullet plug wasn't large, but that wouldn't matter, because the effect was huge. Taz felt her entire body stiffen beneath his touch as the vibrations lit up nerve endings she'd likely forgotten about. The grin on Kip's face made Taz chuckle silently—geez, when was the last time he'd laughed during a scene? These two were a joy to work with. Taz couldn't remember a scene he'd enjoyed as much as this one. It was clear Kip and Caila were comfortable with each other, and that confidence made them open to tonight's experience. Groaning inwardly, Taz wondered what the hell was behind this sudden onslaught of Hallmark moments. They needed to get this done before he broke out in a fucking romantic show tune.

Chapter Three

NATE LEANED AGAINST the doorframe, watching Taz and Kip wind Dr. Caila Cooper up like an eight day clock. The little vet was teetering on the edge and would likely scream the walls down when her Master finally let her come. Damn if he didn't have a soft spot in his heart for the sweet woman. Finding her asleep in her freezing Jeep had kicked his Dom protectiveness into high gear. On some levels, Nate was convinced he'd always feel a sense of responsibility for the diminutive little animal doc.

Caila's pleasure filled scream filled the air, and Nate smiled to himself as he watched Kip lean his head back and groan. The youngest Morgan might have thought Caila was the only one who'd needed this evening's distraction, but Nate knew better. Kip struggled to live up to his family's expectations, and the toll was higher than he'd ever admit. His friendship with Kip had made Nate a better brother in many ways. Watching the youngest Morgan interact with his four older siblings highlighted the competitiveness between Nate and his own brother. It also showed him how destructive it was in the long term, so he was working to bring that pattern to an end.

If they were going to share a submissive and make her their wife, they needed to work together in all things. There couldn't be any secrets between them, and there would never be room for competition or jealousy, either. Making his way to the bar, he caught Landon's attention. While he waited for the bartender to finish the order he was filling, Nate scanned the area, always alert for any problems brewing among the club's membership.

Landon Nixon had been tending bar at the club since it opened and was one of Nate's few close confidants. Landon's family was well-respected and one of the oldest in the state. They'd made a fortune in both lumber and mining two generations before Landon was born. God knew the man didn't need the money he earned tending bar part-time at the club. But the part-time gig gave his friend a much-needed outlet for his kink. Landon's parents might have moved to Florida, leaving the family home to their only child, but out of sight didn't equal out of mind. The elderly couple still kept close tabs on their only child. Their continued presence in the society pages was the only reason Landon made the effort to keep his kink away from the public eye.

"What's up, boss?" The grin on Landon's face was a sure sign he'd already lined up a play partner for later in the evening. He hoped Landon had also lined up his own replacement, because Nate didn't want to pinch hit. It wasn't that he couldn't tend bar, but he was hoping to find a sub to play with himself. Watching Taz fuck Caila's sweet mouth had made him envious and damned horny—not a good combination.

"I wanted to check on Kodi. Things going okay?" He'd recently rehired the pretty dark-haired waitress— something he and Taz had sworn they wouldn't do. Nate wanted to know how it was working out with her back on-board. He'd hesitate to put her on the payroll because they had a clearly outlined policy for employees terminating their employment. Basically, it said if someone quit without giving the proper notice, he or she was gone for good.

The quiet young woman had intrigued Nate when they'd hired her the first time, but the heavy demands of building a business kept him from exploring the attraction. That lapse had been particularly frustrating to him when she'd simply disappeared without so much as a word just a few months after being hired.

Despite his curiosity about what caused her sudden disappearance, Nate had questioned the wisdom of skirting the policy they'd put in place. He finally relented because Rosie had pled the young woman's case until he'd given in. When he'd discussed it with Taz later that night and discovered his brother had also noticed something special about Kodi, Nate took it as a sign he'd made the right decision. And Rosie's insistence she belonged at the club had been so out of character he'd found it impossible to ignore.

Landon didn't hesitate in his answer to Nate's inquiry about Kodi. "Things seem to be working out fine, but she's been awfully quiet. Did you ever find out what happened?" Landon looked around, making sure she wasn't close before adding, "Did she ever say why she took off last year?"

Nate shook his head. "Not really. I finally gave up waiting for her to explain and asked her point blank. All she'd say was it was a family emergency. I wouldn't have let it go if Rosie hadn't walked in during our conversation. Kodi fled and Rosie pleaded with me to go easy on her—called her a frightened little bird who belonged here." Landon raised a brow—a silent question Nate wasn't sure how to answer. "I'm not aware of any connection between them, but that doesn't mean it doesn't exist."

"What? Not up to speed on Rosie's extended family?"

Not hardly. Hell, it would take a fucking genealogy site to keep track of Rosie's family. "No. Hell, she has twelve siblings. *Twelve!*"

"A BAKER'S DOZEN. Isn't that supposed to be lucky?" Landon laughed as he wiped down the counter. When the other man looked up and frowned at something across the room. Nate turned to see what had caught his attention and made his friend's brow crease. It was easy to see he was studying Kodi, but Nate wasn't sure what had caused his concern. Landon's voice was suddenly filled with uncertainty when he asked, "Wasn't her hair darker when she was here before? I remember thinking it didn't match her skin tone, and it's even more off-kilter now."

Nate turned to Landon, knowing the surprise had to be showing clearly on his face. "Is there something you've failed to mention, Nix?"

"Screw you, Ledek. I'm allowed to notice shit. You Special Forces types aren't the only ones who notice details. Besides, my ex-girlfriend yipped all the time about women coloring their hair the wrong *season colors.*" Watching Landon make air quotes with his fingers made Nate shake his head. "Took me fucking forever to figure out she was talking about." Nate must have looked confused, because Landon sighed in frustration. "And here I thought you were the smartest guy I knew."

"Who the hell told you that?" Leave it to his little brother to choose that moment to join the conversation. Looking between Nate and Landon, Taz grinned. "What finally opened your eyes, Nix?"

Glaring at Landon, Nate practically growled, "Would you just get to the fucking point before she makes her way over here again?"

"Who?"

"Kodi. Now shut up so I can find out what the hell our resident fashionista knows about her hair." Landon scowled at him as Taz shook his head in confusion. Oh, yeah, just another night at Mountain Mastery. Taz gave him a one finger salute and stepped behind the bar to make himself a drink.

"I was telling Mr. Charming here how I thought her hair was darker when she was here the last time. Even then, it wasn't right for her skin tone. I wondered why she was coloring her hair at all, because I figured her real hair color was probably something much prettier than the mousey brown she was wearing. And now it's even lighter and looks even less attractive. She's also lost a bunch of weight. The uniform she's wearing is the same one she had before, and she spends a lot of time trying to keep the damned thing from sliding off."

Nate frowned as he watched Kodi yank her short skirt back up twice while wiping down a table across the room. "She didn't need to lose any weight." Granted, he hadn't ever played with her, but she'd always looked perfect to him. She'd only worked for them for a few months when she disappeared, so he hadn't had time to get to know her. Now that he considered it, Nate realized he knew virtually nothing about Kodi Green aside from what he'd read in her background check. Thinking back, he wasn't sure there had been anything in the report about family—he made a mental note to pull her bio out of the file later and take a closer look.

Kodi turned and began weaving through the crowd,

making her way back to the bar. When she lifted her eyes, meeting his gaze, Nate felt a blast of heat engulf him as a surge of electricity passed between them. The charge made the dark hair on his forearms dance in the air and his scalp tingle. He was certain she'd felt it too when she stumbled. Kodi would have fallen if Donovan Gibbs, one of the club's Dungeon Monitors, hadn't steadied her. Van spoke with Kodi for a moment before releasing her and giving Nate a questioning look. Nate shook his head, as much to clear the after-effects of the jolt to his brain as to assure Donovan there wasn't a problem.

TAZ HAD HIS back to the room, but he felt the flash of heat searing through Nate as if it had moved through his own body. Spinning around to see what had happened to his brother. Taz saw Nate staring across the room at Kodi Green. "What the hell's going on, Nate?" His words hadn't been loud enough for her to hear, but Taz was attuned to his older brother and knew Nate heard the underlying concern.

For the first time since they were kids, Taz heard Nate's unspoken response. *"I don't know. She looked at me, and it was like getting hit in the chest with a thousand volts of white heat."* Nate's silent communication was interrupted when a woman at the back of the club started screaming *red*. The club's safe word was cause for at least one of the owners to become involved, but before Taz could volunteer, Nate was already making his way through the quickly gathering crowd. *"Watch her. Don't let her leave. I'm not sure what happened, but I damned well plan to find out. We need to be careful, I'm worried we'll spook her if we aren't careful."*

Kodi's shoulders lowered marginally when she saw Nate moving away from the bar. Taz frowned, wondering why she'd been so nervous. Had she felt the same punch of heat Nate experienced? *Interesting. Very, very interesting.* Pasting on a big smile, Taz stepped closer to the bar and held out his hand for her tray. "You are one busy lady this evening, Kodi. Are the members behaving themselves?" When she gave him a wary look, Taz smiled and set the tray on the bar. "Are you having any trouble with unwanted advances? Remember, members aren't supposed to approach you while you're on duty."

A soft flush colored her cheeks as she lowered her gaze. "No, Sir. No one has said anything to me. I'm not really the type of woman men hit on." The last sentence had been uttered so quietly Taz almost missed it.

Is she fucking serious? Not the type?

Taz heard Landon snort next to him and shot him a quelling look. Nix raised his hands in mock surrender and grinned. Shaking his head, Taz looked back to Kodi. He held out his hand for her order and moved quickly to gather what she needed. Setting the bottles of water and beer on the tray, he gave her a soft smile before sliding it across the bar to her.

"I saw you drive in early this afternoon, Kodi. Did you get a chance to eat before we opened?" She ducked her head and shook it once in answer. Keeping his voice even to disguise his frustration, he said, "After you deliver those drinks, come back, and I'll make you one of my world-famous ham and cheese omelets. High protein for energy and one of the few things I can make on a hot plate." The truth was Taz was a surprisingly accomplished cook if grilling steaks and vegetables counted as cooking.

As an empath, he could feel her internal struggle. A part of her felt like she should politely decline his offer, but she was hungry—*really* hungry. Hell, Taz was picking up echoes of her stomach cramping just thinking about food. It was a test of his control to flash her a flirtatious smile and not demand that she eat something immediately. Turning to the large glass fronted refrigerator, Taz began pulling out the ingredients he'd need. He felt the moment he'd won as something between relief and resignation moved through her. Smiling to himself, he quickly began grating cheese and dicing a large slice of ham.

As soon as she was out of earshot, Taz looked at Landon. "I know we're busy, but see if you can't talk one of the unattached subs into helping out for a while. My brother and I are going to have a chat with Kodi while she eats." Landon nodded then made a beeline for the small sitting area where the subs congregated when they were looking for a Dom for the evening. With Landon's California surfer looks and easy going personality, Taz was putting his money on him returning with a starry-eyed sub in tow within five minutes.

Taz was almost finished with the hastily assembled meal when Nate stalked back up to the bar. "Where is she? You were supposed to watch her. I told you to not let her out of your sight."

"Calm down. She should be back any minute. I tempted her with food, and I don't think she's going to disappear—at least not until after she eats." Nate shook his head in disbelief and began scanning the room. Taz firmed his voice and glared at his brother. "Don't scare her, Nate. She's already intimidated by you."

Nate swung his gaze back to Taz, looking like he couldn't believe what he'd just heard. "What the hell are you talking about? Why on Earth would she be intimidated by me? I'm a charming son of a bitch if there ever was one."

Taz rolled his eyes and chuckled.

"Well, Master Nate, I understand you didn't ask me specifically, but since it seems like an open question...perhaps I can shed some light if you'll give me permission to speak freely." Nate and Taz both turned to look at the sub standing beside them. Laughing, they both shook hands with her Dom. Senator Karl Tyson shook his head in resignation and chuckled softly.

"Love, I think Nate and Taz know you well enough to be fairly certain you'll find a way to share your opinion even if they say no."

Taz wanted to laugh out loud at the mutinous look on her face. Dr. Tally Tyson was one of the best surgeons in the western half of the country. She'd been a resident at Georgetown University Hospital in Washington, DC when she'd met the freshman senator. According to mutual friends, she'd quickly fallen in love with both Karl and his home state of Montana. Tally hadn't hesitated to move west despite the fact her husband would spend a large portion of the year on the east coast. She was smart as a whip and submissive only to Karl and Landon, who often acted as their third.

To her credit, Tally observed the club's rule against speaking without permission and waited patiently for Nate and Taz to give her a nod of approval. She immediately turned to Nate and grinned. "Master Nate, you are a big guy, and you have this aura of authority that borders on....well, it almost shouts 'Don't fuck with me.' People aren't really sure how to take you. Now, those of us who pay attention know you are a softie on the inside."

Taz covered his snort of laughter with a cough, but it didn't fool anyone, least of all Nate, who shot him a withering look. *Fuck you, big brother. She's got your number, and we both know it.*

Tally waved her hand in the most overacted piece of drama Taz had seen in a long time and patted Nate on the arm. "Don't worry. Your secret is safe. There are only a couple of subs who are wise to you, but we won't rat you out." Her small shrug was far too casual, and Taz bit back another grin at her feigned disinterest. "Besides, we like watching the others snivel and squirm; it ensures you aren't focused on making the rest of us toe the line. That would really suck, by the way."

Taz wanted to lean his head back and roar with laughter at the shocked look on Nate's face. The whole conversation was so fucking bizarre considering the circumstances he could only shake his head...until she shifted her attention to him. *Well, fuck.*

"Master Taz, the only time subs are intimidated by you is when they've done something to put themselves in danger. Even those who didn't witness Brinn's spanking heed the lesson because word spread far and wide." Taz mentally flinched at the reminder of the paddling he'd given one of the club's uncollared subs after watching her dodge between cars downtown one afternoon. She'd been warned on multiple occasions about various risky behaviors—many of which he suspected were attempts to gain attention. He'd used the incident as a lesson emphasizing the importance of submissives taking care of themselves. Taz had heard the little daredevil hadn't sat comfortably for several days the following week, but he also knew she'd given up jaywalking.

He must have looked smug, because Tally huffed and

shook her head. "Thanks a lot for that, by the way. I went to lunch with her a couple of weeks ago, when it was raining so hard you could hardly see across the street. There wasn't a car anywhere in sight, but she made me walk all the way to the flip-flapping corner to cross a deserted street. There wasn't an umbrella in the world that would have kept us dry, and I looked like a drowned rat by the time we got to the bistro." The mock glare she gave him made him chuckle.

Karl looked toward heaven and sighed. "So, you're telling the owners of the club they are intimidating, because they do exactly what sexual dominants are supposed to do? That hardly seems like Earth shattering information, pet. And frankly, it's unlike you to waste everyone's time with drivel." Taz grinned at the man's unspoken challenge. Karl played his little sub perfectly, and they all knew it.

Tally gave her Dom a look that was sure to get her the paddling she was looking for before turning back to Nate. "Okay, here's the 411 on Kodi. Please be careful with her. It was hard for her to find the courage to come back here and ask for her job back. I think this was the closest thing she's had to a home in a long time, and I'd hate to see her lose it." Everything Tally had just said surprised him, including her use of the military slang for pre-mission information. Where had the lovely Dr. Tyson learned *that* term?

Nate didn't respond for several seconds, and Taz watched the play of emotions move over his face. Tally finally became uncomfortable with the silence and continued, her tone much quieter than before. "Look, I can't say anymore. Technically, I've already shared more than I should have."

Taz raised his hand to keep her from continuing and nodded.

"Thanks for your input, Tally. I appreciate your honesty. Loyalty among the submissives is something I appreciate. Doms work together for your benefit, so it's only reasonable the subs would team up to thwart our efforts."

Taz was relieved his brother had chosen that moment to lighten the mood, because Kodi was finally making her way back to the bar. All she'd see was the four of them engaged in conversation, and Tally's smile would put her at ease. Leaning closer to her, Taz asked, "411? Spill, sweet sub. I'd be very interested to hear where you learned that particular term."

She grinned up at him. "I'm an Air Force brat, Sir. Hooah."

Karl wrapped his hand around her arm and shook his head. "Come on, trouble. You're going to pay for the glare you gave me a few minutes ago."

Taz chuckled as he watched her eyes dance in anticipation. Refocusing on what she'd said, he understood why Kodi had been reluctant to return to the club to ask for her old job back. Walking away without so much as a phone call wasn't the way to leave a good impression. But he had to admit he hadn't considered how desperate she must have been to ask for a chance to return. Picking up the plate he'd made for her, Taz moved from behind the bar and motioned for Nate to follow him. It was time for them to find out what was going on with Ms. Kodi Green.

Chapter Four

K ODI'S HEAD WAS spinning as the two club owners led her out of the main room. The usual sounds associated with a kink club faded quickly when the door closed with a solid thud behind them. She'd never been in the short hall leading to a small circular staircase. Heck, she hadn't even realized there was a door there until Taz slid it silently to the side. The few feet between the door and the stairs provided even more between buffer them and the club. Soon the only thing she could hear was her own heartbeat thundering in her ears. By the time she'd walked up the steps and watched Nate open the office door, Kodi was weaving on her feet. She wasn't sure what was causing the black dots dancing in her vision, but damned if they weren't getting bigger by the second.

She heard Taz's soft curse just as the block dots began merging. "Take a damned breath, Kodi."

Nate spun around to look at her and glared. She wondered what he was so surly about just before she felt his large hands wrap around her upper arms. "When was the last time you ate, Ayasha?"

Who?

Taz appeared at Nate's shoulder and laughed softly. "He called you *little one*, pet. The endearment is from the language of our ancestors. My brother has honored you

30

with a name from the ancients."

She blinked trying to bring him into focus. *Maybe if I can see him clearly, I'll be able to figure out what he's talking about.*

The next time her mind registered a coherent thought, Kodi realized she was sitting with a plate of food balanced precariously on her knees. "If you don't eat, I'm going to feed you myself, sweetheart. I can literally feel your confusion, and it's not going to clear until you have something in your stomach. Eat and then we'll talk." Master Taz's voice was soothing and she wondered for just a minute if the rumors about him could possibly be true. He'd said he could feel her confusion, and that fit with the stories she'd heard when she'd first worked at the club months ago.

The first bite of the enormous ham and cheese omelet melted in her mouth, and her stomach growled in appreciation. She wasn't sure she'd ever tasted anything so good. She wasn't sure how he'd managed to keep the omelet hot, but it was perfect, and she ate the entire thing without pausing.

"I'm not sure I've ever heard someone moan in appreciation of a ham and cheese omelet before, Taz. You're obviously a magician when it comes to eggs." Kodi was surprised to hear Nate's teasing tone. She'd never seen him be anything but professional.

"I think it's more likely a statement about how hungry our little butterfly was than an endorsement of my cooking expertise. But then again, I've been wrong before, and I did really slave over that hot plate."

Kodi looked up at Master Taz, relieved to see the smile on his face. His eyes were sparkling with humor, and she felt herself relax for the first time since she'd noticed Nate watching her downstairs.

Earlier, when her eyes met Nate's across the room, it felt like the world had narrowed to a pinpoint. For a few seconds, nothing existed but the two of them. Then she'd felt a sizzling awareness flash through her. It had been so intense she'd nearly fallen. If one of the Dungeon Monitors hadn't caught her, Kodi would have face-planted in front of God and everybody.

The first time she'd worked at the club, she'd managed to fly under Nate's and Taz's radar because they'd been focused on building their business. But now, something about their attentive looks told her things would be much different this time. *You can't afford to let down your guard. They won't understand why you didn't tell them about Koi. SEALs stick together like glue.* Just thinking about her brother brought on a wave of sadness so strong Kodi felt tears burn the backs of her eyes.

Blinking them away, she played off her sudden change of mood. "That was fantastic. I'm not sure I've ever tasted anything more satisfying." She ducked her head in embarrassment when she realized the sexual innuendo of her words. Her cheeks burned, and her eyes closed in mortification. *Just shoot me now. They're going to think I was flirting with them.*

She'd seen them play with subs occasionally and had heard they rarely played with the same woman more than once or twice. The last thing she needed was a broken heart and to be unemployed...*again.* She was already struggling to find a warm place to sleep at night. As long as they didn't get the late season blizzard all the local channels were buzzing about, she should be able to make it to spring. Living out of her small SUV was a pain in the ass, but so far, no one had noticed she showered and changed at the club before her shift.

The money sitting in her bank account in Denver wouldn't do her any good until she could afford to drive down there and sign the paperwork. It didn't matter how quickly the balance grew if she couldn't get her hands on the money. She'd finally found her calling, and the rewards were still out of her reach. Hopefully, her ancient laptop would hold out until she could scrape together enough money to replace it, but at this point, that seemed like a longshot. Every time she booted it up, Kodi sent up a prayer for it to work.

The flash drive she used to save her work was the last thing her brother had given her before he'd disappeared. She didn't even care it was almost filled with his pictures and files. She used it to save her work in addition to her online storage. She'd heard too many of her peers telling tales of woe when they lost entire projects after their computers shot crap. Eventually, she would need to sort through his files. Maybe she could find some sort of clue about what he was up to. This recurring disappearing act of his was getting old, especially when he turned up injured and she had to drop everything to take care of him.

The soft stroke of a warm finger down the outer curve of her cheek brought Kodi back to the moment. She blushed again at being caught daydreaming. Looking up into Nate Ledek's dark eyes, she wondered if she'd ever met anyone as multifaceted as the man watching her so intently. She saw the corners of his mouth turn up ever so slightly; it was the only indication he'd given her he'd been patiently waiting for her to return to them. *Good God, Gertie. You've seen what happens to subs who zone out from distraction.* Doms loved it when their subs hit subspace, but they were usually pretty pissy if the sub drifted off into la-

la-land on her own because she wasn't paying attention during a conversation.

"I'd love to be able to hear what you're thinking, Ayasha. Your emotions play over your face like a marquee, but knowing how you're feeling doesn't tell me what brought it on."

Oh, damn.

"I hope I'm not that easy to read. That wouldn't make me very mysterious, would it?" She wasn't very adept at flirting, but the heat in his eyes told her she wasn't a complete failure, either.

Taz stepped closer and stared down at her. His arms crossed over his chest and his legs spread shoulder width apart making him look more like a Greek God than the owner of a kink club. *Holy hat racks, talk about intimidating.* "If you think subs are allowed secrets, we haven't done a very good job training you. Perhaps you are need of a little refresher?"

Uh oh. She'd been grateful they hadn't made her repeat the club's mandatory training when she'd returned, but now it looked like her luck might be running out.

Who was she kidding? The fact they'd rehired her had been an enormous blessing. There wasn't a chance in hell she would complain about having to retake the class. She hoped they'd let her fit in around her working schedule, though...damn, she really couldn't afford to miss any work.

"Okay. I guess that's fair. When is the next class? Can I still work until then? I really need this job. Maybe I could work extra hours to make up for those I'd miss to attend the training sessions? All of my limits are still the same. Nothing's changed there, so that should make it easier, right? You aren't going to fire me, are you?" Kodi was working herself up into a genuine "tizzy" as her dad used to say. But the whole thing felt like she'd pushed a snow-ball off a mountain. Once she'd started talking, everything just kept getting bigger and faster. And the worst part was both men were staring at her like she'd lost her mind. *Yes, indeed, that's not out of the realm of possibilities considering what a cluster-fuck your life has been the last couple of years.*

FOR THE FIRST time in recent memory, Nate found himself struggling to process what the sub in front of him had said. He and Taz both prided themselves on their ability to sense where things were going during a scene. Their intuitive abilities ordinarily allowed them to stay several steps ahead of the woman they were topping. But Kodi had so totally missed Taz's point it had blindsided him. From the look on Taz's face, he hadn't fared much better.

"I have to give you credit, sweetness; you've rendered Master Nate speechless. Hell, I can't remember the last time that happened."

Nate wasn't sure Kodi would hear the amusement in Taz's voice, but he certainly hadn't missed it. Shooting a quelling look at his younger brother, Nate watched Taz's eyes dance with mirth. *Asshole.*

Taz tilted his head, turning his face back to the Kodi, a slow grin tugging up the corners of his mouth. "No, Kodi, you are not being fired. And, I had something else in mind for your refresher course."

Nate had taken her left hand, holding it between his own much larger mitts, his thumb brushing over her wrist in slow, teasing circles. Her pounding pulse told him she was excited, and he was thrilled with how perfectly her body was responding to them. She wasn't trying to pull back, so he knew she wasn't afraid—apprehensive, yes—but he could live with that. Hell, he preferred a certain level of trepidation, because it enhanced the senses—ensuring the sub absorbed every nuance of a scene. And even though they weren't going to fuck her tonight, Nate was sure even as inexperienced as Kodi was, she'd be aware things had shifted between them. She might be inexperienced, but she'd worked in the club long enough to recognize a scene when she saw one.

"Wha...what do you mean?" Her eyes were the color of rich milk chocolate and getting darker by the minute as her body's sexual responses kicked into high gear. Oh yeah, she definitely felt the same zing with Taz she'd experienced with him earlier. Nate's gifts weren't as strong as his brother's. He needed touch to connect, and even then, it was a rare person he could tune in to. He could hear bits and pieces of her frantic worry about losing her job, and that wasn't the direction he wanted this discussion to go.

"Stop worrying about losing your job, Ayasha. We've already assured you that you are not being fired. We won't ever lie to you." When she dropped her chin to her chest, looking at the place where his hands held hers safely nestled between his own. Nate could sense her confusion. She didn't understand why the small gesture made her feel secure. He got the odd feeling she was trying commit the feeling to memory. Years of Special Forces missions had shown him how uncertain the future was; but knowing Kodi was experiencing uncertainty on such an emotional level made him want to wrap her in his arms, shielding her from the world.

Nate lifted her chin until she was forced to meet his

gaze. "You and I both felt something downstairs, pet. What my brother and I want to do is explore that *something*. Let's find out where it leads. Desire shines in your eyes, but you have to be brave enough to take a chance."

"It takes courage to set your fears aside and go after what you want, Kodi." Taz paused for a minute, letting the subtle truth of his challenge sink in. "Nate's right. We won't ever lie to you, but we won't always tell you everything we're planning, either. There are times when anticipation of the unknown amplifies response. It's a powerful aphrodisiac for many subs." Taz knelt in front of her, taking her right hand and enclosing it in the same way Nate held her left. "My brother and I are attending a play party at the Morgan's on Saturday. We'd like for you to go with us. It will give us a chance to spend some time together."

Nate knew why Taz hadn't touched Kodi until this moment. Once his brother made any kind of skin to skin contact with someone, he often felt the connection for a long time—even if he didn't want to. Sheltering her delicate hand between his own told Nate how interested Taz was in Kodi. Nate felt her response the instant their hands touched—the spark of electricity between them had been strong enough to carry through to him.

They'd never dated any of the subs who worked for them for a reason. In a regular business, a relationship between an employee and the boss was a bad idea—in a kink club, it was a short road to disaster. Nate and Taz had also agreed they wouldn't spend time outside the club with subs they played with to keep them from being misled. They seemed to be batting a thousand today with rule breaking. But the older they'd gotten, the less they played—it was as if they somehow sensed they were close to finding their *one*.

Nate watched his brother's brow furrow, but the small *tell* disappeared so quickly he wondered for a few seconds if he'd imagined it.

Kodi took a deep breath before answering—her voice so soft he could barely hear her. "I don't know if that's a good idea. I'm not really...well, what I mean is, I'm not very good at socializing, so parties aren't that much fun for me. It wasn't something my parents encouraged, so I just didn't ever master the whole small talk thing. Besides, I'm not even sure what happens at a play party."

Now Nate was frowning. too. Even without any special gifts, he'd have been able to see she was lying. When he looked at Taz, Nate saw the flicker of annoyance in his eyes. *Oh yeah, she is definitely going to pay for that whopper later.*

TAZ DIDN'T ORDINARILY allow subs to lie to him, particularly when it was so blatantly obvious. Hell, he certainly hadn't needed any of his gifts to see the longing look that flashed in her eyes when he first mentioned the party. Her story about not enjoying social events was clearly a cover—but for what? He'd bet his half of the club she was no different from most women. She probably loved parties, even if most of the men he'd ever talked to avoided regular parties like the plague. But this wasn't an ordinary *party*—not by any stretch of the imagination.

After listening to Doms and fellow soldiers grumble about social occasions for years, Taz had come to a few conclusions. Married men attended social functions because they knew their wives loved them and getting laid was a sure bet when their women were happy. Guys with girlfriends avoided them, if possible, because they felt it gave their women ideas about ownership. Single men attended for the free booze and access to happy women. Everyone knew hostesses invited all their single friends. Those ladies were also enjoying the free bar, so it usually worked well for everyone. What he didn't know was why Kodi would deny herself the chance to attend a party when he could sense how much she wanted to go.

"Tell me the *real* reason you don't want to go, sweetness. Let me remind you we are still in the club, even if we aren't downstairs. We don't consider our living space part of the club, but the rest of the building—including this office—is subject to all the same rules pertaining to honesty as you'd follow in the main room or one of the private playrooms." He saw her eyes widen when she realized the implication of his words. She'd signed several documents as part of her employment contract with the club. One of those was a standard membership agreement complete with all the usual requirements for honesty and full disclosure.

Their employment and membership contracts were plainly written to avoid any misunderstandings. He knew the rule about honesty was easy to understand. Ironically, it was also one of the rules Dominants and submissives had the most trouble adhering to. It was difficult to force people to be honest with themselves and their peers when the club's kink community struggled even more to accept themselves than their straight vanilla counterparts.

Society imposed an absurd number of *norms* on adult sexuality, which was an oxymoron if you asked Taz. How could anyone determine what was *normal* or appropriate for another person to enjoy? He believed the only taboos in adult sexual behavior were those that were nonconsensual or hurt someone else in a way not designed to bring both parties pleasure. Anything else between consenting adults was fair game.

Nate studied Kodi with an intensity Taz had never seen before. His brother's dark eyes were completely focused on her, but there wasn't any censure in his gaze, only curiosity. "Let me tell you what I see, Ayasha. Maybe it will open the door to your honesty." Nate waited for her to nod her agreement before continuing. "I see a beautiful woman who appears to be as attracted to us as we are to her. I think there is a simmering cauldron of desire bubbling just below the surface, but for some reason, you don't think you deserve the fulfillment the lifestyle could give you. You've chosen to work in a kink club because it lets you experience Dominance and submission in a way that feels safe—even if it's only a shadow of what it could be."

Taz saw her eyes fill with tears. Nate's observations had obviously been accurate. He knew from experience it was hard to hear the truth when you already felt like you weren't doing your best. "It doesn't have to be like that, sweetness." He saw her eyes widen and watched her pupils dilate. *Perfect.* He'd piqued her interest. "But first, tell us why you lied about not wanting to go out with us." Taz deliberately rephrased their invitation—maybe he was playing dirty by pointing out she'd turned down a date with her bosses, but at this point, he didn't care. Whatever was holding her back, he and Nate would help her work through it.

Grasping her hand, he felt the sudden surge of emotion flowing through her. It was so strong he was certain it had come from the depths of her soul. She was filled with yearning but embarrassed because she didn't have anything appropriate to wear. Of all the potential entanglements he'd considered, a dress hadn't even made the list. Damn, it had been too long since he'd had a steady girlfriend if he hadn't at least considered the possibility.

Fuck me. There isn't any way to approach this without causing her further humiliation. He suddenly understood the aghast looks Doms got when they lectured subs about embarrassment not having any place in a D/s relationship. When she dropped her gaze to her lap, Taz tugged on the collar of his shirt and mouthed *nothing to wear* to Nate. His brother's nod was almost imperceptible before his smile turned wicked.

Nate looked inordinately pleased the problem was so easily handled. Taz knew his brother loved nothing more than taking a woman shopping. Nate swore the smell of new clothes was an aphrodisiac to most women and dressing room sex was some of the best anyone could experience. *"It's all those mirrors, little brother."* Taz accompanied Nate on a few of his expeditions, but personally, he didn't see the appeal of fucking a woman when she was more worried about drawing unwanted attention than soaring over the moon. "If she's thinking about anything but her pleasure, you're doing it wrong," was Nate's often repeated response.

When they were teens, Taz had been busy attending every martial arts class his dad could enroll him in. Taz had been a trouble magnet in school, and their dad had insisted he channel all that excess energy into a variety of self-defense disciplines. At the same time, Nate had been learning the finer points of retail debauchery. The real irony was Nate's already impressive flirting quickly became world class seduction skills.

Nate would make it a shopping experience unlike any other Kodi had known, but he wouldn't fuck her. It was important to establish a strong bond as a triad before making love one-on-one to a woman they planned to share. However, if Nate felt the same pull with Kodi he was feeling, it wouldn't hurt to remind him they needed to take her together the first few times.

Shaking off how far ahead of himself he'd gotten, Taz looked at Nate and wanted to groan at the look on his brother's face. Damn. He recognized that look even though he hadn't seen it in a long while. Anytime Nate was listening in on Taz's thoughts, he'd get a knowing look that told Taz he'd been made.

Chapter Five

KODI LOOKED BETWEEN the two club owners who'd been starring in her romantic fantasies since before she'd even met them. She wasn't sure if her brother's stories had painted the two of them as heroes or if her young, romantic heart had filled in the blanks. But she'd heard the admiration in her older brother's voice whenever he talked about them, and her overactive imagination had always envisioned them as her personal knights in shining armor. But the reality she'd found when she walked into Mountain Mastery all those months ago had been so much more delicious.

Now she was at a total loss. How was she supposed to interpret the knowing looks passing between them? She was sure there had been some sort of silent communication, and whatever it was didn't seem likely to bode well for her. Her lack of experience with men would be glaringly obvious to these two experienced Doms in thirty seconds flat if she didn't figure out what was going on.

What do you expect? You're a virgin pretending to be an experienced submissive. You've used your brother's stories to fuel your childish fantasies of who Nate and Taz Ledek are...without paying particular attention to the facts. And you're working in a kink club where it's impossible to think about anything other than sex, because you're surrounded by it four nights a week. Oh yeah, she was surrounded by sex alright. Hot, seductive, scream-the-walls-down, mind-altering acts of sexual depravity that made her crave their touch more every single damned shift.

Each night she worked, Kodi watched couples, three-somes, and more—in every conceivable gender combination—engage in sexual acts that probably should have scandalized her. But they didn't. The things she'd seen might have embarrassed her a time or twenty, but only the most extreme acts made her turn away. She'd already done plenty of reading about the lifestyle before she'd applied at the club, so she'd been somewhat pre-pared. And if her brother ever realized she'd found his stash of books, there would be hell to pay. The e-reader he'd gotten her one year for Christmas was filled with erotic romance novels, also. Probably not the use he'd envisioned when he bought it, but it wasn't something she planned to share with him, either.

Kodi accidently discovered her brother was a sexual Dominant while still in college. Koi always crashed at her small condo when he was on leave, and she'd loved the time they spent together. During her senior year, she'd skipped her last class on Friday because she'd been so anxious to see if he'd made it *home*. The scene she'd walked in on had surprised her, but she hadn't been repulsed.

Koi had been dressed in faded jeans with a tight black t-shirt stretched over his broad chest. The naked woman bent over the back of Kodi's faded floral sofa was sobbing in apology; even though Koi didn't appear to be buying it. Kodi tried without success to step back out the door without being seen. Her brother turned toward her before she'd managed to escape. His eyes widened in surprise, but no shame reflected in the dark orbs. Somehow, she'd found the courage to pepper him with questions later.

He'd been honest in his answers about the lifestyle, and understandably evasive about his personal kinks. Koi had also declined to comment on the woman Kodi had seen way too much of earlier in the apartment. Her brother's straight forward, honest answers to her questions fueled the fire of her already smoldering interest in ways nothing else had. The two of them had discussed things several times over their few days together before he'd gotten the call they'd both known would eventually come, pulling him away from her once again.

Koi had woken her up long before daylight to tell her good bye, and the last thing he'd said before walking out the door was a warning to not go to a club he hadn't personally approved. The irony of his words wasn't lost on her. *Who on God's green Earth asks their brother for a recommendation to a kink club?*

During the next year, she'd gathered bits and pieces of information during their email exchanges before finally deciding to make her way to Mountain Mastery. She should probably feel guilty for milking Koi for information, but she didn't. In fact, she had gotten the distinct impression he was harboring secrets of his own, making it easier to push her own shame and guilt aside.

Refocusing on the men standing in front of her, Kodi took a deep breath. She'd always prided herself on being honest with herself and others, but damn it all to hell, this wasn't good. No, this definitely had disaster written all over it. Separately Nate and Taz Ledek were intimidating as hell. When they were together, it was something akin to being plunged into a deep pool of testosterone without knowing how to swim. They were so far out of her league she felt like a Peewee player suddenly thrust into the

World Series. If she agreed to go to the party, they'd burn her to the ground, leaving nothing but ashes in their wake. But if she didn't go...she'd always wonder *what if*, and that would be far worse.

Fuck a fat duck, she wanted to go to that party, even it wasn't a good idea for a lot of reasons. She'd mentally run through her clothing and hadn't come up with anything acceptable; and God only knew she didn't have the money to buy anything sexy enough to wear. Well, that wasn't entirely true...she had the frick-fracking money. She just didn't have *access to it*. Her trust fund was tied up in a lot of legalese, waiting for Koi to be home long enough to sort it out. And since it didn't appear Uncle Sam was going to share her brother anytime soon, she was relegated to waiting...again. And to make matters worse, her overactive imagination was finally starting to pay off, but she couldn't get her hands on any of the money she'd earned from her first foray as an author.

Who was she kidding? The Ledek brothers probably only invited her because they thought she was easy. God knows she'd heard that line more than once while working at the club. She felt Taz's grip tighten on her hand just as he made the strangest sound...*Did he just growl at me?*

Nate was on her other side, chuckling. "This would probably be a good time for us to tell you about Master Taz's special gift."

Special gift? Oh, shit. Evidently those rumors she'd heard about him being able to read minds were true. She'd always assumed he was just well trained in reading body language. *It's not actually possible to know what someone else is thinking, is it?*

"The short answer is not ordinarily. But nothing about this situation is shaping up to be *ordinary*." Taz's words shocked her all the way to her toes.

Kodi was on her feet before she realized she'd moved, and by the stunned looks on their faces, the two Masters were equally surprised.

Nate was the first one to stand. She took an involuntary step back when he moved toward her. "Stop, Ayasha."

Her body responded to the command before her mind had a chance to process the words. Freezing in her tracks, all she could do was stare as Nate spoke.

"Do you believe either of us would hurt you?" Before she could answer, he took a small step forward and continued, "I want to remind you honesty is paramount in all D/s relationships—it doesn't matter if its casual or committed."

"No, Sir." The words came easily, because deep down, she was absolutely certain neither of them would ever hurt her...at least not physically. "But it's disconcerting to know Master Taz can hear my thoughts." Kodi was sure those words would go down in some sort of history book listing gross understatements.

Nate nodded his approval. "That's a good start. Now we all need to get back to work. But first, I want to hear you say you will go to party with us this weekend. You and I will go shopping tomorrow morning. My brother and I have certain...*expectations* when it comes to how we want our date to be dressed."

"Or more accurately, undressed." Taz was grinning at her with a wicked gleam in his eye. "There are certain things we don't want you to wear." The heat in his gaze as it moved down her body before slowly returning to her blushing face sent a bolt of heat straight to her sex. Kodi sent up a silent prayer he wouldn't see how much his words affected her, but doubted either man missed the flush she felt flaming over her cheeks. Nate's eyes had never left hers, the look so intense she couldn't hold back the shudder moving up her spine.

One of the reasons she'd originally come to Mountain Mastery looking for a job was the stories she'd heard about the co-owners, but she'd also wanted to learn more about the kink community. Her brother's tales about his fellow soldiers had always fascinated her. However, there had been a special reverence in his voice anytime he'd talked about Nathanial and Tashunka Ledek. Kodi assumed this club would be one of the few Koi would approve, so she'd ignored his warning to let him screen her choice.

He'd raised seven kinds of hell when he learned what she planned to do, but her decision had been easy to justify because he hadn't specifically forbidden her from *working* in a club. Not surprisingly, he hadn't been impressed with her distinction.

After their parents died, her brother became her self-appointed guardian even though she'd already been a legal adult at the time. She'd never been sure how he'd managed to get home so quickly after her mom and dad's accident. The truth was she'd been so relieved when he walked through the door she hadn't asked.

Koi had always been her hero. He was a decade her senior, and in many ways, he'd raised her. Perfect son, Koi's arrival had been planned...probably down to a gnat's ass knowing their obsessive-compulsive mother. Kodi had been an unexpected and unwanted surprise, something her mother had never let her forget. She could still hear her mother screeching at her for every stretch mark, bump, and bulge marring her perfection. Priscilla Green never considered that her lifestyle choices might be partially responsible for her fluctuating weight. *Yeah, because cocaine, wine, and cocktail party cuisine couldn't have possibly been a factor.*

Koi had been aptly named. He was every bit the panther his Choctaw name implied. He'd been a Navy Seal until he'd been severely injured. When she'd gotten the call, Kodi hadn't even taken time to formally quit her job at Mountain Mastery. She'd just packed up her car and been on the road in less than an hour. It was during those long months caring for Koi that she'd written the book now making its way steadily up the erotic romance charts. *Damn it to donuts, I wish I could get my hands on some of the money that damned book is earning. It's getting too damned cold to sleep in my...*

Blinking rapidly, Kodi realized how far her mind had wandered and how dangerously close she'd come to mentally picturing the place she'd been sleeping for the past few months. The knowing look in Master Taz's eyes almost made her flinch. "Why is it so cold in your room, sweetness?"

"Cold in my room?" She'd been so distracted by thoughts of her brother she hadn't realized she'd also been worrying about sleeping in her cold car. *Craptastic.* She'd heard about Master Taz's penchant for punishing subs who put themselves in danger, and it wasn't anything she was wanted to experience firsthand.

"You don't like sleeping where it's cold. Why is it so cold in your room?" He crossed his thick arms over his chest and stared at her intently. Damn it, this was going to get dicey if she wasn't careful. Bringing up memories of the basement apartment she'd lived in during her first stay in Montana, she shivered remembering the nights she'd slept in layers of clothing trying to stay warm.

"Just thinking about an apartment I used to live in and how cold it was during the winter." *See? I didn't lie. I might have taken liberties with the truth, but I didn't lie.*

Chapter Six

TAZ KNEW HE'D missed something important, but it flashed through his mind so quickly he hadn't been able to catch it. It didn't take any special skill to see she was deliberately bringing up a memory to conceal what she'd really been thinking about, but this wasn't the time to push her. The spanking he'd given Brinn was coming back to haunt him; the look of trepidation on her face was a sure sign she'd already heard the story.

Nate would have an opportunity to check out her place when he picked her up tomorrow for their shopping trip. But first, the two of them needed to make sure she wanted them enough to take a chance. He'd listened to her internal debate about dating her bosses versus her desire to learn more about the dynamics of a D/s relationship. He understood her concern about personal relationships in the workplace—hell, he'd used the excuse himself a time or two. But the connection he and Nate felt wasn't something they were willing to ignore, either.

Looking at his watch, Taz fought the urge to cringe. They needed to get back downstairs to work. It wasn't fair to ask the others to pull double duty while they were holed up in their office with Kodi. Holding out his hand, he waited until she stepped close enough to lay her cool fingers in his warm hand.

Nate stepped up behind her, close enough she would certainly feel the heat of his body blanketing her despite the small space he'd left between them. Taz could tell her that small allowance for personal space wouldn't last long, but why give away all their secrets?

They'd grown up in a family that valued the healing power of touch. Their parents, grandparents, and extended family were all very physically affectionate. One of the things Taz hated the most during his time in the military was the lack of physical contact and affection. Any woman they shared would never lack for physical intimacy. He or Nate would have their hands on her at every possible opportunity.

Taz watched Kodi's eyes widen briefly before glazing over as Nate leaned down to speak against the soft shell of her ear. "I will pick you up at oh nine hundred sharp, Ayasha. I want you to wear a simple shift dress—something that slips on and off easily. You can also wear a thong, but nothing else."

Nate was the picture of patience as he gave her several seconds to absorb the information. Watching his brother press butterfly kisses to the sensitive skin below Kodi's ear made Taz impatient to run his hands over every bare inch of her tanned skin. Hell, who was he kidding? He wanted to taste her, and going back to work with his dick throbbing against his zipper wasn't going to do a damn thing to take the edge off his desire.

Nate finally spoke again after seeing Kodi's small shiver. "The only correct response is, 'yes, Sir.' As soon as we hear those two words, we're all going back to work before my brother and I succumb to temptation and strip you bare. I think we all know, if that happens, none of us will get back downstairs anytime soon."

Taz wanted to roll his eyes at the understatement. Hell, if they started now, they'd be lucky to get back downstairs before Nate was supposed to pick her up tomorrow morning. Once they got her between them, it wasn't going to be easy to sate their desire. Fuck it. He was going to have to hit the locker room and take a cold shower before his balls exploded.

NATE FELT KODI'S neck muscles tense beneath his lips when he'd told her what time he would pick her up. *What the hell was that about?* As soon as she whispered her acquiescence, they led her back downstairs. Nate watched as Kodi moved around the club in a daze. Her eyes were hooded, and her movements stilted. Good to know he and his brother weren't the only ones dealing with an overload of unsatisfied lust.

"Nate, a word, please?" Karl Tyson's words jarred him back to the moment, and Nate was stunned to find the man standing so close. Hell, he'd been an operative for years, and no one had ever gotten that close without him being aware they were approaching. Christ, no wonder his peers got their asses handed to them on missions when women entered the picture. All the blood that should have been feeding his brain was pooled below his waist.

The two of them moved to the bar, and Nate watched a wicked grin move over Landon's face when he saw them approaching. "I thought you had plans, Nix? Don't tell me you let a sub slip through your fingers."

"Oh, ye of little faith. I'm just waiting for my back-up to finish paddling his sub. Seems she decided to be less than forthcoming about a rather large scrape on his new truck. Unfortunately for her, the repair shop called the wrong number to let the owner know the truck was ready to be picked up. That call brought down little Jessie's house of cards. I doubt the sweet sub will be able to sit comfortably enough to drive for a few days, so the fresh paint on Nick's truck should be safe for a while." Landon looked like he was enjoying the story enough the delay in his own playtime wasn't an issue.

Shaking his head at Landon's nonsense, Nate returned his attention to Neal. The man's smile lit up his entire face. "What's up, Neal? I'm going to assume from that shit eating grin you haven't had some sort of problem at the club."

"No. No problem, but I wanted to ask if you and Taz have invited Kodi to the Morgan's play party this weekend?" Nate must have looked as surprised as he felt. *Fuck me, the NSA could learn a thing or two from the rumor mill in a kink club.* "Listen, I'm not trying to snoop, but I have a great idea if she's going to be your date."

Well, this is starting to sound interesting. Wonder what the good Senator has up his sleeve?

Nodding, he was surprised when Landon spoke up. "Hot damn, I haven't had the limo out in forever." Nate had seen the Nixon's car collection and smiled when he thought about taking the Hummer limo his dad had acquired in some bizarre business barter. Landon's mother hadn't been impressed with what she called the brothel on wheels, but her son loved the outrageous seductive ambiance.

"What's the plan?" Nate was fairly certain he didn't need to ask considering the gleeful looks on his friends' faces. *Great Goddess, have some dignity guys. Doms are supposed to be intimidating, not looking like five-year-old children on Christmas morning.*

"What's going on? And why does our local Senator look like he's just won the lottery?" Taz stepped up beside Nate and leaned against the bar, nodding his thanks when Landon handed him a bottle of water.

Nate and Taz listened as Karl outlined what they'd planned for the trip. The limo's vibe would be perfect for a quick scene. The time constraints would assure Tally and Kodi were properly wound up by the time they arrived at the Morgan ranch. Nate was aware Landon acted as Neal and Tally's third. It was an arrangement that appeared to be working well for all three of them. Nate often wondered if the arrangement wasn't at least part of the reason his friend didn't pursue a permanent relationship with a submissive of his own.

The feisty doctor had gotten herself into a lot of trouble when she and Karl first joined the club because she'd only submitted to her Dom. Tally hadn't felt the need to hold her tongue with other Doms, and her curvy backside had paid the price more times than Nate wanted to remember. Karl had known he needed help, and despite his laid-back, California surfer charm, Landon Nixon was as sexually Dominant as any man Nate had ever met. The two men were finally beginning to make a bit of progress with Tally, but it hadn't been smooth sailing.

"I know Tally doesn't have many friends outside the medical community, and my guess is Kodi could use a friend as well. Any time we've been here since her return, I've noticed she's been...different."

"Different how?" Nate wanted to grind his teeth together in frustration. How had he managed to be so inattentive to his own staff? Noticing details was supposed to be one of the things Doms excelled at. Now he wondered if he hadn't confused creating a successful business with creating the atmosphere where the business would succeed on its own. He and Taz had envisioned a self-sustaining business. They wanted to expand, but the goal had always been to eventually have plenty of spare time to concentrate on the family they'd always hoped to have. How skewed had their focus been?

"Fragile, skittish. It's like she is waiting for everything to collapse around her. I'm not really sure how else to describe it." Karl's observation was startling and humbling at the same time. It was humbling to admit how distracted he'd been. Jesus, Joseph, and sweet Mother Mary, how had he missed something that important?

Landon leaned a hip against the backside of the bar and crossed his arms over his chest in a deceptively casual move. "Something is definitely going on with her, but anytime I've tried to make small talk, she bolts. I get the impression she is worried I'll ask questions she doesn't want to answer. I'd love to push her simply because I know there's a problem and I want to fix it. As a Dom, it's damned hard to let that sort of thing slide, but as a coworker, there are lines I'm hesitant to cross. Between the four of us, we should be able to handle two little subs within the confines of a limo."

Nate wasn't entirely convinced, but kept his reservations to himself. Hell, if he'd been as inattentive as it appeared, he might need help crossing the damned street.

The four of them finalized their plans quickly before Tally or Kodi made their way to the bar. Nate was looking forward to spending time with Kodi tomorrow for several reasons, but now the time seemed to hold more potential. The connection he and Taz felt was too important to risk making any mistakes. One of the things their ancestors' stories had always emphasized was the significance of a lost opportunity.

The words of the elders spoke in his mind. *A door to another's heart may only open once...be watchful...be vigilant.*

Chapter Seven

T HE NEXT MORNING, Kodi coasted her beat up SUV into a parking place behind the club. Double checking to be sure she'd gathered everything she'd need, she closed the door with a quiet snick and moved toward the building. She'd already made the mistake of leaving her lotions and potions in the car a few days before, and she hadn't enjoyed the consequences. *Muck it, smearing ice cold lotion over warm skin has to be one of the worst tortures known to mankind. If they really wanted information from prisoners of war, they should abandon waterboarding and use cold lotion torture.*

Keying in her security code at the back door, she jumped up and down in place trying to stay warm while waiting for the soft beep indicating the door was finally open. She'd been so worried about oversleeping she'd barely slept at all. Of course, the fact it had been positively artic inside the crappy SUV hadn't helped. Covering a wide yawn, Kodi moved silently down the dark hall and slipped into the back entrance of the ladies' locker room.

Calling the opulent space a locker room was almost laughable. The sitting room was larger than the living room in her childhood home, and their lockers were large enough to hold an NFL player's gear. Unloading her arms, Kodi leaned back against the counter to kick off her boots.

Damn her feet were cold. It didn't matter she was wearing three pairs of socks under the ugliest snow boots she'd ever owned.

Stripping quickly, she stepped under the warm spray of the shower. Groaning as heat replaced the bone-chilling cold, Kodi started to sing softly. She loved the acoustics in the club's large showers. Later in the day, the cleaning crew would have the music cranked up while they worked, but right now, her voice was the only thing filling the silence. The sound of falling water amplified her voice as she sang *Try Everything* by Shakira.

Kodi had been stunned when the club's owners asked her to attend the Morgan's party as their date. It had taken her a while last night to wrap her head around the fact the Ledek brothers finally noticed her at all. But she'd finally concluded, if she wanted to learn more about D/s relationships, she couldn't afford to waste this opportunity.

Wrapping her hair in a towel after finishing her shower, Kodi stayed in the warm enclosure to smooth scented lotion over her damp skin. The sweet citrusy fragrance lifted her spirits even more than the upbeat words to the song. Kodi was surprised how much she was looking forward to spending the day with Master Nate. She'd never gone shopping with a man aside from her brother.

Dancing her way out of the shower, Kodi was lost in the energy flowing around her. She was so completely immersed in the moment she didn't notice the man leaning casually against the doorframe to her left...until he spoke.

NATE HAD BEEN standing in front of his office window

when he noticed Kodi's battered vehicle limping into the employee parking lot behind the club. *Why had she coasted in?* Turning to the bank of security monitors lining the wall, he watched her gather things together and then barely latch her car door. She was obviously trying to be quiet, and he found himself curious what the little sub was up to. When she keyed in her security code, Nate made a mental note to check and see how often she was coming to the club before her shift. Something about the entire situation seemed *off*, and Nate wasn't quite sure what the problem was.

Tracking her progress through the darkened club, Nate watched her enter the ladies' locker room. They'd never installed any security monitoring equipment in either locker area in the interest of members' privacy—those two areas were the only parts of the club the security team couldn't see from a remote location. His curiosity on full alert, Nate made his way downstairs and stepped into the sitting room they'd set up to give the club's female members a place to relax.

Greeted by the sweet swells of a female voice, Nate sucked in a breath as Kodi sang about her commitment to try everything. If there was ever a Freudian moment with a submissive, this was it. He wondered if she knew how telling her song choice was. Nate loved the hopeful tone he heard; the giddiness underlying her sweet vocals made him smile. She always seemed so focused and serious when she was working. It was a pleasure to get a candid look at the woman he and Taz were drawn to.

Moving to the door of the shower area, Nate leaned a shoulder against the doorframe and crossed his arms over his chest. Envisioning Kodi naked on the other side of the frosted glass wall sent a surge of heat clear to his soul. The vision also sent blood thundering to his rapidly hardening cock. Fuck it. At this rate, most of his blood was going to pool below his waist. He wasn't going to be able to form a complete sentence if he didn't rein in his libido.

Leaning against the frame, Nate listened to Kodi's lilting voice singing about not giving up and being brave. He was in awe of the Universe's perfect timing. The Great Goddess of his ancestors never ceased to amaze him. Things always fell together perfectly—when he was wise enough to step back and put his fate in her hands. Opening his mind, he let the music wash over him as he tried to listen to his own internal voice.

In seconds, Nate was staggered by the realization Kodi was seeking a connection that went far beyond the physical. If he and Taz were going to reach her—*really* reach her—it would be through intimacy, not sex. Oh, the sex would be a big part of the reward, but it wouldn't be what tied her soul to theirs.

Again, he was reminded how little he knew about the woman showering nearby. He'd planned to review her file before meeting her this morning, but that would have to wait. Right now he had a deliciously naked woman to question—he wanted to know why she'd come to the club to shower rather than getting ready at home. Something about the situation was sending up entirely too many red flags for him to ignore.

She'd turned off the water, but hadn't stepped out of the enclosure yet, making him wonder what she was up to. When a sweet floral scent riding billowing clouds of steam rolled over him, Nate realized she was applying something designed to make him insane, so he continued to wait patiently. It was going to take him a few seconds to call some of his blood back to his brain anyway. Hell, he was already teetering on the edge of control, and he hadn't even *seen* her yet.

Nate felt the air leave his lungs in a heated rush when Kodi stepped from the shower. She'd twisted a towel on top her head, but everything else was exposed to his appreciative view. Her face was flushed from the heat, and moisture glistening on her tanned skin. Fuck, the woman was a straight up goddess. A little too thin, perhaps, but that was something he and Taz would remedy in good time. Nate frowned when he realized she hadn't noticed him. They'd need to teach her to be more mindful of her surroundings. He wasn't aware of any specific security risks surrounding them, but that didn't mean he was willing to take any chances.

Watching her toss the towel aside to let her raven-colored hair fall in soft waves down her back sent another surge of blood to his cock. Shit, he was going to black out from a diminished blood supply to the brain if he didn't stop the peep show antics and take control of the situation.

"Good morning, Ayasha." Nate deliberately kept his voice level even though the deep tone of dominance would be impossible for her to miss. He had to hold back his smile when she turned to face him, her eyes wide in surprise. Letting his eyes travel slowly over her naked form, Nate made no attempt to conceal his pleasure. "You are stunning, love."

When she scrambled to reach for a towel, Nate shook his head. "Don't." The sharp command had the desired effect—her hand opened reflexively, letting the damp cloth slide silently to pool on the warm tile floor. He was suddenly more pleased than he should be he'd gone to the extra expense to heat the floors throughout the club. Kodi's nipples might be tight buds of puckered pink flesh, but it damned well wasn't because she was chilled.

"I am very much enjoying what I see. You're not allowed to deny me this pleasure." Damn, he loved watching her pupils dilate wider as he spoke. Using his shoulder to shove himself from his leaning position, Nate took measured steps toward her. He could practically hear her mind spinning, assessing whether to stay or flee. And he'd bet his last nickel she was also scrambling to come up with a plausible cover story before he'd even asked her why she was showering here instead of her own home.

When he was standing in front of her, Nate brushed the backs of his fingers lightly over the tips of her nipples. She sucked in a quick breath as her eyes became half-lidded with desire. "What a special treat I've come upon this morning. I hadn't expected to see you naked until at least noon. I'm pleased the day is off to such a good start." Seduction came second nature to Nate, but this situation required an entirely new level of finesse.

Leaning forward, so close he knew she could feel the heat of his body blanketing her, he didn't touch her. The only thing caressing her was his breath brushing against the tender skin below her ear. "You are beautiful, Ayasha. Listening to your sweet voice, so full of hope and determination as you sang about reaching out for what you need—that's heady stuff for a Dom, pet."

Pulling back, Nate was thrilled to see the flush moving over her chest as her body responded to him. She didn't understand yet, but she'd just had her first lesson in bondage, and he hadn't even touched her. She'd been held still with nothing but the power of his dominance and his voice. The woman was a natural submissive, even though her lack of training was easy to see. He wondered if she understood what a potent combination those two things were for the right Dom. Nate would teach and Taz would push—they would be everything she needed as a submissive.

When he saw her begin to lean forward, he stepped back. "I want to look at you. Turn for me—slowly, very slowly." When she didn't respond, he crossed his arms over his chest and widened his stance. "You have two choices, Kodi. Obey or use your safe word." *Begin as you intend to go.* The words echoed through his mind, a subtle reminder he needed to earn her trust one step at a time. A large part of her trust would come on the heels of consistent guidance and predictable consequences. As skittish and untrained as she was, Kodi would need to know there were benefits for compliance and consequences for disobedience.

Blinking at him, she frantically tried to process his words. He knew she wasn't deliberately ignoring his directive. Realizing she was overwhelmed was the only reason he hadn't given her a warning swat. Goddess above, just thinking about how his palm would warm her ass to a deep shade of rose made his cock throb in response. When she murmured an apology, he shook his head. "Don't apologize. The correct response is 'Yes, Sir' and then follow the direction. Let's try again."

Repeating his original instruction, he saw understanding reflected in her eyes rather the vacant look they'd held earlier. She nodded, whispered, "Yes, Sir," then turned ever so slowly around. He didn't take a breath until she was facing away from him for fear she'd see how fragile his control really was. *Fuck me. I want to see her hair spread over my thighs as her lips wrap themselves around the head of my cock.* The thought had no more than moved through his mind than he felt his phone vibrate in his pocket.

Nate leaned forward to press a kiss against her shoulder, halting her progress. "Wait right there while I admire this side, too. Lord have mercy, you take my breath away." Slipping his phone out of his shirt pocket enough to read the message he was sure was from his brother, Nate bit the inside of his mouth to keep from laughing out loud.

What the fuck? You were supposed to take her shopping? How the hell did she end up wet and naked? They'd been told their telepathic connection would strengthen when they found *the one*, but the sudden shift was still a surprise. Taz had always been more gifted, but Nate heard echoes of Taz's chuckle filter through his mind.

Not wanting to take the time to type a reply, Nate refocused his attention on the woman standing in front of him. If Taz couldn't pick up anything from their conversation, he'd simply have to wait until Nate had time to answer. He saw goose bumps move over Kodi's skin and knew he'd lose a precious moment if he waited any longer. There was a narrow window of opportunity between lustful desire and confidence-stealing insecurity. Nate didn't want to add unnecessary hurdles to what was already going to be a challenging morning.

Skimming the calloused pads of his fingers along the soft slope of her shoulder, Nate leaned forward to press kisses along the same line on her other side. "Your skin smells good enough to eat, and it's silky smooth beneath my touch." Watching her muscles ripple beneath the skin made his cock jerk in anticipation. "My brother and I will touch you every chance we get, Ayasha. You're standing still when I know you're reeling. I'll reward your patience soon."

Moving his fingers farther down her back, Nate zeroed in on the dimples just above her ass. "These are one of my favorite places on a woman's body. So sensitive—one of the body's main energy pathways runs very near the surface here, allowing a deeper connection with touch." This time the shiver he saw move over her was edging toward chill, so it was time to move things along.

Cupping her shoulders, he turned her until she was once again facing him. "If I don't stop touching you, I'm going to kiss you until we're both so lost in the pleasure all common sense evaporates from the heat. And I'm not fucking you in a locker room…at least not the first time." He grinned at her and chuckled when she blushed.

"We'll chat while you get ready. Don't bother with clothing. I have that covered." When she dropped her gaze to his empty hands, Nate smiled. "No, I didn't bring the dress down with me. We'll be taking the elevator up to the apartment as soon as you're ready." He heard her quick inhalation, she was probably concerned about who else might be wandering around the club. She didn't ask the question he could see in her eyes, and he was enormously pleased with that small show of trust.

Nate motioned for her to proceed as he leaned against the marble counter. When she reached for the blow dryer and a brush he knew would straighten her hair, he shook his head. "Leave the waves, pet." Her eyes went wide in surprise, making him laugh. "Those are a major turn on for me, sweetness. My imagination is coming up with some very creative ways I'd love to use those beautiful tresses, but we'll table that discussion for now." He'd never seen her with her hair down, and he was shocked to see how long it was.

"What is your natural hair color?" The question surprised her, and Nate hoped she'd be startled into answering before giving herself a chance to edit.

"It's dark, sir."

"Why do you lighten it, Ayasha?" He had the feeling it wasn't something she was comfortable doing. Since women typically have the best sense of what looks good on them, he was curious about her motivation.

"It started when my brother went into the military. He was worried about people targeting me because of my connection to him." He didn't say anything when she paused. He'd learned a long time ago about the value of silence when asking questions. She shifted nervously as he continued to watch her work through what he assumed was an abbreviated version of her beauty routine. In his experience, it was a rare woman who hit all their usual steps while a man watched.

When he didn't press, some of the tension left her shoulders, and Nate saw her take a deep breath. "My brother is a little over the top sometimes. Looking at us, no one would doubt we're related. Coloring my hair was a way to get him off my as...backside." He chuckled at her quick save and gave her a quick nod to let her know he'd noticed. "I'm not saying he doesn't have any reason to be concerned, because he rarely talks about his time serving our country. But I can tell you I've never had any reason to believe I'm at risk. And to be perfectly honest, I'm tired of dancing to that tune."

This conversation was filled with landmines, but he wasn't going to launch into that discussion now. He'd dash off a note to Phoenix Morgan later and see what he could find out about her brother, but right now, he wanted to change the direction of the discussion. Keeping her off-center was going to be key in helping Kodi stay out of her own head. "I've made you a spa appointment for later today. I'll ask your stylist to return your hair to its natural color."

"I can't go to the spa." The alarm in her voice made the words squeak out, surprising him. He didn't respond aside from a raised brow indicating he wanted her to continue. "I can't afford a spa appointment, Sir. I'm already...well, I'm struggling to catch up financially...so anything extra isn't happening. Saving everything for a place to..."

Nate watched her go deathly pale when she realized what she was saying. *Well, isn't that interesting? Another small piece to a fascinating puzzle.*

Chapter Eight

K OI GREEN LEANED against the rock wall of Alexandria's Fort Qaitbey listening to the soft waves of the Mediterranean Sea lap against the shore. Big surprise, his contact hadn't shown up. He'd tried to tell his handler the man was blowing smoke up their ass, but the man charged with Koi's management and safety in the field had been steadfast in his refusal to listen. How a former operator buried deep in the hollows of the Pentagon thought he knew more about Koi's contacts than he did was one of the great mysteries of working for Uncle Sam.

Adding to his annoyance was the news his sister's name was pinging alerts all over the fucking internet. Somebody with a lot of contacts was running searches on his younger sibling, and he was damned anxious to find out what was going on. Christ, Kodi could walk into trouble with her eyes wide open and never be the wiser. She'd always been one of those rare people who assumed people had her best interests at heart until they proved her wrong, and they frequently did.

Koi ran interference for Kodi when he could, but now that he was working for the Agency, he was out of the country even more than he'd been as a SEAL. It was almost impossible to keep up. He needed to have some time stateside so he could set up a support network for her, but getting there was proving to be difficult. He hadn't been thrilled about his transfer, but his last injury had made returning to his SEAL team impossible.

When Kodi told him a publisher had accepted her first novel, he'd been thrilled for her. Well, as thrilled as any big brother could be when his younger sister decided to write an erotic romance. He'd never dreamed the damned publisher would cheat her out of so much of the money. The woman responsible was going to pay for what she'd done to undermine Kodi's budding career. But he'd learned long ago, revenge was a dish best served cold. No doubt the old hag thought she'd gotten away with stealing thousands of dollars from a newbie author. He had news for her.

Kodi didn't know he was no longer a SEAL. One of his conditions for the move had been that his sister could still contact him in the same way she had since before their parents' accident. It had taken her so long to recover from their loss Koi hadn't wanted to do anything to rock the boat. He'd secured her trust fund, giving her a healthy allowance each month, arranged for her expenses to be paid, and then submerged himself in the shadowy world of international intelligence gathering.

Shoving away from the wall, Koi pulled his phone from his pocket and frowned at the number of alerts scrolling up the screen. It was time to get his ass home. *Damn, little sister, what the hell have you gotten yourself into?*

KODI SHIVERED AT the sound of Master Nate's voice outside the small boutique's dressing room. She'd been surprised when he'd let her browse the first store without interference. He hadn't hovered over her, but she'd been keenly aware of him watching her. His dark eyes followed as she looked through the racks of dresses, and the one time she'd stepped out of his line of sight, he'd shifted immediately. The perceptive tilt of his head told her he'd known she was testing him. When she'd shrugged, Kodi had seen him chuckle at her attempt to be nonchalant.

"Ayasha, I'm coming in." Not a request. Not even a question...just a statement of fact. It didn't really matter since he'd already seen her naked this morning. She was still trying to sort out how she felt about their earlier encounter. Ordinarily, she'd have been mortified, but his voice had enthralled her. She was still waiting for him to press the issue about why she was showering at the club. He'd asked once and watched her carefully as she walked through the mine field of truth.

Kodi's justification? It damned well was too cold to shower where she'd been staying. Of course, the small bath house at the lake outside of town wasn't heated, so it was no big surprise it was cold. Late fall in Montana could be frigid, and this year had been brutal. When she'd arrived at her usual campsite late last night, Kodi had been disappointed to see they'd locked the building for the winter. Damn, she hated peeing outside.

A stinging swat to her ass brought Kodi out of her thoughts. Blinking up into dark, assessing eyes, she realized Master Nate must have been speaking to her, but she had no idea what he'd said.

"Tell me what you were thinking about, Kodi. And don't you dare lie to me like you did this morning." *Oh, shit.* "Oh, shit, indeed. We'll be chatting about that later, because Taz also wants to hear you explain why the address you listed on your employment agreement is a vacant lot."

For a few seconds, Kodi couldn't breathe. She felt the dress she'd been holding slide from her fingers, but she couldn't make her fingers close. *Why is the room getting darker?*

NATE WAS GOING to kick Taz's ass for what happened with Brinn. Dammit, as soon as he'd mentioned Taz wanting answers, Kodi had fucking stopped breathing. She was practically blue by the time he'd gotten her to take a damned breath. This wasn't the first time he'd seen fear in her eyes when Taz's name came up. Now he needed to find out exactly what she'd heard, because the truth wasn't flattering to his brother, but it shouldn't provoke stark terror, either.

Nate was grateful he'd had the foresight to send her file to Phoenix Morgan last night. It had saved him the effort this morning after he'd found her showering at the club. Phoenix's call a few minutes ago, had confirmed what Nate already suspected—she'd lied about where she was living.

Misleading them as employers was different from lying as their submissive. He suspected Kodi was living out of her car after seeing the pictures Landon had sent showing the older model SUV's interior. How had she crammed so much in such a small space? Thinking back on her answers this morning, he realized—while she hadn't lied—she'd danced very carefully around the truth.

Once he'd been convinced she wasn't going to hold her damned breath again, Nate pulled her into his arms. Damn, she fit him perfectly, and he was thrilled when he felt her relax into his embrace. Her breasts pillowed against his lower chest, making him long to feel her bare skin sliding against his own. When she pulled back, he allowed her to put just enough distance between them that he could look into her eyes.

"Stop worrying about my brother, pet."

"Please don't let him hurt me. I don't like pain. I can't even imagine why anyone does." Her voice trembled over the words, and Nate fought back the urge to challenge her comment about pain. He'd met very few submissives who didn't enjoy at least a bit of pain. As the flip side of pleasure, pain often intensified the effect of pleasure. In his experience, the contrast between the two sensations amped up a submissive's release exponentially.

"He'd never hurt you, Ayasha. You need to hear the jaywalking story from Master Taz and Brinn. Kink clubs have rumor mills just like the outside world. And our strict rules of confidentiality often allow the rumors to rage wildly out of control because the people *in the know* aren't allowed to correct those who are speaking out of turn." He'd warned Taz the disaster with Brinn was going to haunt him. And now, realizing it was a roadblock with Kodi, the whole thing pissed him off.

"When I said, we'd talk about the situation, I meant exactly that. We'll discuss it, and I hope you find we're both far more reasonable than you've been led to believe. You're interested in learning more about D/s relationships, so we'll consider it a teachable moment. The only thing more important than your happiness is your safety, pet. Don't forget that."

Kodi nodded, telling him she understood, but he shook his head and waited. She'd worked at the club long enough to know verbal responses were required. He saw understanding in her eyes before she whispered, "Yes, Sir. I'll try to remember."

He smiled and brushed a sweet kiss over her lips. "Perfect. Now, as much as I will always love seeing your clothing lying on the floor because it means you're naked and nearby,"—he flashed her a predatory grin before picking up the black dress from the floor—"I want you to try this one on for me." It was one he'd asked the sales clerk to take to the dressing room while he'd been on the phone with Landon. His friend hadn't hesitated to break into Kodi's junker SUV and then growled his frustration at what he found. The pictures he'd forwarded had spoken for themselves.

From what Landon reported, she had a tent and bedroll along with a couple of pots that had obviously been used over an open fire. God dammit to hell, didn't she know how dangerous it was to camp alone? The one consolation was the small caliber handgun stashed under her seat. She was going to be surprised to find her belongings had been moved into the small spare bedroom in their apartment. He didn't have any intention of letting her sleep in that small bed, but it was important to at least make it looked like they were giving her space.

Leaning against the wall, Nate watched Kodi slide the dress slowly down over her hips. The dress hugged her curves like a second skin, the back dipped so low it exposed the tempting dimples at the top of her ass. When she turned to face him, it wasn't the dress that stole his breath—it was the look of wonder in her eyes. For the first time in years, Nate felt another person's emotion wash over him in a wave so strong it almost took him to his knees.

He'd learned to block empathetic emotions when he'd joined the SEALs. The bombardment of feelings could be paralyzing when so much death and destruction surrounded him. Freezing on a mission would have gotten him and everyone on his team killed.

Sucking in a breath, Nate let his gaze caress every inch of her. The woman standing in front of him was completely different from those he was usually attracted to, at least physically. She was petite, slender, and her breasts would fit easily in his hand. He'd always preferred tall, well-rounded women with tits big enough to fuck if the urge hit him.

The realization everything he'd thought he wanted in a woman had suddenly shifted slammed into Nate's chest with the force of a sledgehammer. His entire life, he'd heard the elders in their community speak with reverence about the power of spiritually enlightened moments when truth was revealed. But nothing he'd learned had prepared him for the shocking reality. He'd known when it was time to walk away from the SEALs—he'd felt it to his bones, and he'd always considered that his moment of connection. Now, he knew better.

Kodi was looking at him, worry painting her expression as he stood there with his mouth hanging open, lost in his own introspection. Pulling his thoughts back to the moment, Nate pasted on a smile he hoped conveyed all the ways he was considering peeling her right back out of the garment. "I knew it would look good on you, but even I didn't know it would render me speechless."

"Do you really think it's appropriate for the party? It's awfully short. Do you really like it?" She was tugging the hem of the dress down, which made the low-cut neckline slide from provocative to scandalous. *Win-win* in Nate's opinion.

"First and most importantly, I do indeed like it—more than I can tell you. This is another teachable moment, Ayasha. When your Dom takes you shopping, he is the one you are trying to please. Neither Taz nor I would ever dress you in something we thought would embarrass you. Even in a scene, we won't use humiliation, because it's not something you need, and it certainly isn't something I enjoy." He wasn't above embarrassing her a bit to make a point, but he'd never understood how true humiliation could build anything but animosity in a relationship.

She shivered as her gaze dropped to the floor.

"Eyes on me, pet. We can't learn about each other without seeing into the windows of the soul." Kodi raised her eyes to him, and he felt the connection between them sizzle and draw tighter with each beat of his heart. He knew they'd have plenty of obstacles to overcome, but each one they cleared brought them one step closer to where they needed to be.

"Thank you for the explanation, Sir. And for your patience. It's one thing to read about the lifestyle and something entirely different to live it. I thought I'd seen enough at the club to make me understand it, but now I'm sure that's not the case."

Nate nodded. There was something about her words that struck him as *incomplete*, but he didn't have time now to get into a deep philosophical discussion about how D/s relationships served the needs of both the Dominant and the submissive.

Sliding his hands inside the hidden openings over each breast, Nate enjoyed her startled yelp. "Did I forget to mention this dress has several bonus features for those of us who enjoy touching our lovely submissives without making them undress completely?" He massaged the soft globes until he felt them swell and her peaked nipples press against his palms. Goddess above Kodi was so responsive she took his breath away.

Stepping back, he gave her a wicked smile. "Let's get you out of that lovely dress before I push you up against the mirror and have my wicked way with you. I'll take it out front, and we'll be ready to find you the perfect pair of shoes after lunch. Then you've got a spa appointment that will probably take up the rest of the afternoon." He'd already made all the arrangements for her pampering and would return to his office in the club while she was being waxed and buffed to a sparkling shine.

Laughing at himself for his typical male thinking, Nate silently thanked Tobi West and Gracie McDonald for standing their ground and insisting he and Taz scrap their "lame attempt" to incorporate a spa into their club. The two women had gone toe-to-toe with him about the expensive upgrades to his original design, promising him the benefits would pay for themselves in two years. And damned if Mountain Mastery Spa hadn't gone into the black at twenty-two months. At the rate the business was growing, they should probably consider expanding it into one of the larger buildings behind the club.

Nate led Kodi to his truck and lifted her effortlessly into the passenger seat. Reaching over to secure her seatbelt, he brushed a kiss over her soft, moist lips. What started out as a sweet moment quickly accelerated into a heated claim, a promise of things to come. When he finally pulled back, her lips were nicely swollen from his efforts. Before closing the door, he leaned close once again to whisper against her ear. "You test my control in ways I'd never dreamed possible. Open your legs for me, pet. I want to play a bit on our way to lunch."

Chapter Nine

T AZ HADN'T PLANNED to join Nate and Kodi for lunch, but the vibes his brother was sending out were so damned distracting he wasn't getting a damned thing done anyway. Watching them walk into the small Italian eatery, Taz smiled to himself when he noted how flushed her cheeks were. If he knew his brother, Nate had played with her while driving across town—just enough time to get her primed, but not enough to give her the relief she needed. *Perfect.*

She slid into the booth, and he pulled her closer until their thighs were touching. "I want you close, baby. I'm anxious to hear about your morning." When she stiffened, he frowned at his brother.

"Let's order first, and then we'll talk." Nate was focused on the menu, but Kodi was looking at her hands twisting in her lap.

What the fuck's going on? Landon had already updated him on what he'd found in Kodi's car. He'd been in touch with Nate on and off all morning, so he felt like he was up to speed, but the woman sitting next to him looked positively terrified.

By the time the waiter had taken their order and delivered their drinks to the table, the tension radiating from Kodi was almost palpable. Taz looked over her head, giving his brother a look that would be impossible to misinterpret. *What the hell is wrong with her?*

"It seems our sweet sub has heard about the incident with Brinn. She's afraid of you, brother."

What the fuck? Is he serious? Of course, he's serious. Nate was always solid.

Taz turned in his seat so he could face her and sighed. The stories about what had become known as *The Brinn Incident* had spiraled out of control at the fucking speed of light. Kink clubs were hot beds of gossip, but this incident had been embellished to the point even *he* barely recognized it anymore.

"Kodi, I promise there is a lot you don't know about Brinn's punishment. And if I had to guess, I'd be willing to bet what you *do know* has been so exaggerated it doesn't even resemble the truth. The rules about confidentiality, so I'm sure you understand why I can't tell you anything specific without Brinn's permission. I'll talk to her and ask her to explain what happened. There is a backstory, and I assure you everything that happened was consensual. And the bottom line is, no one has ever suffered more than they could endure under my hand. I have very strict personal limits when it comes to punishments."

Relieved when she nodded, he brushed her hair back over her shoulders with his fingers. "What I can tell you is I've never hated a scene as much as I did that one. I don't enjoy that level of play. Nate and I have both circumvented punishments that intense. But sometimes circumstances dictate we have to color outside the lines. Typically, we avoid playing with subs who feel the need to top from the bottom."

"I appreciate that you want to explain, but I'm not sure I want to hear about you having your hands on another woman…well, either of you actually."

Taz was so stunned by her words he felt his mouth drop open as his brother's roaring laughter surrounded him. Warmth filled his chest when he realized somewhere deep inside, she was already beginning to see them as hers—and damn if that didn't make his whole day.

Nate turned her to face him, grinning like the cat who'd swallowed the canary. "Ayasha, you have no idea how thrilled we are to hear you say that. Just for the record, we aren't going to want to hear all the details of your previous sexual encounters, either. Well, unless something has been particularly traumatic. If there are triggers we need to know about, we'd like to hear about those so we don't cause you any emotional harm."

Even though Kodi didn't get a chance to answer, Taz felt a wave of embarrassment wash over her. The waiter chose that moment to appear with their meals, so the opportunity to ask her what was going through her mind was lost, but he filed the information away for later. He'd wondered about her previous sexual experience, but now curiosity gave way to a need. Something Nate said had definitely flipped a switch.

As they finished the meal, Taz realized how much he'd enjoyed their casual conversation. Kodi was remarkably easy to talk to. She'd laughed about shopping with Nate and shivered at his description of the dress she'd be wearing to the party. It was Taz's turn to shiver when they started talking about shoe shopping. The only part of that discussion he was interested in was the result.

Taz escorted Kodi outside and waited while Nate settled her in the truck. After closing the door, Nate turned to him. "Have you heard from Phoenix?"

"Not yet, but I'm sure things are chaos up there today.

If I know Coral, she has them all running around like chickens with their heads cut off getting everything ready for the party. I also called Micah, but they were in the air, so I don't expect to hear from him until they land in Missoula. Everything is upstairs, and her vehicle has been secured in garage." At Nate's questioning look, Taz felt his frustration surface. "I thought Caila's car was a fucking safety hazard until I saw Kodi's. But after I read the letter on her front seat, I think I understand some of the problem."

"What are you talking about?" Nate glanced back at Kodi, holding up one finger to let her know he'd be there in just a minute before returning his attention to Taz. "Cut to the chase. I'd like to keep her as settled as possible, and waiting while we chat isn't going to help.

"Seems she has some money in a bank in Denver, but they won't let her transfer it electronically until she comes down and personally signs the paperwork. I doubt her car will make it that far. I'm guessing she was trying to earn enough money to get a place of her own first, since it's getting too damned cold to camp out."

Nate didn't say anything for several seconds, but his disbelieving stare spoke volumes. He finally shook his head and sighed. "She may fight staying in our apartment, but I won't lose this battle. All morning, I've felt the connection between us grow stronger. You'll spend some time alone with her this evening and see what I mean." He'd walked partway around the truck before looking back at Taz. "She's the one, brother. You and I both know it, and on some level, I think she feels it as well."

Taz simply nodded before stepping back into Kodi's view. He blew her a kiss and watched her laugh before returning the gesture. Even through the tinted glass, Taz could see the sweet pink blush painting her cheeks. He found himself looking forward to his time alone with her this evening. The spa treatments they'd set up for her this afternoon would leave her too sensitive for any sexual hijinks, but that didn't mean he couldn't begin building the intimacy between them.

He hoped the time he'd spent with her during lunch helped put her mind at ease, because the last thing he wanted was for her to be afraid of him. No connection—no matter how strong—could survive that sort of pressure. Submissives who were frightened of the Master's reactions were rarely honest, because their fear overwhelmed their desire to please their Dominant.

KODI HADN'T THOUGHT anything could be more embarrassing than her annual physical exam with her gynecologist...but oh how wrong she'd been. Having a complete stranger smear wax over every inch of exposed skin surrounding her pink bits was worse...far worse. Add to that humiliation the pain of having every single hair yanked out by its roots, and it had been the perfect storm for an afternoon in hell. She was grateful the young technician had gone to such lengths to make her feel at ease. The three large glasses of wine she'd guzzled had also gone a long way in easing her discomfort.

When she finally stepped back into the lobby of the club's spa, Kodi was surprised to see Taz leaning against the wall near the door. Impossibly tall and ruggedly handsome, she sucked in a breath as she let her gaze skim over him. The wine had made her bold, and she didn't bother to shutter her interest. "Well, aren't you looking all sexy and fine, Master Taz? To what do I owe this unexpected pleasure?" She was proud of herself for spitting it all out without slurring...much. *Yeah, that wine might not have been such a good idea after all. I don't think those were wine glasses. In college, we called those fishbowls.*

His knowing smile lit up his entire face. "I must say, you are in better spirits than I thought you might be. Deanna must have taken good care of you."

Oh, yes. Yes, indeed. Good care for sure. Maybe I should have eaten the san...witch. Kodi felt herself frown and then realized Taz's head was leaning back as he roared with laughter.

"I do believe we've just discovered the way to get the unvarnished truth from you, baby. I'm glad the staff let me know what to expect. Otherwise, I might be worried." He pulled her into a crushing hug before waving goodbye to the receptionist and leading Kodi out of the spa. "It's a good thing you have the night off, baby. I'm not sure Landon would be thrilled with one of his best servers showing up sloshed."

"Nope, I'm good. I need to get ready for work, but I have to tell you walking isn't all that easy. You won't believe what those ladies did to me. Holy hell, Herman, I'm bald as a billiard ball. Uncle Fester's head doesn't have anything on me." She stopped walking and considered her words. "Wait, I think I got that mixed up. I don't think those two go together."

He had her pressed against his side, his arm wrapped tightly around her, and she felt him shaking with laughter. Taz gently urged her forward and she was grateful for his help since walking wasn't as easy as it usually was. "No, baby, I think you're mixing up *The Addams Family* and *The*

Munsters. Gomez goes with Uncle Fester and Herman goes with Grandpa."

"But Gomez doesn't start with an H. That messes up my alliteration." She'd stopped again and looked up at him with what she hoped was sober sincerity. But if the ghost of a smile she saw in his expression was any indication, she hadn't been successful. He was trying valiantly to not laugh, and she finally let herself giggle at his failed efforts. "It's not nice to laugh at people who are inbreeded...imitated...well, fuck it. Drunk."

It took her brain a few seconds to process the heat coming from her ass. "Did you swat me? What the heck former?" Frowning, she shook her head. "What the heck forest? Damnit. Why?"

"Your language. The only time I want to hear the word fuck cross those pretty lips is when you are begging my brother or me to do just that." She studied his stern expression for several seconds before heaving a huge sigh.

"Is that some sort of a SEAL thing? Because I have heard that same nonsense from my brother." Using her hand to mimic talking, she blundered on. "Blah, blah, blah. Do as I say not as I do. Boys can say bad words, but girls should be sweet and demure. Sugar and spice and all that drivel."

He shook his head, and before she realized that was happening, he'd scooped her up in his arms and was striding confidently toward the elevators leading to their private apartment. "We'll go over the rules again later when your head is in the game. For now, I'm going to get some food in you. We'll talk while you eat."

"I'm supposed to be at work in...oh, hey, what time is it? Master Nate took my phone before I went to the spa. He said I was supposed to relax. Like that was going to happen with some woman smearing hot wax all around my girly bits and then ripping out the hair by the roots. That hurts, you know. I'm glad Deanna doesn't share your disdust...disagree...well fu..dge. Disdain for cursing, because I rehearsed all the dirty words I knew...more than once." His chest vibrated with laughter as he pressed his palm over the control panel.

"So your brother is a SEAL?"

Kodi felt herself stiffen at the question. Dammit, she wasn't supposed to tell people what her brother did for a living. "Duck. I'm not supposed to tell anybody that. How about you forget that I said that? You can forget one little thing, can't you?" When he didn't respond, she knew it was a lost cause. SEALs were too smart for their own good if anyone asked her...which they never did. And being a Dom made him a double threat. "Anyway, I'm supposed to be at work soon. I need to go to my car and get my uniform. Maybe I should do that before I eat so it warms up. I hate putting on cold clothes."

Taz set her on her feet after stepping from the elevator, but she was too stunned to move. They'd kept many of the old warehouse's features downstairs, so the completely modern décor of their apartment shocked her. Gray marble floors seemed to stretch out forever before butting up against a wall of windows facing the Rocky Mountains. The sun had set behind the range, but there was still enough light to make that side of the room appear more like a spectacular painting rather than a wall of glass. The sky was painted with several shades of blue to violet. It was truly spectacular.

"Wow. This is...oh, my, I don't even know how to put it into words. Your home is beautiful."

"Thank you, baby. We love this space. It took us a long

time to get it just right." He linked their fingers together and pulled her into what could only be described as a chef's dream kitchen. He settled her on a tall stool facing a granite counter with instructions to "stay put." She tried to take in her surroundings, but her gaze kept returning to the man moving around the kitchen with a quiet grace belying his size. He reminded her of a jungle cat, no wasted movement. Every motion efficient and productive.

"If you don't stop looking at my like that, I'm going to forget the spa staff's admonishment about tissue sensitivity." He slid a plate of crackers, cheese, and fruit in front of her along with a small bottle of water. "Eat up, baby. I've been looking forward to spending the evening with you, and I'd like for you to be conscious."

"I'm conscious. I might not be lucid, but I'm awake." She giggled and stuffed a cracker into her mouth before she said anything else stupid.

"Your shift has already been covered this evening. And for now, I don't want to hear anything else about money. I'm more interested in getting you settled." Taz's eyes were so dark it was difficult to tell what was iris and what was pupil. They were black pools of passion that she could see women falling into without a second thought.

"What do you mean by settled? I'm going to be on Master Landon's shit list, you know. And I've seen how that works out for people. He can be a real hard ass for a guy who looks like a beach bum, I gotta tell ya." When she heard his snort of laughter, she looked up to see him smiling down at her.

"I'm going to let the language pass this once, baby, because I happen to agree with you." He winked at her, making her almost swoon off her seat into a blob of goo. Quirking a brow at her, he continued. "By settled, I meant fed and comfortable. We're going to have a chat, and I want you to be able to focus on one topic for more than a hot minute."

Kodi didn't know what to say. She was as surprised as he was by her behavior. "I'm sorry. I don't have much tolerance for alcohol. And I'm nervous. If we're going to hang out for a while, can I go get a change of clothes from my car?"

"Why are your clothes in your car, baby?" Taz's voice was pitched low enough to be considered almost seductive, but there was a thread of steel in his tone that set off warning bells in her head. She'd heard that same tone from Koi, usually when he already knew the answer to the question he'd asked. "I can practically hear your mind trying to figure out how to spin your answer, Kodi. Don't. Just answer me. Honestly."

Chapter Ten

TAZ TRIED TO catch as many of the bits and pieces floating through Kodi's mind as he could. But with her thinking fragmented by stress and alcohol, it was difficult. He caught a reference to him sounding like her brother, and he stored that piece of information for later. Their initial inquiry to their military contacts hadn't yielded any results, but that didn't surprise anyone. It was common for Special Forces operators to bury family information deep in hopes of keeping their loved ones safe from potential threats. God knew he'd made his share of enemies over the years and still worried about them targeting his family.

When he reminded her to stop trying to frame her response, Kodi sagged and tried to look anywhere but at him. "Look at me, baby." There was a brief hesitation he wouldn't ordinarily tolerate, but it was too early in their relationship to expect anything else. She needed to get through this first test of trust before he'd be comfortable imposing the rules of D/s interactions. If she'd admit she had nowhere to go, it would be easier to convince her to stay with them.

Pulling her small hand between his, Taz felt her pulse pounding under his touch. Indecision and fear of being viewed as a failure was easy to read in her emotions. "I understand you've been taking care of yourself for a long time. But maybe it's time to take a chance and let someone else help. Everybody needs a little help now and then. Why are your clothes in your car, sweetheart?"

"You saw my car, didn't you? You already know what's in there." He didn't respond since she'd answered her own question. Taking a deep breath, she blurted out the truth. "I haven't been able to save enough money for an apartment yet. I'd been camping out, but the camp ground closed the bath house, so now I don't even have a place to pee. I really hate peeing outside. The cold wind blows right up your who-ha. I've been sneaking into the club early to shower. That crazy old bat at the bank in Denver won't let me transfer my money here unless I show up in person. What the hell is with that anyway? And there's a glitch with my trust fund, so until my brother surfaces again, I'm not getting any money from that, either. I've sold everything I could sell. And by the way, your staff needs to check the back storeroom at night to make sure no one is sleeping there, because...well, it's possible to hide there. Probably shouldn't have told you that, but what the hell, I'm already in so deep it's not like it matters now."

She'd pulled her hand from between his and was on her feet before he realized she'd moved. Damned quick for a woman still fighting her way out of an alcohol fog. She stumbled back a couple of steps before lifting her chin in a move he suspected was more about instilling herself with confidence than it was a show of strength for his benefit. "I'll be going now. Sorry this didn't work out. You guys don't need a train wreck for a sub. There are plenty of available women who would be overjoyed at the chance to work with you."

"Do. Not. Move." His voice cracked like a whip, the

sound bouncing around the room, freezing Kodi in her tracks. He knew she'd responded before her mind processed the order. "First of all, you are not a train wreck because you've been caught in a quagmire you didn't create. Second, we don't walk away from people we care about because the going gets a little bumpy. And last of all, we expect you to let us know when you need help. Hell, we'd expect it out of any of our friends or employees. And we damned well expect it from the woman who's agreed to explore the mutual attraction crackling around between us like fucking electricity."

Of all the reactions, he'd anticipated, seeing her sway on her feet wouldn't have even made the list. When her eyes became unfocused, he realized she was holding her breath. God dammit to hell, what he'd taken as compliance was abject terror. She was petrified of him, and once again he wanted to kick his own ass for the debacle with Brinn. He made it around the counter just as she started to slide to the floor.

Taz pulled her into his arms and moved to the living room. He could have demanded she take a breath, but he'd already frightened her more than he'd intended. Christ, he needed to get this misunderstanding cleared up sooner than later. Picking her up was enough to break through her momentary freeze. He was relieved to hear her pull in several gulps of air before he settled her on his lap. Her body trembled in his arms, but he didn't let her go. Letting the silence soothe her would go a long way toward calming her down.

Once he felt her relax against his chest, Taz stroked his hand up and down the length of her spine. "Thank you for being honest, baby. But the lesson I want you to learn from this is that it's okay to ask for help. I strongly suspect our local banker can help you handle the woman in Denver."

Kodi pulled back just enough to look up at him. "Really? I didn't think there was a way around her silly rule."

"How could you have known if you didn't ask? Do you feel comfortable asking your brother for help?"

"Yes. He's always helped me. My parents weren't thrilled when I came along, so most of my care fell on his shoulders even though he was only ten. He has always taken care of everything for me. That's why I dropped everything to go to him when he got hurt last year. He needed me for several months while he completed his rehabilitation." She dropped her gaze and sighed. "I felt horrible walking out on my job here. But when I got the call that he'd been injured, all I could think about was getting to him as quickly as possible."

When she started trembling again, he pressed his finger to her lips. "My brother and I will want to hear all about that soon enough, sweetheart. But not tonight. I've been looking forward to spending the evening with you and chatting about your brother isn't exactly what I had in mind."

He lifted her chin so he could press his lips against hers. Warmth spread through him like a ray of sunshine. Tracing the seam of her lips with the tip of his tongue, Taz moaned in satisfaction when she opened to him. Pushing forward, he didn't leave any part of her sweet mouth unexplored. "Good God, baby, you're going to test my restraint tonight. I know you're too sensitive to fuck, but if you're not careful, I'm going to throw caution to the wind."

Her grin made his heart clench. Ordinarily, he wouldn't be thrilled about a woman flashing him a big smile after he'd told her how much he wanted to be inside her. But there was something about Kodi that made him long to see her happy. His grandmother's words echoed through his mind. All the times she'd tried to explain how the connection would change everything reminded him how little of what she'd said he'd actually taken to heart.

Taz helped Kodi to her feet and shifted his hard cock as he stood beside her. When her eyes went wide with surprise, he laughed. "Yes, that's what you do to me, baby. But no, I'm not going to act on it—at least not tonight." He saw a flash of insecurity play across her pretty face, and he sighed. "Don't doubt for a minute how much I want you, Kodi. That's why I'm taking you to your room to shower and change while I finish warming up your dinner. It'll give me a minute to convince my cock patience is a virtue."

He'd led her several steps toward the hallway leading to the room where her clothes were now neatly tucked away before she skidded to a halt. "Wait. Did you say 'my room'? I don't have a room. How could I have a room in your apartment? Houston, we have a problem. Damn, what the holy heck was the alcohol content of that wine anyway? I'm babbling, aren't I? Holy Hannah, I could have sworn you said I had a room."

Pressing his palm to her lower back, Taz eased her forward. "That is exactly what I said. Sleeping in your car is not an option, baby. Not only is it unsafe—for too many reasons to list– it's also unnecessary. We have a spare room, and it's yours for as long as you want it." He leaned down and nipped the shell of her ear playfully before adding, "That isn't to say we won't be more than happy to share a bed with you. In fact, we're looking forward to it. But we won't rush you. For now, we intend to enjoy your company and help you learn more about dominance and submission."

"But...oh fudge, you already knew I'd been living in

my car before I told you. You weren't very upfull...full-out...outside...dammit."

"Upfront?"

"Yes. That." Goddess, she was adorable when she was trying to scowl at him.

"We didn't actually know, but we certainly had reason to believe so. And I'll remind you the address on your latest employment contract is a vacant lot. So you might want to hold back on frowning at me for not being forthcoming." He cocked his brow in challenge and was pleased to see her blush a lovely shade of crimson.

Stepping aside so she could enter the bedroom, Taz was happy to hear her soft gasp. "It's lovely. I want to protest being managed, but I can't seem to muster the strength to complain about such a wonderful gift."

"Thank you for being gracious, baby. Many submissives don't understand how much their Doms enjoy spoiling them. When they refuse gifts, it's an insult that degrades the relationship."

"I'd never want to take advantage of someone's generosity. But you're right; it's too cold to sleep in my car. I should have asked for help. This room is bigger than the apartment I had when I lived here the first time." She heard her voice catch and bit her lower lip to keep from crying.

He and Nate needed to remember how little tolerance Kodi appeared to have for alcohol. Her mind was bouncing all over the place, but he had a plan to refocus her on their evening together. "I'll give you ten minutes to look around, and then I want you to meet me outside the door." Grasping her chin gently between his thumb and forefinger, Taz turned her so she was forced to look at him. "Do you understand the instructions, sweetheart? I don't want there to be any question later."

Kodi's eyes were wide and had lost some of their earlier lack of focus, but she still wasn't functioning at one hundred percent. He wanted to be certain she understood this was the beginning, even though he intended to ease her further into a scene in a few minutes. She'd had a lot thrown at her in a short amount time, so he wanted to make sure she was keeping up. "Yes, Sir. I understand." He nodded and stepped out of the room, closing the door behind him.

Taking a deep breath, Taz checked his watch and made his way quickly to his own room. He wanted to check that everything was in place. When he and Nate renovated the warehouse, the one area where they hadn't spared any expense was their apartment. The kitchen was restaurant quality, and their private bathrooms were personal retreats designed to be their oasis of warmth during the long Montana winters. Both spaces had enormous garden tubs large enough to accommodate three or more people comfortably, but his own space focused more on healing than Nate's.

The hours Taz spent training exacted a heavy toll on his body, so he'd chosen more intense pulsing jets in both the tub and the shower. A six-foot-long floating stone wall featuring a line of gas-fueled fire separated the bathtub from the rest of the room. The partial wall gave the space the illusion of privacy he needed after a strenuous workout. A large walk-in shower had multiple deep-tissue massaging jets mounted at shoulder and thigh level. The rest of the room was geared more toward function than aesthetics.

Nate had chosen to create a tropical oasis in his shower, complete with a twelve-foot-tall rock waterfall. Hell, the flowering plants lining the walls had cost a small fortune.

But Taz's favorite feature was the insulated glass wall facing the Rocky Mountains. The narrow lighted ledge they'd added to the exterior of the building prevented anyone on the ground from seeing inside, yet didn't interfere with the spectacular view of Montana's nighttime sky. Taz couldn't wait to press Kodi's naked breasts against the glass and fuck her until she came screaming his name. Goddess, if he didn't stop thinking about sliding piece A into slot B, he wasn't going to make it back down the hall in time to meet Kodi.

Everything was set out and ready in his bathroom, leaving him to light the fireplace and candles before starting the water. The warmer held his favorite towels, and the soft strains of relaxing music drifted around the room. Taz returned to his closet and removed his shoes and socks before padding barefoot back to the kitchen. He slid their dinner into the oven then walked toward her bedroom with two minutes to spare. He was surprised to see Kodi already standing in the hall wringing her hands.

"I didn't want to be late, and I don't have a watch." She might have been talking to him, but her eyes were locked on his bare feet. He fought back his amusement. He'd seen every conceivable kink over the years, and who was he to complain if she liked his feet? Personally, he loved women's legs while Nate was all about their bare backs. When he'd seen the picture of the dress Nate had chosen for Kodi to wear (however briefly) at the party, he hadn't been at all surprised it would leave her back exposed to their touch. And he'd been more than a little pleased to learn the little black dress was short enough to display her amazing legs.

Taking her hand, he gave it a gentle tug. "Come." He didn't say any more as he led her to his bathroom. He didn't pause as they entered his bedroom, but he felt her fingers stiffen in his. "This is my bedroom, but it isn't our destination. The spa staff provided me with detailed instructions on your care, and I intend to do everything I can to make you as comfortable as possible. After this, we'll move to the media room and watch a movie while we eat. Nate won't be able to stay away for long, so I expect he'll join us sooner rather than later." When she didn't respond, he turned, studying her as she took in the room.

"It's unbelievable. Really. I've never seen anything like it...even in magazines. I'll bet you have women clamoring to come up here." Her soft words were a mixture of awe and hesitation, and that misconception was one he was going to correct straight away.

He tipped her face up to his and shook his head. "The only woman who has been past the guest room is our housekeeper. Family members and a few close friends who have been invited for dinner are the sum total of our visitors. We've never brought any of the subs we've played with up here. And just so you know, that wasn't accidental. It was on purpose and by design. We wanted to make sure the woman we were both attracted to wouldn't be subject to any residual sexual energy."

She blinked at him in surprise before gifting him with a smile he would have sworn lit up the entire room. "That's amazing and very Zen-sounding, Master Taz. I would have never thought of it exactly that way...but you're right. The leftover energy would be a downer even though it might not be obvious what was causing it." He didn't protest when she returned her gaze to the room, taking in every-thing with wide-eyed wonder. "You went to a lot of trouble to make this a place of peace and healing. Is it a therapeutic space for you? I know you do a lot of training. Is that why you designed it this way?"

Taz was stunned. He was genuinely shocked. How had she learned about his training? "You've surprised me, baby.

It seems you know more about me than I was aware, and I'm not used to being caught unaware." Christ, how had he lost control of this situation? It was past time to take back the reins. Crossing his arms over his chest and making a point to widen his stance, Taz let his eyes travel over her. She shuddered under his intense scrutiny and goose bumps raced over her exposed skin. *Perfect*. It was time to begin. "Strip."

She blinked at him in surprise before he saw worry replace the warm interest that had been in her eyes moments ago, "Did I do something wrong?"

"No, you didn't do anything wrong. If anything, you are almost too good to be true." He turned her until she was once again facing him before continuing. "Nate and I will rarely allow you to question our orders. But I'm going to give you a pass this time because I realize it was an abrupt change in direction. It's something we'll do often, because we will enjoy keeping you guessing. But you're new to the lifestyle, and it's important for us to build a solid foundation of trust. It's equally important for you to learn how things work. So, I'll answer this one question, and then I want your immediate compliance." He waited for her to nod in agreement before he lifted his hand to trace the tips of his fingers along her lower lip. "You surprised me. That doesn't happen often. It derailed me for a moment, and I want to get this evening back on track. And, baby, let me assure you, getting you naked is my top priority. Now, lose the dress."

Chapter Eleven

NATE LEANED AGAINST the wall watching Brinn stomp away from the bar in a fit of anger. He was sure her display of disrespect was for his benefit; what he didn't know was what had set her off or what he was going to do about it. She'd been a problem almost from the moment she joined the club. Bottom line was she set new standards in topping from the bottom. He and Taz disagreed about how to handle her, and in truth, their indecision hadn't done her any favors.

"She's in rare form tonight." Landon's amused voice sounded from behind him. He hadn't done anything to temper the sarcasm in his tone. Nate knew his friend didn't care for the spirited sub, but he'd never been sure exactly why Landon disliked her.

"Any idea what's put her in this mood?" If she had a reason for acting out, he might be more inclined to go easy on her. He didn't usually tolerate employees or members bringing an attitude into the club, but there were times life's issues were just too much to ignore.

"She's been like this since she found out Kodi wasn't working tonight. Or maybe I should say, since she found out Kodi is upstairs with Taz." Nate swiveled his attention quickly to Landon. "Don't look so surprised, boss man. Everybody knows you don't take subs into your apartment, so this is hot news."

Growling, he looked around the room. "How the hell did anyone find out she was upstairs?" Shit, even as he asked the question, he realized how stupid it sounded.

Landon's loud laughter filled the room before he started shaking his head, letting Nate know his friend considered him a dimwit. "Just guessing, I'd say someone saw her get in the elevator with your brother, unless I missed a memo."

Smart ass. "Very helpful, asshole." Taking a deep breath, he watched as Brinn stepped up to the other end of the bar and set her tray down on the bar with enough force to tip over the two of the empty glasses she'd been carrying.

"She just made the misstep I've been waiting for." Nate watched as Landon stalked to the other end of the bar, his long stride eating up the distance in record time. The man might look like a laid-back California surfer, but he wasn't to be trifled with. Nate often wondered how his friend had mastered the panther-like grace he'd shown on several occasions. Maybe they'd get a chance to talk during the party. Nate suspected there was a lot more to Landon Nixon than met the eye.

"Brinn, you've been acting like a spoiled brat all evening. Explain." Landon's tone was glacial, and the snarly sub hadn't missed the menace in his tone. Nate couldn't hear her reply, but it hadn't done anything to ease the fury radiating from Nix. "Strip." Her compliance was anything but immediate, but she finally pulled her short dress over her head and tossed it against Nixon's chest.

Nate heard Landon curse in French. *You've gone too far this time, sub.* He doubted she understood how far over the line she'd stepped, but she was about to find out. Most of the submissives at the club saw Master Landon as a playboy with plenty of free time and expensive toys. They didn't know the ruthless businessman lurking just below the surface.

"Go find Master Rafe. Tell him I'd like to speak with him immediately. You will accompany him back to the bar. If I'm busy, wait. Do not leave the club without speaking to me first."

When she paled, Nate bit back his laughter. Rafe was one of the club's few sadists. He would be more than happy to take a pound or two of flesh. Very few of the club's members knew Master Rafe was, in fact, Dr. Rafe Newell, a well-respected plastic surgeon whose practice in San Francisco attracted elite clientele from all over the world. He piloted his own jet, allowing him to visit the club at least twice each month.

Taz and Nate met Rafe years ago in a club on the east coast. The three of them stayed in touch, and when he and Taz decided to open Mountain Mastery, Rafe had been one of the first charter members to sign on. He refused to play in his home city, wanting to avoid any uncomfortable encounters with patients—many of whom he claimed were in the lifestyle. When Nate had asked him how he could be sure, his friend had rolled his eyes. "Can you recognize Dominants and submissives outside of a club setting?" When he and Taz both acknowledged it wasn't difficult. Rafe had laughed. "I assure you, those traits are magnified when they're in my clinic."

Master Rafe was an expert at dispensing pain, but Nate had never seen him take a sub further than his or her limits. His knowledge of the human body and understanding of its pain cues made him one of the few sadists Nate had ever trusted enough to dispense punishments in his stead. Once

Brinn scurried away, Nate motioned for Landon to step closer. "Tell Brinn she either submits to Master Rafe's punishment or she's suspended for a month." Nodding to the laptop they kept behind the bar for the club's Masters and Dungeon Monitors' use. "Be sure to double check her limit list. I don't want there to be any mix-ups."

When he saw some of the fire fade from Landon's eyes, Nate smiled. "We're going to have a chat one of these days about your dislike for Brinn. I have a feeling there is an interesting story buried in there somewhere." The man's eyes narrowed, but he didn't respond. Nate made a mental note to follow up and find out what the mouthy woman had done to cause such a rift. "But right now, I've got other priorities. You've got this under control, and I've already let the Dungeon Monitors know they're on their own for the rest of the evening."

Landon's expression finally softened before he gave Nate a wicked grin. "Enjoy your time with your little sub. I'm not sure what I'm looking forward to the most—the Morgan's play party or the drive up and back."

Nate nodded and laughed because he damned well knew their plans for the road trip were going to upstage the party.

Nate was stopped by club members so many times before he'd reached the elevator he was damned frustrated by the time he stepped inside. Once the doors slid closed, he took a steadying breath before laying his palm over the reader. There was no reason to expose Kodi to his foul mood, so he made a concentrated effort to push away everything downstairs.

Reminding himself about the message he'd gotten earlier from Taz saying she hadn't balked at staying with them, he was again both pleased and surprised. But he wasn't going to borrow trouble by trying to figure out why she'd been so cooperative. *Could be the fact it's fucking colder than hell and no sane person would want to sleep in their car.* Pushing his inner cynic aside, Nate stepped into the apartment. As anxious as he was to check in with Taz and Kodi, he wanted to shower and change first.

Fifteen minutes later, he stepped silently into the media room and paused long enough for his eyes to adjust to the dim light. Kodi was curled up against Taz, her tear-filled eyes focused on the movie screen. She hadn't seen him enter, but Taz turned to him and grinned. How she'd talked his brother into watching a chick-flick was a question Nate wasn't sure he wanted to have answered. *Good Lord, is that a box of tissues on her lap?*

"What is our little sub wearing, brother?"

Kodi had been so engrossed in the movie she hadn't noticed his approach until he spoke from beside her. She squeaked in surprise and jumped to her feet, the box of tissues on her lap tumbling end over end onto the floor. The dishes on the side table told him Taz had fed her, and Nate was relieved she'd eaten. He'd been concerned when Taz explained how affected she'd been by the wine.

Slapping her hand over her heart, Kodi swayed unsteadily on her feet, causing Taz to pull her down onto his lap. "Geez, Nate. You scared the shit out of her. What the hell?"

Before he could answer, she looked up and shook her head. "No, it's okay. I should have been paying attention. Holy Hermanettes, my brother used to do that sort of thing to me all the time. He was always grinching at me for not being aware of my surroundings if I was reading or watching TV."

Hermanettes? What the fuck was that? And sweetheart, I

*won't be painted with the brother brush because my intentions
are anything but brotherly.*

"I didn't mean to startle you, Ayasha. And I'm sure Taz
appreciates the fact you feel safe enough with him to focus
all your attention on the movie. I know I'd see it as a
compliment. But I'm still wondering what you're wearing.
In fact, I'm wondering why you're wearing anything at all.
Strip."

KODI STARED BLANKLY at Nate for several seconds before
moving her gaze to Taz. Warm fingers grasped her chin,
pulling her attention back to Nate. "First lesson, sweet sub,
my brother and I work together for your benefit. We won't
allow you to play one of us against the other, nor will we
involve you in any disagreement we have about what's
best for you. In return, you'll respect and obey us equally.
If you have questions about how this will work, we'll be
happy to sit down with you and discuss it later. But right
now, I want to see the results of your afternoon at the spa."

Nate's words were spoken in a deep tone that made
her entire body feel as though it was being electrified from
within. Every cell was suddenly crackling with energy, the
sensation so strong she wondered for a moment if they
could feel it, too. "It's part of the connection, baby." Taz's
voice from beside her made Kodi shake off the strange
feeling, but her mind was still scrambling to process Nate's
words.

Working in the club meant she'd seen plenty of nudity.
She'd realized this was coming, so she wasn't completely
blindsided. Why was she hesitating? After all, Nate had

seen her completely bare this morning. And she'd taken a bath with Taz earlier this evening and the only awkward moment had been when he'd seen her shoulder. For some reason he'd seemed oddly drawn to the small crescent shaped scar on her shoulder. So why was she stalling? When Kodi lifted her shaking fingers to the placket of the shirt Taz had given her to wear, the insides of her wrists brushed over her tightly peaked nipples. She sucked in a quick breath at the brief stimulation.

"Taz's white shirt wasn't hiding your body's response. Those pretty nipples beaded beautifully the first moment I walked into the room. But I want to see your bare pussy. Have you ever been waxed before, Ayasha?" The depth of his voice with its slow cadence, and tempting timbre almost made her forget he'd asked her a question.

"No, Sir." Her answer sparked fire in his eyes, and she was glad he hadn't tried to hide his desire. The look he was giving her infused Kodi with courage...knowing she had that effect on him was heady stuff. The last button slipped free, and she let the soft cotton slide off her shoulders.

"Great Goddess, you are beautiful, Ayasha. Your skin is glowing. Soft as silk and as smooth as glass." His step forward left her within reach, and he trailed the tips of his fingers down the center of her torso. A trail of goose bumps followed, and she felt herself shiver despite the warmth in the room. "The light from the flames loves you. It dances over the surface of your skin in a sweet caress."

Taz stepped behind her, anchoring her in place, his hands wrapping around her hips. The tips of his fingers tightened against her protruding hip bones. "We're going to help you regain some of the soft curves you lost while you were away from us." His words were spoken against the sensitive slope where her neck and shoulder met, making her shiver in response.

"Spread your legs, baby. Show Master Nate those pretty, bare pussy lips. I'll bet you're already wet, the folds safeguarding heaven swelling in anticipation." Good grief, Taz's voice was every bit as mesmerizing as Nate's. She didn't stand a chance.

She shifted her stance, opening her legs, but Nate's eyes never left hers. "Your body recognizes its Masters, even if your mind hasn't caught up. Although I suspect it isn't far behind." Taz pressed himself against her back and placing the palm of one hand against her lower abdomen. She felt him take a step back, forcing her to lean against him. The position put her on display for Nate, and he didn't try to hide his appreciation. "Look at those dusty pink nipples, drawn up so tight and begging for my attention." The tip of his finger circled the areola of first one breast and then the other until she was trembling in Taz's arms.

"She is shaking like a leaf, and you've barely touched her. Our little firecracker is going to go off like the Fourth of July." She heard the smile in Taz's voice along with something that sounded a lot like admiration. It was probably too much to ask that they'd like her enough to stand by her if the truth ever came out.

Kodi had started writing to stem the monotony of sitting for hours in waiting rooms while Koi was shuffled between doctors and physical therapists. The tedium had been making her brain numb. Plucking bits and pieces from the stories her brother had shared about his fellow Special Forces operatives and their missions, she'd spun a tale to keep herself from expiring from boredom.

The fictional characters were a combination of the most intriguing characters Koi talked about with a heavy emphasis on the two men she'd worked for. Nate and Taz intrigued her in ways no other men ever had. Walking away from her job at Mountain Mastery had been one of the hardest things she'd ever had to do. Even though she hadn't worked there long, it had been the first time she'd gotten an inside look at the lifestyle she felt drawn to.

Thankfully the Ledek brothers had been too busy building their business to notice her infatuation, because it had given her the opportunity to observe them. Oh sure, she'd watched everyone at the club, but her attention had always come back to Nate and Taz. There was something special about the way they treated the people around them...almost as if they were all on the same team or members of their extended family. A very quirky, extremely kinky family who accepted each other unconditionally. It had been the reason she'd wanted to return when Koi recovered and returned to work.

Kodi was sure no one had been more surprised by the book's success than she'd been. Her first foray into the literary world, and she'd made a big splash. She'd also made some big mistakes. Trusting a small indie publisher in Colorado had been her biggest mistake. The wicked woman was only paying her a fraction of the royalties she'd earned. Unfortunately, the old hag knew Kodi didn't have the financial resources right now to fight her. Kodi had sent Koi a desperate message asking for his help, but hadn't received an answer the last time she'd been able to check her email.

A sharp slap to her bare ass made her jump. Her squeak was more from surprise than the heat spreading rapidly from the stinging cheek of her ass to her sex. "Where were you, Ayasha? I've spoken your name twice and addressed you indirectly as well, all without the slightest hint of response."

Good grief! No wonder he's pissy. A snort of laughter from behind her made Kodi stiffen. *Okay, this empath thing is going to be a pain in my ass...literally.*

Chapter Twelve

TAZ NOTICED A recurring pattern with Kodi. The deeper she was submerged in her own head, the more difficult she was for him to read—*probably because her mind works at the speed of fucking light*. It wasn't that she skipped between subjects—it was simply the remarkable speed at which she processed information. The images, impressions, and echoes of sound he usually relied upon simply flew by too quickly for him to be able to pick them up. Phoenix Morgan was the only other person he'd ever met whose mind worked that quickly, and he'd been a member of Mensa since he was a damned kid.

If they kept her focused in the here and now, she broadcast her thoughts as clearly as if they'd been spoken aloud. For now, they'd need to keep her grounded in the present if he was going to be able to press what many might consider an unfair advantage. He'd never seen his gift as a shortcut, because he understood what a heavy burden it could be. It had taken him a long time to learn how to block the energy enough to be comfortable in large groups. The constant bombardment of the emotions swirling through crowds was not only exhausting, but it had also been distracting enough he'd been in trouble at school almost from the moment he walked through the doors.

Taz was more grateful than he could ever say for his father's insight. His dad had recognized his young son's struggle for what it was and used Taz's natural affinity for martial arts as an outlet. The intense physical activity provided a way for Taz to channel all the frustration bubbling to the surface. Learning to control his anger had gone a long way toward teaching him how to shield himself from the tumultuous swirl of emotions assaulting him anytime he'd stepped into a public place.

The only person in his family he'd never been able to read was his elderly grandmother, whose gifts were even stronger than his own. Nana-son's gift was far more predictable and controlled than his own. She'd assured him his gift would further develop after he found "his one." He'd never been convinced—until now.

Smoothing his hands over Kodi's soft skin, Taz bracketed her hips, holding her tightly enough to she couldn't misinterpret the message. Feeling her muscles quiver beneath his touch gave him a ridiculous sense of satisfaction. He could hardly wait to bind her in ropes and chains. Leaning close, he whispered against the soft skin below her ear, "Answer his question, baby? Where did that quick mind of yours wander off to? And who is cheating you?"

Her response was lightning quick. She tried to pull out of his hold, but he'd been ready. "Stop and think, Kodi. Are you acting or reacting? Are you afraid of us or afraid of being vulnerable?" Kodi went completely still. Even those pesky voices inside her were quiet for the first time since Nate and Taz explained they wanted to claim her as their own. The silence was almost eerie, but it also told him he'd hit the nail on the head.

After several long seconds, she finally spoke. "From the moment I started learning about dominance and submission, there was something deep inside me that recognized it as what I'd been looking for. Reading about it was almost frightening, because I often wondered if someone had been waltzing through my fantasies taking notes. It was like finding a lost piece to a jigsaw puzzle. That may be part of the reason your ability to…well, hear what I'm thinking makes me so nervous."

"It shouldn't. And someday soon, it won't. If you will open yourself up to it, you'll be able to take comfort in the security of knowing we'll be able to fulfill you in ways you've never dreamed possible. And you'll understand it's possible because we're able to sense the hopes and dreams you may not even know are lurking in the dark corners of your consciousness." Taz wondered if Kodi realized Nate was touching her while he was speaking. His brother stroked his hands over her shoulders, tracing a path all the way to her wrists before reversing until he tunneled his fingers around her neck and through the silky strands of her hair.

Taz moved his hands to her waist and wanted to growl in frustration when he realized his fingers and thumbs practically touched. How much weight had she lost while she'd been gone? How badly had her brother been injured that he didn't notice his damned sister fading away before his very eyes?

Nate leaned forward and pressed a kiss against her forehead before continuing. "There's no room for secrets or deceit in *any* successful relationship. But honesty is particularly important when D/s is involved. If safe, sane, and consensual are the guiding tenants of kink, then honesty is the Golden Rule."

Pausing to let his words sink in, Nate tipped her head back, making her hair brush softly over Taz's bare chest.

Each slide of the silken strands left a trail of blazing heat behind. "Factor in that what we're proposing is poly-amorous makes the stakes exponentially higher." Taz noticed Nate had kept his voice pitched low as he spoke. He'd modulated his tone to convey the seriousness of his words. One of the things Taz admired about his older brother was how rock solid Nate was—*always*. The one word consistently used to describe him? Steady.

Nate had been a respected team leader in the SEALs, and there wasn't anyone in the world Taz trusted more. "But...this"—she gestured between them—"is so new that the intensity of it feels a little invasive. Kind of like you're peeking in my windows before our first date."

Taz released her to move to the side. He wanted to see her facial expressions when he spoke. "I can't say that I've ever considered my gift in quite those terms, but I can see why it might feel that way. Typically, I'm not proactive in connecting with people. It just happens. But I have made more of an effort with you because *you matter*. In fact, you matter more than anyone else ever has. The chemistry between us is extraordinary, and realizing you feel the same connection to my brother pushes things toward phenomenal, baby."

"Taz is right, and we want to learn as much about you as we can. But we also want you to be comfortable. Trust takes time. If it feels like we're rushing you, it's only because we've been waiting a long time for this connec-tion." When she shifted on her feet, Nate took her hand, pulling it up to press kisses over her knuckles. "One of the things we'll always require is your honesty. In turn, we'll endeavor to always be honest with you. We need you to let us know when you're feeling overwhelmed. In time, we'll know you better than you know yourself; but until then, we're going to depend on you being brave enough to speak up."

Her nervous laugh didn't do anything to make him feel better, because the smile she'd given them hadn't reached her eyes. It was time to turn a corner in this conversation before she forgot where they'd been headed. *Good Lord, how did we get so far off track?*

KODI'S MIND WAS spinning so quickly she was having trouble keeping track of the conversation. Her lack of experience with men had never been something she considered a disadvantage until this moment. *Like any woman has enough experience to wade through the emotional quagmire the Ledek brothers create?* Individually, they were a lot, but together, they were overwhelming. She was trying to catalog her feelings; making mental notes and sketching out possibilities for her next book helped her organize her thoughts. She didn't want to risk annoying them any more than she already had with her distraction, but the feelings their dominance brought out in her were too much to ignore.

"There you go again, Ayasha. I'd advise you to step off whatever bus you're getting on, because there will be no more mental field trips for you this evening."

Mental field trip? Well, that about covers it, I guess.

Before another distraction could take root, Nate dropped to one knee in front of her and skimmed the tips of his fingers over her newly waxed mound. The touch was feather-light but so full of promise her knees almost folded out from under her. She swayed on her feet and was surprised when Taz's arms wrapped around her, pulling her back against his solid chest.

When did he move?

"Ninjas. Oh…"

"Ninjas? What are you talking about, baby?" Taz's warm breath brushed over her ear like a lover's touch.

"You move like ninjas. Silent and probably just as deadly when you want to be." She felt him smile against the sensitive skin below her ear and shuddered.

"In our line of work, stealth is a survival skill. But I'll admit, I think it's one that may come in handy with you as well. I think there may a lot to learn by watching you when you don't have your guard up." Taz's words might have unsettled her if Nate's fingers hadn't been waltzing over her sensitized girly-bits, making her tremble. She didn't doubt for a minute they would use those stealth skills to spy on her, and it probably wasn't going to end well…at least not for her. But the truth was, she just couldn't manage to care—not at this moment.

Taz's hands were now cupping her breasts, rolling her nipples between his fingers and pinching them until they were stiff peaks throbbing in time with each beat of her heart. His lips trailed a line of kisses along the top of her shoulder, paying special attention to the small scar he seemed drawn to and leaving a trail of need in his wake. But it was Nate's fiendish fingers, sliding through her wet folds, that were stealing her sanity.

Kissing her denuded mound, he whispered against the soft skin. "I can smell your arousal, Ayasha. Your cream is soaking my fingers, testing my control in ways I'm unaccustomed to. I have to keep reminding myself we must wait, but the temptation is growing at a dangerous rate."

She was leaning fully into Taz's hold, her legs no longer capable of holding her upright. Their combined touches were enough to drive a woman to the brink, but Nate's seductive voice pulled her dangerously close the edge. Kodi wondered if it was possible to come just from hearing a hot guy talk about sex. She tried to scrub the thought from her mind, but Taz's soft chuckle told her the effort had fallen short.

"Trust me, baby. We're going to make it our mission in life to discover all the ways we can make you come. Personally, I can't wait to watch you unravel beneath me. See your eyes go wide when the first wave of orgasm crashes over you." Taz gave her nipples a hard pinch, and she felt a wash of fluid soak her sex.

"She just soaked my fingers, brother. I'd say our sub likes hearing our plans for her. Let's send her over, and then we'll all cuddle on the sofa."

Oh yes, yes, yes. Sending me over is a wonderful idea. Her silent agreement was her last cognitive thought before Nate slid his finger deep inside her. One thrust against her G-spot and his command—"Come for us, Ayasha. Come now."—was all it took for the world to explode around her in a kaleidoscope of sparkling color. Arching her back, pressing into the heated palms flattened over her breast, Kodi heard a woman's scream but didn't register it had been her own until her throat burned from the effort.

In the back of her mind, Kodi wondered if she would survive sex with these two men. Her thinking was already fractured, and they hadn't even fucked her. Her heart was hammering in her chest so hard she thought it might burst and pulling air into her lungs was almost impossible. But the pleasure had been so incredible she let the worries melt away and slid silently into the darkness.

KOI DISCONNECTED THE call with his handler. For the second time in as many hours, he was uncomfortable with the way their conversation had ended. The man he was supposed to be able to trust above all others had always been solid until this trip. But something about this conversation had ice cold slivers of doubt spreading over him. Questions rolled and tumbled through his thoughts like a raging river filled with hidden hazards beneath the murky sludge of deceit.

Stepping out of the shadows, he walked down the shade side street marveling at Alexandra's fusion of the ancient and modern world. The city's architects and engineers had the unique ability to incorporate the beauty of their history as they moved progressively forward. It was too bad their politicians didn't maintain the same level of respect for the safety of their citizens.

The information broker he'd been supposed to meet with had disappeared, and Koi didn't hold much hope the man would be found alive. The handler's cavalier attitude about their missing source made the hair on the back of Koi's neck stand up. One of the many things he'd learned as a SEAL was to trust his instincts. Failure to heed those internal warnings never worked out well.

Being the suspicious bastard he was, Koi pulled a second phone from his pocket. He still wasn't sure who was responsible for the ambush of his SEAL team, and until he was, he'd continue covering his own ass at every possible turn. When he'd first joined the Special Forces, his Team Leader and the man's twin brother had taken Koi under their wings. Kyle and Kent West had retired two years later, but Koi had never forgotten the lessons they'd taught him.

During their last mission, they'd told the members of the team about their plans, including putting together a private team specializing in hostage rescue and private protection. He hadn't done a good job of staying in touch with them over the years, but he was sure the phone number he had was still valid. Koi had learned the value of keeping contacts a long time ago. You never knew when you were going to need a favor. Rumor had it the Wests had recruited Micah Drake. If there was anyone in the private sector who could dig deep enough to find a rat, it was Drake—the man's computer skills were legendary.

By the time Koi made his way to the fountain in Antoniades Garden, he'd decided to ask the Wests to check on Kodi as well. He'd always tried to keep his sister shielded from the worst of his work, praying he'd be able to prevent the violence from touching her. Kodi's innate goodness and submissive nature made her an easy target. The alerts flooding his phone were disturbing, but his handler's casual inquiry about Kodi rattled him more than he wanted to admit.

Chapter Thirteen

NATE LOOKED AT the limp woman cradled in Taz's arms and grinned. "She is more responsive than any woman I've ever known. She almost came from the conversation alone, and the instant I touched her G-spot she exploded." He'd been surprised when he'd encounter the thin barrier of her virginity. It hadn't been completely intact, but there was enough remaining that he knew she'd never taken a man. He'd used his little finger to avoid tearing the remaining membrane, because it was her gift to give. It was important she made the decision rather than having it taken from her.

He had to adjust his throbbing cock before the zipper of his pants left a permanent stamp along his length. Nothing tested a Dom's control like feeling a sub come over his hand and then not being able to find his own pleasure. Christ, he might have to take another shower—this one a lot colder than the one he'd taken a few minutes earlier.

"Saturday is going to be fun. I can't wait to see her naked on her knees watching Karl and Landon fuck Tally." They planned to leave early enough in the day to allow them to enjoy the ride north to the Morgan Ranch. Taz simply nodded, but his eyes blazed with heat, and Nate knew his brother was looking forward to seeing her reaction as well.

She finally started to stir in Taz's hold after they'd settled on the sofa. He cuddled her close for several minutes, softly praising her for the pleasure she'd given them earlier. Before she had a chance to ask the questions he saw shining in her eyes, Taz shifted her onto his lap. "I'm going to make us something to snack on. I'll be back in a few minutes. After you've eaten, we'll let you get some sleep. I have a feeling you haven't been getting much rest lately." Nate wouldn't have known she flinched at Taz's words if he hadn't been holding her. She'd appeared stoic, but the observation had clearly affected her.

"Why am I still naked?" Her sudden question surprised him enough to elicit a sharp bark of laughter.

"Because it pleases us." Nate let the simplicity of his statement settle into her mind before adding, "We'll keep you naked as often as we can, Ayasha. It's something you'll get used to—eventually. There will probably come a day when you'll be more comfortable out of your clothes than you are in them." Using the tips of his fingers to trace the edge of one areola before moving to the other, Nate gave her a wolfish grin. "Being able to touch you is pure pleasure. And I can assure you, we'll touch you at every opportunity."

Nate looked forward to the day when she'd step off the elevator and strip without being prompted. He wanted her to be comfortable with her body and to trust them to protect her from any negative criticism or disparaging judgment of others. Having every inch of her exposed to their view and accessible to their touch was something he would always enjoy.

"There are so many rules. I'm not sure I'll ever remember them all. It's easy for me to get lost in a project

I'm working on and everything else fades to the background...even rules."

Nate pulled her lower lip from between her teeth and shook his head. "That luscious lip belongs to us now, and we don't want it damaged." He smiled at her, hoping to ease her tension. A lot of couples observed a very strict set of rules in the D/s side of their lives. Hell, he'd known Dominants who set up rules they knew a submissive couldn't possibly follow so they'd have reason to punish them. That wasn't how he or Taz operated—it never had been. The way he saw it, forcing someone to fail was something you did to your enemies, not a woman who'd given you the most valuable gift in the world—her trust. And a betrayal of trust was the key ingredient in any recipe for a relationship disaster. Without a firm foundation of trust, there wasn't a polyamorous relationship in the world that would weather the storms of social judgement. And, from what he'd seen, those relationships never lasted long.

Using he hand to cup her chin, Nate forced her to meet his gaze. "You're spending too much time worrying, and that's our fault. We're here to help you. It's our job to guide and nurture you as you learn, pet. You'll make mistakes...everyone does. And you'll be held accountable for those mistakes, but you're really over-thinking that part of the dynamic."

She was worrying her lip again and there was renewed tension in her muscles as she worked everything over in her mind. It was time to distract her. There were plenty of ways Nate was certain would work, but the first dozen things on his list would lead to him sinking as deep inside her as possible.

Taz must have been listening in, because he chose that moment to step back into the room, carrying a tray loaded with sandwiches and fruit. "Come on. Let's finish our movie while we eat. We'll catch Nate up on the plot. I'm sure he's dying to find out about Meg Ryan's email." Nate didn't have any idea what his brother was talking about, but he found himself smiling at Kodi's sweet giggle.

The rest of the evening passed quickly. When Kodi started to fade, they stretched her out between them. Nate was grateful when the chick-flick she'd been watching ended and they switched to an action movie. Kodi's tears at the end of the romantic comedy she'd been watching with Taz had made his heart ache despite her assurance they were happy tears. *Happy tears? Good Goddess.* He was suddenly grateful his mom had explained the concept to him when he'd first started dating. The first time Nate took his high school sweetheart to a movie and she'd cried all the way home, he'd been in a near panic before kissing her goodnight at her parents' front door and sprinting back to his car.

Threading his fingers through the silken strands of Kodi's hair, he smiled when she burrowed closer, pressing her face against his lower abdomen. "How did we miss the connection when she was here the first time?"

Taz's large hands were gently massaging her small feet as he critiqued the explosion scene of the movie. "How on Earth does Hollywood get their facts so skewed? If they'd really used that much C4 they'd have blown the entire first floor." Shaking his head in disgust when the movie's hero slid to safety a split second before the blast, popping the door neatly off its hinges, Taz turned his attention back to Kodi. The genuine affection in his eyes was easy to see. "I'm not sure how something so important slipped by us, but I'm sure nana-son will have the answer. If I had to guess, I'd say it's all about timing. We weren't ready. Hell, we were ass deep in alligators trying to get the club up and running. I swore there were days I might actually meet myself coming in the door as I was leaving."

Nate understood too well. They'd worked sixteen to twenty hours a day for months on end without taking a single day off. There had been many nights he'd been so tired he'd fallen asleep standing up in the shower. He'd come awake gasping as ice cold water rained down over his freezing skin. They'd lost several employees during their first year in business, because they hadn't known enough about screening or watching for signs of discontent. Now their turnover rate was almost zero. Kodi was the only former employee they'd ever rehired, and she had Rosie to thank for their decision.

They wrapped her in the soft throw they kept on the back of the sofa when she'd started to shiver. He'd loved having her completely bare, but the supple fabric molded perfectly to her curves, so it did little to conceal the temptation beneath. Turning off the gas fireplace, Taz watched Nate cradle Kodi in his arms and move toward the guest room. "Damn, I hate that we're putting her into a cold bed all alone."

"Fuck, I hate that I'm going to get into a cold bed all alone." Nate loved the feel of a naked woman cuddled against him while she slept. He usually left their beds before dawn, but there was nothing quite like snuggling a warm, sexually sated woman after a few bone-melting orgasms. Despite his cock's shrieking protests, he'd settle for the skin to skin contact without the sex if it meant the chance to hold Kodi all night.

"Couldn't agree more, but since we didn't talk to her about it before she fell asleep..." Taz let his words trail off, but Nate understood and agreed. Once she agreed, she'd sleep with one or both of them every night. But until then, they were playing from an entirely new sheet of music.

Taz turned down the bed and waited while Nate laid her gently on the soft mattress before tucking blankets around her. She shivered, her eyes fluttering open just enough to register he was close. "I love this dream." He'd barely heard her whispered words, and he smiled at his brother. Taz was grinning like a cat looking at a bowl of cream—pure desire and anticipation.

Leaving a soft nightlight glowing so she wouldn't wake up disoriented, they made their way back to the kitchen. Grabbing a bottle of beer, Nate leaned back against the kitchen counter, looking out into the inky darkness beyond the large kitchen window. In a few hours, sunshine would flood the kitchen with the first rays of morning light. He knew he'd regret not getting every minute of sleep he could, but his mind was spinning too much to rest.

Turning his attention to Taz, Nate said, "Phoenix called earlier. He said he has a lead on the author of the book—seems our notes helped him narrow down the possibilities pretty quickly. I hope he has an answer soon. We need to find out who the author is and what her connection is to us. I'd hate to think about Kodi getting wind of this and being hurt by our appearance in some damned romance novel—no matter how hot the story is. Hell, she might think we've actually been with the woman who wrote it." Just thinking about how she might react made his stomach turn over.

Taz nodded his understanding then grinned. "She is really amazing. I was almost speechless when I picked her up at the spa and saw her hair. I hate to admit it, but Landon was right. The natural dark color makes her glow." Sighing, he shook his head and laughed. "Fuck. I'm turning into a sap."

It was just the break Nate needed. He leaned his head back and laughed. "Never thought I'd live to see the day, and as much as it pains me to admit it, you're right. Dammit it all to hell, there's going to be no living with Nix now."

Nate tossed his empty bottle into the trash before heading down the hall to his room. He looked in on Kodi and smiled. She'd kicked free everything but the sheet, which was now hovering just above her newly waxed mound, leaving her breasts open to his view. Standing in the open doorway watching her sleep, he didn't feel the least bit guilty for his voyeurism. They'd been waiting for her so long he wanted to enjoy every moment.

He and Taz had promised to let her have tomorrow to herself. They had business to attend to until the club opened in the afternoon, but as soon as her early shift was finished, they had plans for her. It was time to find out how deep her submissive streak ran. They'd use a tour of the club to find out which kinks turned her on. He and his brother would work together, one escorting and the other observing. It was a perfect way to test her responses, and by the end of the night, they would have enough information to make Saturday's trip memorable for everyone. Sending up a silent prayer of thanks for finally bringing her into their lives, Nate made a mental note to give Rosie a big hug and slip a nice cash bonus into her purse when she wasn't looking.

PHOENIX LEANED BACK in his chair and chuckled. After the

Ledek brothers' call for help, he'd downloaded the book in question. Holy hell, he now had a much clearer understanding of why erotic romance was so popular. He'd found a few personal references and revelations Nate and Taz had missed. No doubt they'd been struck mute after the first couple of chapters. Damn, he would have loved to have been able to watch their faces as they stumbled into the first description of the *Native American answer to Adonis* description. The two club owners were never going to live that down—at least, not if Phoenix had anything to say about it.

Watching information scroll up the screen as his program searched for possible matches, the one thing he couldn't get past was Nate mentioning that Kodi said she couldn't access her trust fund until her brother got home. Something kept niggling in the back of his mind, but every time he felt like he was getting close to remembering what sparked the recognition, he was interrupted. He'd been working on background checks for the Prairie Winds team, maybe there was something there he was hitting on.

Leaning back in his chair, Phoenix let everything he'd learned about Kodi stream through his mind while his computer searched for links to the information he'd entered about the author.

Letting his thinking drift, Phoenix kept coming back to the knowledge the author was playing a game of hide and seek she couldn't possibly win. From her writing, he could tell she was certainly bright enough to understand she wouldn't be able to hide forever. But it was the element of longing threaded through the words that made him realize she'd written the book during a time of stark loneliness. Closing his eyes, Phoenix worked to fit the pieces of the puzzle together. When things didn't align, he shifted his mental perspective and started again. The words *Occam's Razor* drifted through his mind just as soft warm hands slid over his face in a caress so gentle it stole his breath.

Without opening his eyes, Phoenix wrapped his fingers around Aspen's wrist and pulled her hand to his mouth, pressing a kiss against her palm. "Sweet wife of mine, to what do I owe this unexpected pleasure?" She rarely interrupted him when he was working, so he was sure there a reason for her visit.

"I missed you." The simple declaration had him opening his eyes to study her expression. "You worked late last night and were gone by the time I woke up. We'll all be so busy this weekend I know I won't get any alone time with you, and..."

His usually logical and focused wife had ridden an emotional roller coaster during her entire pregnancy. After their child was born, he'd seen her slowly return to herself. There were still moments—like this one—when he realized she was still fragile and her vulnerability squeezed his heart. It seemed like a cruel trick for nature to play on a woman who had one of the sharpest strategic minds he'd ever encountered.

Pulling her around until she was sitting on his lap, Phoenix let his broad hand stroke up and down the length of her spine. "Are you ready for a weekend away from our noisy bundle of joy?" His heart turned over when he saw her eyes glassy with unshed tears. Holding her face between his hands, Phoenix studied her carefully. "Don't cry, Athena." When the first tear breached her lower lid, rolling silently down her cheek, he kissed it away. "You're killing me, baby." Picking her up, he moved out the door and down the hall to their bedroom. Coral had once described pregnancy and the first few months of motherhood as being taken hostage by your own hormones. He hadn't understood at the time, but the truth of her words had become crystal clear over the past several months.

Laughing to himself, Phoenix realized his attempt to sort out the question about the author had just been interrupted again, but this time, he didn't care. Work could wait. He had something far more important to attend to...

Chapter Fourteen

KODI SET HER tray on the bar, relieved her shift was finally finished. The club was unusually crowded for a Friday night, but that hadn't been the problem. Her issue was with her traitorous body and the two men who'd tracked her every movement all evening. They might have given her the day to herself, but they hadn't let her out of their sight since returning upstairs at five o'clock.

She'd made good progress on her next book without the distractions of the local library. And since she didn't have the password to connect to the internet, she'd spent the entire day working. The reality of how much time she wasted surfing social media was humbling at best and downright terrifying at worst. Pushing that realization forcefully out of her mind, she decided it was best to ignore it for now. *God only knows what Taz would do with that piece of information.* Shaking her head at her wayward thoughts, Kodi realized submitting her next book was going to require finding an excuse to go to the library alone or asking for their password. Dammit to rotten moth balls, both of those options held inherent dangers.

Warm arms encircled her just before she could slide all the way into full-blown panic. "What's got you teetering on the edge of a meltdown, baby?" Taz's body heat and sweet words immediately set her body on an entirely different course. She'd enjoyed the light dinner they'd shared upstairs, even if the healthy fare had been sorely lacking in all things flavorful. What was it with former SEALs and their almost religious avoidance of all things tasty? You'd think it was a crime to eat anything with salt or sugar in it. His soft chuckle brought her back to his question. "Come on. We'll hit the snack table, and I'll hide you from Nate's view while you indulge in a couple of sinful delights."

Tugging her along behind him, Taz led her to the spread of sweet treats. True to his word, he stood in front of her while she ate two finger sandwiches and a chocolate petit that melted on her tongue. The rush of sugar drowned out all the sounds of sex surrounding her, and Kodi felt a moan of satisfaction vibrate from her core.

"Want to tell me why our sub is moaning in front of the snack table like she's about to come with a smear of chocolate on her lips?" Nate's voice startled her out of her convection induced trance, and she took a stumbling step back.

Shit! I can't believe I closed my eyes and let him sneak up on me. Wait, how did he get in front of me?

"I'm not sure I've ever seen anything quite like it. She didn't even realize I'd stepped behind of her. I don't know whether to give her more to see if she can actually orgasm from chocolate or paddle her ass for being so unaware of her surroundings." Taz's teasing tone made her smile, but Nate's look was another story.

"I'm leaning toward the spanking. She needs nutrition, not sugar. I don't want her crashing on us later." He was standing so close she could feel the heat of his body washing over her skin. The urge to press herself against him was almost more than she could resist. Leaning her head back so she could see his expression, Kodi felt Taz step close behind her. Nate's voice may have sounded stern, but his eyes were dancing with mischief. Exhaling a sigh of relief, she used the tip of her tongue to slowly lick the offending smear from her lips.

Nate's eyes dilated, shining with unmasked desire. "Keep teasing me, Ayasha, and you'll find yourself naked on the first available flat surface. With one thrust, my cock will be buried so deep inside you I'll be able to feel your heart beat." She gasped as raw need flooded her entire body. Her pussy clenched, and she sent up a pleading prayer the rush of fluid to her sex didn't make a public appearance.

"I think our sub might be more of an exhibitionist than we suspected, brother." Taz's sex roughened voice sent goose bumps over the surface of her skin. Kodi was grateful for the pounding beat of the music, because it masked the thumping of her knees knocking together.

"Let's go." Nate's growled words were a warning that her teasing had pushed him further than she'd intended.

Repeat after me, Kodi...do not poke the bears. Looking back over her shoulder as Nate pulled her away from the refreshments, Kodi was surprised to see Taz hadn't moved. The sexy wink he gave her made her want to go back and throw herself into his arms, but Nate's large hand was firmly wrapped around her wrist, and Kodi doubted anything short of the apocalypse would break his shackling hold.

Realization of how much she liked that small tease of bondage made her stumble. The stilettos she wore as part of her uniform were always a test to her limited agility, but she'd never come so close to falling until now. Nate caught her before her knees collided with the concrete floor. His gaze assessed her so intently it felt like a hot caress. "You're so beautiful. I can't wait to see you bound for my pleasure. There won't be any part of you I won't know intimately. I'll taste every square inch."

He knelt in front of her and slipped the shoes from her feet. Massaging first one tired foot and then then other, his strong hands infused renewed energy into her entire body. "Oh, my God in heaven, that feels amazing." She hadn't intended to say the words aloud, but they slipped out before she could call them back. He used the tip of his finger to trace a line along inside of her thigh as he stood back up, much closer now than he'd been before.

"I'm taking you to the locker room. Outside the door, you'll strip and hand your uniform to me. Then you'll go inside and put on the dress in your locker—nothing more. Do you understand?"

Did he say strip? Outside of the locker room? In the club's main room?

"Yes, that's exactly what I said, Ayasha." Kodi wondered if he'd heard her thoughts or if she'd carelessly spoken really out loud...again. "Kodi, I asked you a question and I expect an answer."

"Yes, Sir. I understand." She heard the airy tone in her voice and knew he hadn't missed it when the corners of his mouth tipped up. They were in front of the locker room door a few seconds later, and she wondered how she'd managed to walk across the expansive room without realizing it. When he turned to her, arms crossed over his broad chest and watching her expectantly, she didn't hesitate. Reaching behind her to unzip the short skirt, Kodi watched his eyes drop to her breasts as they pushed toward him. The skirt slid silently to the floor, and she considered making a show of bending to retrieve it before remembering his earlier warning about teasing.

The short halter top was easy to untie and landed at her feet with a subtle rustling of fabric. With her breasts bare, the cool air of the club brushed over her heated nipples, making them draw into tight points and throb with her desire for him to touch them. She closed her eyes and pulled in a deep breath, hoping to calm her racing heart. When she reopened them, Nate was holding her clothing, his eyes blazing with lust. He used his free hand to press her thong against her soaking pussy, the damp fabric broadcasting how wet she was already.

"Take off your thong and hand it to me, pet." She was so caught up in the spell of the moment it took her a second to register his words. It was a command. There was no doubt about that, but beneath the surface was an unspoken invitation she couldn't ignore.

Hooking her thumbs under the narrow elastic at her hips, Kodi skid her palms slowly down the outside of her thighs. Bending at the waist, she slipped the wet piece of silk off then laid it carefully in his outstretched hand. The fire in his eyes gave her a perverse sense of accomplishment. Who knew she could tempt the devastatingly handsome man standing so close his masculine scent surrounded her?

"Well done. Now, go inside. As soon as you're ready, return to me. I'll be right here waiting."

Stepping into the expansive locker room, Kodi felt a wave of insecurity wash over her. What the holy hell had she just done? She'd never flaunted her body in public before, and even though it felt right at that moment, self-doubt was now creeping into her mind like a slow moving fog.

Ducking into one of the restroom stalls, she pulled in

several deep breaths, trying to slow her breathing. She'd been so focused on pulling herself together Kodi hadn't realized she wasn't alone until the sound of women's voices jarred her back to the moment.

"They'll fuck her and then send her packing. There isn't a chance in hell she can handle Nate, let alone Taz. Their kinks run deep, and she's nothing but a piece of trailer trash. Have you seen what she drives? I'm surprised they don't make her park off-site to avoid the embarrassment."

"Don't be a snob, Brinn."

Kodi didn't recognize the second woman's voice, but assumed it was the curvy blonde she seemed to pal around with. Since Kodi often left the club immediately after her shift, she didn't know many of the submissives personally. Looking down, she realized her hands were trembling as she fought to push the other woman's harsh words from her mind.

"I'm not the one working in a place I don't belong. You and I both know she wouldn't be able to get through the first level screening for club membership if she wasn't waiting tables like an attention-craving college student. Mark my word, the Ledek brothers will push those monster cocks of theirs into every available hole and then send her on down the road. It won't take them long to figure out those tits are fake."

"Crass, Brinn. Very, very crass." Brinn heard one of the stall doors slam and recognized Tally's voice immediately. "Do the club's owners know you are talking like a jealous hag about the woman they consider theirs? Because I can't imagine them being thrilled with the sewage you're spewing." The disdain in Tally's voice was easy to hear, and Kodi felt tears burn the backs of her eyes, realizing she'd come to her defense.

Looking down, Kodi realized her feet were visible beneath the stall. Sitting down, she pulled them up to her chest and held her breath, hoping no one would know she was inside. After a few tense moments, Brinn's nasally voice broke the silence. "Come on. I'm not going to listen to Miss I'm Married to a Senator flap her gums."

Brinn was relieved to hear the women leaving the room as Tally's voice once again filled the smaller space. "That's Dr. I'm Married to a Senator, you ignorant bitch." A few seconds later, Kodi heard the door between the locker room and the club's main lounge open and close. After a few seconds, Tally spoke again. "You can come out now. They're gone." *So much for hiding.*

Kodi self-consciously stepped from the stall. She was relieved to see Tally was also naked, even though she appeared oblivious to the fact she was completely exposed. The other woman studied her for a few seconds before frowning. "Which one of them spun you up and then sent you in to the lion's den?"

Kodi blinked a couple of times before the question fully registered. "Master Nate. I'm supposed to be getting dressed, but I wanted a minute to calm down."

Tally's smile didn't reach her pretty, blue eyes. "How'd that work out for ya?"

"Not so great, actually." She started to move back into the locker area before turning her attention back to Tally. "Please don't tell anyone about this. It was humiliating, and I'd prefer to just pretend it didn't happen." She was asking for a huge favor. Secrets didn't seem to last long around the club. But her nerves were too raw right now to risk a rehash of Brinn's harsh words.

"I won't say anything unless I'm asked, but for the record, I think you're making a mistake. Ignoring how hurt you feel will only give it more power over your heart." The other woman was right, but that didn't mean she was capable of dealing with it right now. When she didn't respond, Tally stepped closer. Nodding once, the other woman gave Kodi's upper arm an affectionate squeeze before she turned and walked from room.

On shaking legs, Kodi moved quickly to her locker. The dress they'd left for her wasn't at all what she'd expected. Heck, even calling it a *dress* was being charitable. It was little more than a series of colorful silk scarves fastened to wide piece of elastic she assumed was supposed to hold everything up. Shaking her head, Kodi stepped into the dress and pulled it up over her breasts. "Holy crap. If I breath, my nipples are going to play peek-a-boo with everyone in the club. And that's not even mentioning the fact a brush of air is going to expose all my pink bits and my bare ass." Taking a deep breath, a nervous laugh bubbled free. "Better than being completely naked, I guess. And for God's sake, Kodi stop talking to yourself."

"I don't know. I find it informative and enchanting at the same time." Nate's deep voice behind her was such a surprise Kodi yelped and slapped her hand over her heart so it wouldn't beat right out of her chest. "We really are going to work on your awareness, Ayasha, but not to-night." She watched him take measured steps toward her, surprised when her fear slipped away as he came closer.

His fingers tunneled through the scarves with unnerving accuracy to stroke the underside of her breast, the calloused pad of his thumb pressing against the tight peak of her nipple. "It looks beautiful on you. Peek-a-boo or not, it's going to give us the access we'll need for everything we have planned." Locking her knees to keep them from folding out from under her, Kodi felt herself sway toward him. Nate reached past her, pushing the door of her locker closed as Kodi took a steadying breath. "Come. I'm anxious to get started."

Started? Oh boy.

Chapter Fifteen

N ATE HAD BEEN worried when he saw Brinn and Keri walk out of the locker room. He'd have never sent Kodi in if he'd known Brinn was also inside. When Tally stepped out a few minutes later looking annoyed, he'd started to question her, but he'd been interrupted. One of the newer Dungeon Monitors had stepped up to tell him they were ready for the tour. The younger man had given him a thumbs-up before disappearing into the crowd. Deciding to check on Kodi himself, Nate slipped into the room just in time to hear her comments about the dress they'd chosen for her.

Damn, it had been a struggle to resist pulling the pretty scarves back off her and parading her through the club stark naked. As much as he would have enjoyed it, he'd had to remind himself she wasn't ready for that yet. He'd seen how hard it had been for her to strip outside the door, and he'd been damned proud of her bravery. There would be time for lengthy discussions later. But right now, he needed to get started on the plan he and Taz had worked on most of the day.

Kodi nodded when he indicated it was time to leave, but he didn't miss the small shudder that moved through her when he pressed his palm against the upper curve of her ass. The intimate touch was a connection that vibrated all the way to his soul. He moved her to the front of the crowd gathered to watch the first scene. He held her close, her back pressed against his front.

Nate chuckled when she stiffened. "Yes, Ayasha, that hard on is for you. I find myself in a perpetual state of arousal when I'm with you." Nate hoped like hell relief was on the horizon. Otherwise, he'd be taking another freezing shower in a lame attempt to deflate his erection without taking himself in hand like a horny teenager.

The Dom on stage was flogging his submissive, the thudding of the leather strands leaving her upturned ass a deep shade of rose. "Notice the way he checks on her? He's watching every nuance of her body language. The position of her body, restrained over the spanking bench, legs spread wide, gives her Dom—and us—a close-up of the sweet nectar coating the petals of her sex. She's so wet he'd be able to sink balls deep in her without any friction at all. Her soft mews of need are music to her Dom's ears."

Moving his hand between the scarves, Nate let the tip of his finger slide between her legs. Damn, he wanted to shout in triumph when he found her as drenched as the woman on the stage. "This is definitely something we'll try." He turned her so she could see his satisfaction as he slid the finger wet with her cream between his lips. "You're as sweet as a ripe peach, and I'm not sure I'll be able to hold my desire for you in check if we don't keep moving. We have more to show you. Let's go." His voice was rougher than it should be, but he was pleased he'd been able to speak at all.

The next scene was one he fully expected her to recoil from, and she did—immediately turning her face away from the stage. As empowering as it was to know she'd sought shelter in his arms, he didn't move her away from the humiliation scene. "Tell me why this didn't appeal to you, pet." He needed to hear her reasoning, and he suspected she'd better understand her own feelings if she was forced to explain them to him.

"It turns my stomach to see people treat each other so disrespectfully. I'm not passing judgement on their kink, but it isn't anything I would enjoy." He watched her carefully as a small shudder moved through her. Breaking their gaze, she looked around before turning her attention back to him. "Where is Master Taz?" The uncertainty in her voice made him realize she'd misread his brother's absence.

"He is watching us. One of the most powerful elements of a polyamorous relationship is having two sets of eyes and ears carefully monitoring your every response. We'll never discount what you tell us, nor will we overlook the significance of what you *don't* say." He could easily tell when she'd fully registered his meaning; her soft gasp made him smile. "Before long, my brother and I will know your body better than you do. We'll map each spot and memorize the response our touch elicits—whether it's our fingers, tongues, or cocks."

He wasn't sure she realized he'd been walking her backward toward the next scene. Once he'd maneuvered her into place, he turned her, pulling her against his chest. Nate heard Kodi's soft gasp when she saw the submissive suspended in a shibari rope harness. The ties were much more basic than the intricate patterns of the ancient Japanese art form the rope master preferred. Nate appreciated the effort he'd made to keep the presentation simple and less intimidating. Even in its simplest form, the knotted patterns took considerable time to complete, so the woman displayed beautifully was already deep in sub-space when they stepped close.

Glancing up at Taz, Nate found his brother grinning like a kid shown a sweet treat. While they both enjoyed rope restraints, Taz was particularly fond of them. He swore natural fiber ropes connected the Master and submissive to Mother Earth, enhancing the experience for both.

Nate's reasoning was simpler; he preferred to avoid the damage to delicate skin that metal handcuffs and chain often caused. And he loved the temporary marks left by rope. Those tell-tale markings usually faded in a few hours, but the lingering psychological effect was a reminder to the sub of her surrender. Nate found himself looking forward to caressing those ligature marks after a scene as he whispered to Kodi how proud and honored he'd been when she'd given him her trust.

"Your body is vibrating with interest, Ayasha. Tell me what you see." Nate wanted to hear the words, even though he worried they'd likely snap the last thread of his control.

"It's art in motion. A celebration of beauty. I saw Taz do a demo once and..." Kodi went completely still in his arms, and he knew what she'd stopped herself from revealing.

"Did you see yourself in my brother's ropes, pet? Did you wish it was your soft skin his rough palms stroked as the ropes tightened around your bare breasts?"

"Yes." Her voice was breathy as she stared ahead. He wasn't sure whether she was seeing the scene in front of her or if she'd superimposed her memory of Taz's scene in its place. The brush of air beside him was all the warning he had before Taz stepped in front of them, blocking her view of the Shibari demonstration. His brother's hulking presence startled Kodi, breaking the trance she seemed to have fallen into and making her press back even farther against him.

His eyes were focused on their startled sub, but Taz's word were spoken to Nate. "Let's go. The rest can wait. It's time." Nate wasn't sure if Taz had read something in Kodi that told him it was time for them to claim her as their own or if he was so lust-crazed he couldn't wait to sink into her heat.

Nate was on board, but one of them needed to keep a cool head. They'd always been committed to the guiding tenets of the lifestyle. Safe, sane, and consensual was more than a series of words on the wall above the reception desk. Nate was certain he and his brother would keep Kodi safe, though their sanity might be questionable at the moment. It was Kodi's consent he wanted to hear reaffirmed. Turning her to face him, he looked into her dark eyes and felt like he was falling headfirst into the deep, turbulent pools of need.

"Tell me you want this, Kodi, because once we start down this path, there will be no turning back. We intend to claim you—every part of you will belong to us before the first gold rays of light fill the morning sky. What's your safe word, Ayasha?"

He and Taz stood shoulder to shoulder as they watched her take a deep breath and straighten her shoulders. Nate fought a smile as he watched her gather her conviction around her like a warm cloak, but it wasn't until he saw her chin tilt up he knew they'd won the battle. "My safe word is red, Sir. And, yes, I want this." He should probably call her on the vague answer, but why tempt fate?

TAZ WANTED TO smack his older brother upside the head when he slowed down their exit. He understood the reason Nate's calmer head should prevail, but that didn't do a thing to diminish his frustration. He hadn't needed empathetic gifts to know what Kodi was thinking as she'd watched the shibari demonstration. Her desire was written plainly in every nuance of her body language.

He remembered seeing her standing in the shadows watching his demo not long after the club opened. But he'd been so focused on the rope play he hadn't registered her interest. Hell, who was he kidding? He'd barely registered her existence he'd been so fixated on building a successful business.

Standing across the room watching Kodi's reactions as Nate led from one scene to the next had been its own form of torture. When he saw her reaction to the ropes, the intensity of his desire for her had gone from smoldering embers to a raging inferno in the blink of an eye. Taz was standing in front of her almost before his mind registered he'd moved. And those few seconds of waiting for her to give her consent seemed interminable. Now he was forced to hold back until they could make their way upstairs. They wanted their first time with her to be private. Her trust was still too fragile to risk in a public scene.

As soon as the elevator doors whispered closed, Taz pulled her into his arms. Sliding his fingers through her hair, he tilted her head and took possession of her mouth. He was too wound up to use the finesse she deserved, but when she softened against him, Taz knew it didn't matter.

He suspected there was fire buried beneath her cool façade, and when he felt her hands fist the front of his shirt, he saw he was right. His control snapped between one heartbeat and the next, and he pushed her against the wall, trapping her small body against his own much larger one. Her sweet moan of surrender sent another surge of blood into his cock. He was going to pass out cold from lack of oxygen to his brain if he didn't get her to a horizontal surface.

Pulling back when he felt the elevator come to a stop, Taz was pleased to see Kodi's dazed expression. "The two of you raised the temperature in this damned elevator ten degrees in thirty seconds. I'm sure that has to set some sort of record, but right now, all I care about is getting our beautiful sub naked and spread out on our bed." Fighting his urge to throw her over his shoulder and sprint to the bedroom, Taz stepped back and let Nate lead her down the hall to his room.

When they'd designed their spacious living area, they'd agreed to designate the larger suite on the buildings west side as the master suite. Nate had been using it since they moved in, but they'd always known it would be the room they'd share once they found *their one*. Facing the mountains, the sunset views were spectacular. Their plans to add a large balcony needed to be stepped up now that Kodi was in their lives.

The outdoor space would be shielded from the view of anyone on the ground by landscaping, letting them enjoy outdoor sex whenever the urge struck. An image of her sunbathing naked on the deck filled his mind, making his steps falter. The picture had been so real he wished he could save it to study later, because recreating it had just moved into the top five on his bucket list.

As soon as they stepped over the threshold, Nate

picked up the remote and opened the drapes. He hadn't turned on the lights, but light from a full moon bathed the room in a soft white glow, setting the mood perfectly. "Hand me your dress, Ayasha. Remove it slowly and place it in my hand." They both watch as Kodi lifted her shaking hands to the band at the top of the dress and slipped her thumbs under the elastic. As she slid the garment down, Taz heard his own growl rumbling deep in his chest when it caught on her tight nipples, making her breasts bounce once they were freed from the temporary hold.

"Fuck! You're killing me, baby. I'm going to love seeing those pretty, pink nipples decorated with gold clamps. I'll add gemstones to the dangling chains so every move you make reminds you who those aching buds belong to." Despite her tan skin, a deep blush painted her cheeks. Great Goddess, when was the last time he'd seen any other woman blush?

Kodi laid the dress in Nate's hand, and Taz let his brother settle her on the bed while he pulled what they'd need from a large armoire. There was no way any of them had the patience for any real rope play, but that didn't mean he wasn't going to give Kodi her first taste of being bound for their pleasure. Turning back to face the room, Taz wasn't surprised to see his brother had already shed his own clothing and had Kodi spread out in front of him. Her bare sex glistened with moisture, and he sucked in a breath as the petals of her labia flowered open as Nate kissed her.

"Beautiful. I'm going to remember this moment for the rest of my life, baby. Turning around and being treated to a view of your wet pussy—knowing you are waiting for me to bind your hands to the bed before I sink balls deep in your heat." As soon as his large hand shackled her wrist, every emotion battling in her mind hit him like a cresting tsunami wave. Pulling back, he stared at her, blinking his eyes in disbelief. "Never? You've never had a man? Not at all?"

"What?" Nate's voice was rough, and Taz sensed he'd spoken the words louder than he'd intended. Nate had said a small part of her hymen remained intact, but he'd just assumed she hadn't been with anyone large enough to shred it. It never occurred to him she was a virgin. Kodi struggled against Nate's hold, but he didn't move from where he'd been leaning over her. "Don't move, Ayasha. Not so much as a twitch until we've sorted this out."

"There is nothing to sort out. I want to leave. You're looking at me like I've got some kind of horrible affliction."

Is she serious? The most precious gift in the world is an affliction?

Taz sat on the edge of the bed and placed her hand over his heart. "You surprised me, baby. It had never occurred to me a woman as beautiful as you are wouldn't have enjoyed an active sex life. Were the men who attended your college blind?"

"She had to have attended college inside a convent. It's the only possible explanation." Nate's voice had softened despite his cryptic response. It was easy to hear the affection in his tone, and Taz appreciated his attempt to defuse the situation.

"Knowing we'll be your first is a gift we'll always treasure, but I'm damned glad to find this out in advance." Tossing everything aside, he leaned down and poured everything he was feeling into their kiss. There wouldn't be any bondage or toys tonight—no, this was about making their union special for all three of them. "We're going to cherish this moment forever. There is an unspoken bond between a woman and the man she gifts with her virginity.

145

Knowing Nate and I are going to be the only men to have ever push ourselves into your sweet body... God, baby, I'm not sure I can even express how huge that is."

The silent communication between Taz and Nate was short and to the point. They'd give Kodi the seduction she deserved and make sure tonight was a sweet memory despite any discomfort she was going to feel. Nate's finger had probably already pushed aside most of the remaining membrane, but her untried muscles where going to burn as they were stretched for the first time. Taz was confident he'd be able to distract her enough to negate any pain she might feel at that point.

Nate sat up, and Taz was pleased Kodi didn't follow. Her pulse was still pounding at the base of her throat, but her breathing was less labored, and she seemed to be coming off the surge of adrenaline that triggered her flight impulse.

Taz knew they should reevaluate her willingness. But he wasn't going to give her a chance to say no simply because she was embarrassed. Moving closer, he drew a line along the underside of her jaw from just below her ear to the center of her chin before heading south. When he reached her collarbone, he retraced the path with soft kisses. "I'm going to claim this sweet mouth while Nate finds heaven in your tight little pussy, baby."

Tashunka meant "horse" in his native language, and he'd endured untold teasing about it over the years. But the simple truth was he'd been blessed by the Great Goddess when it came to penis size. Nate wasn't much smaller, but even the smallest difference would likely feel like a lot to a woman who'd never experienced the heated stretch of a cock.

From the look on Nate's face, Taz guessed his older

brother was well aware of the responsibility that lay ahead. There was a mixture of blazing impatience laced over concern flashing in his dark eyes. *Slow and easy, brother. She needs to come at least once before you even think of proceeding.*

Nate's nostrils flared as he moved between Kodi's legs, pushing them wide and staring intently at the rose fully open in front of him. As far as Taz was concerned, the knights of old had gotten it exactly right—a woman's pussy was the most beautiful flower in the world. Soft pink and rose colored petals of flesh swelled and turned deep red when blood filled the tender tissues, opening it up in an invitation as old as time itself.

Keep that poetic shit up and I'm going to get you a job at fucking Hallmark. Pay attention. Our woman is all our focus. Let's see how high we can make her fly with our mouths before we move on to bigger and better things.

Chapter Sixteen

K ODI WAS CERTAIN the world around her had exploded
in a nuclear burst of heat worthy of star creation.
From the moment Nate sealed his lips over her sex, she
fought to draw air into her lungs. The heat of his mouth
and devil-blessed tongue were enough to drive a woman
out of her mind. Somewhere in the dark corners of her
brain, Kodi knew she wasn't supposed to come until they
told her to. She'd been reading erotic fiction for years, and
working in a kink club had provided a front row seat to all
the ways wickedly clever Doms could punish subs who
hadn't been given permission to find their pleasure.

"I'm proud of you for trying so valiantly to hold back
your release, baby. But that's not what tonight is about.
We want you to come as many times as you can. Give us
everything. We're waiting to hear you shout our names as
you fly into space." She was struggling to wrap her head
around his words when he added, "Come for us. Now."
Those simple words were all she needed to shatter. Her
back arched off the bed so far Taz pressed his palm between her breasts, forcing her to lie flat.

A piercing scream echoed around the room, bouncing
between the walls like a mountain echo. Their names shot
from between her lips like arrows circling back to pierce
her heart. By the time the last tremors faded to faint ripples

across her sweat-dampened skin, Kodi's brain was starting to come back on-line, and she wondered if her body would ever fully recover. Hell, she wasn't sure she'd even be able to walk again. *Holy shit, no wonder people are addicted to sex. I'm pretty sure I saw a couple of angels lounging on a cloud as I flew by.*

Nate's soft laughter made her go still for just an instant before she raised her hands, covering her face. Feeling the skin heat beneath her fingers, Kodi knew she was blushing furiously. "Oh, good Lord, please tell me I didn't say that out loud." She felt Nate shift and was surprised when his large body blanketed hers. The skin to skin contact instantly kicked her entire being back into sexual awareness. She didn't know how many orgasms she'd just experienced because they'd overlapped, layered over top each other and keeping her in a state of isometric freeze for so long her muscles were now completely lax.

"Keep your eyes open, Ayasha. I want to be able to see all the way to your soul as I slide into your heat. Remember, you have a safe word. I expect you to use it if you need to."

"If you need him to slow down, baby, use yellow. That will let us know you're getting close to your limit. Nate can adjust your position as necessary."

She didn't respond because just thinking about Nate pushing his enormous cock into her was making her begin to tremble with a mixture of fear and longing. When the tip pressed against her entrance, Kodi was shocked by the heat emanating from the smooth skin stretched tight over the broad head. A fresh flood of moisture flowed all the way from her core. He moaned when the thick syrup moved over him. The sound gave her an immense feeling of satisfaction. The realization that she could affect him so strongly was incredibly empowering. Nothing could have deterred her in that moment.

"Fuck! She just soaked me with her sweet cream." Nate's words set off another wave of heat Kodi was sure started deep in her core.

Taz groaned as he circled her nipple with the tip of his tongue. The dueling sensations were more than her mind could separate, and she gave up trying. Nate's deep voice broke through her thoughts when he turned the conversation back to her. "Pet, Mother Nature's lubricant is better than anything mankind has ever invented. Feeling your body paving the way to heaven is pushing my control dangerously close to the breaking point."

She dug her heels into the mattress in an effort to gain leverage and tilt her hips and force him deeper. "Please."

"Don't move, Ayasha. We have to do this nice and slow. We need to give all those delicate tissues a chance to stretch naturally." Kodi might not be experienced, but she didn't need a full battery of past sexual escapades to recognize the strain in Nate's expression.

"Baby, take deep breaths and relax. Your body *will* adjust, but it takes a few minutes for those untried muscles and tender tissues to accommodate a man as large as Nate." Her eyes dropped to his erection, and she wondered how he was ever going to fit. "Don't worry. We're going to fit together perfectly." The blistering kiss he gave her caught her by surprise. The passion almost masked the twinge of pain she felt as Nate pushed through the remnants of her virginity. Exams by physicians over the years had removed portions of the barrier, but she'd felt the last pieces break away with Nate's possession.

Her body was betraying her...she craved what Nate was offering, but was in equal parts terrified of it. A part of her needed what they could give her, yet she clenched involuntarily around him in a futile attempt to stave off the intrusion. He had to stop several times to talk her back from the edge. His patience tugged relentlessly at her heart. When the first beads of sweat appeared on his brow, she understood how difficult it was for him to hold himself back. "Please don't give up on me."

The startled look on his face morphed into a sweet, almost boyish grin. "Never, Ayasha. Never." His words were spoken just as she felt the tip push against her cervix, making her gasp as heat spread over her. "We'll begin slow, but if you keep flexing those vaginal muscles, I'm not going to be responsible for my actions." His words were clipped, but his smile assured her there was no real admonishment in them.

Feeling him retreat, Kodi savored the feeling of each ridge and bump caressing her tender tissues. The burn from stretching was now molten need rather than discomfort, and the return stroke felt like someone throwing gas on the smoldering embers of her previous orgasm. Her body caught fire in an instant, and she was clamoring for more before she'd even made sense of everything she was feeling.

Taz sealed his lips over hers a split second before Nate kicked things up in both speed and intensity. The air around her sizzled with unspoken communication, and her need to tap into the energy flashed through her so quickly she wasn't sure where the thought had even come from.

Mine! Ours! Two distinct voices rang through her thoughts just before her mind once again shattered in a million pieces of glittering light and she was launched into space.

NATE'S ENTIRE BODY was bathed in sweat as he fought for control. Nothing had ever felt as good as being sheathed in Kodi's blistering heat. His release blindsided him. Hell, he couldn't even remember the last time that had happened. The last time he'd come that soon after entering a woman he'd been in fucking high school. Great Goddess, the woman undid him in ways he didn't even understand.

He'd felt the connection between the three of them just before everything inside him exploded in a cataclysm of pleasure. He knew she'd heard his and Taz's voices in her mind, but he was sure she didn't understand the significance of the moment. According to the legend handed down from his ancestors, the link could only be felt between hearts joined by destiny. When Nate's gaze met his brother's, he saw his own wonder reflected in Taz's eyes as well.

They both felt Kodi was their "one", but Nate expected the confirmation to be more abstract and elusive. He'd never believed it would be so blatant. Sure, their chemistry was off the charts. But attraction didn't always mean the connection was *right* or that it would be lasting. Nate had enjoyed great chemistry with women he didn't feel *connected* to—but this had been something entirely different.

He'd managed to catch most of his weight on his forearms, but he was still pressing Kodi into the mattress. "Ayasha, I'll move as soon as I recover enough that I can trust my muscles to cooperate and my body to respond to my brain. Right now, I'm worried I might crush you if I tried." Taking a few seconds to make sure the next thing he said was worded carefully, he was surprised to see uncertainty in her eyes.

Oh, hell no. I'm going to squelch that insecurity right fucking now. "I'm not sure I know the words to explain how amazing that was. It was far beyond spectacular sex. That was a soul-deep fusion of spirits. And just to be clear, we're never letting you go."

"Baby, I've seen a lot of erotic scenes over the years. I've watched—and yes, participated in—more ménages than I can count. But I've never felt as connected as I did watching my brother make love to you." Nate could feel Taz's anticipation. His brother's need to feel Kodi's sweet body pressed against his own was coming off him in waves. It required a Herculean effort, but he finally managed to lift himself up so Taz could move into his place.

The moment he slid from her body, Nate froze. Leaning back on his knees, he looked down with mixed emotions, watching his seed flow from between the swollen lips of her sex. The pale pink tinge of blood made him cringe, but knowing he'd marked her in such a primal way was oddly satisfying. But the sudden realization he'd failed to use protection for the first time in his life reminded him how careless he'd been with her safety.

"What's wrong? Why are you looking at me like that?" He heard the note of panic in her voice and was grateful Taz kept her from scrambling out from under him.

"You didn't do anything wrong, pet. I'm the one who made a mistake. I failed to protect you. We have access to your medical form in your employment file, but felt it was an intrusion on your privacy to look at it under these circumstances. Which means we should have had a conversation about condoms and birth control prior to this."

She relaxed back against the bed and smiled. "Damn, you scared the duck waddle out of me. I thought I'd lost a vital organ or something. Maybe given birth to an alien or two. Give a girl a break, would ya?" Nate stared at her, his mouth dropped open in shock—as his brother rolled to his back and roared with laughter.

WHILE PHOENIX MORGAN leaned back in his chair with boots propped up on his desk, Micah Drake studied the data spread out in front of him. Phoenix's report was nearly complete, and Micah was mentally filling in the final pieces of intel he'd pulled from various emails after they'd landed in Montana this afternoon. Pushing away from the desk, he turned his chair so he faced Phoenix. "Have you had a chance to look at the documents I forwarded to you a couple hours ago?"

"I have." Phoenix didn't say any more, but the gleam in his eye told Micah the other man had reached the same conclusion.

"Author Keme Meadows is none other than Kodi Green. The same woman Kyle West has been tasked with checking on per a frantic message from her brother, who—I might add—placed that call from Alexandra, Egypt, after his phone lit up from all the inquiries we were doing. Kyle helped put together Koi's transport home, because he was so concerned about her."

"I do believe you've summed things up pretty well. And I'm damned impressed with the alerts he'd set up, because I didn't realize I was in the middle of a mine field until it was too late." Once he'd connected the background searches he'd been working on for the Wests, the pieces had fallen together quickly.

Micah laughed. "I told Kyle to hire him. We've hired so

many of Uncle Sam's best operatives the alphabet agencies have to hire us." Leaning forward to shuffle the papers on the desk with nervous fingers, Micah sighed. "Seriously, who's going to tell Nate and Taz? Because, from what I've heard, they are falling for her hard and fast."

"Drake, is there any pie you don't have your finger in? Hell, I just heard that myself a few hours ago, and I belong to their damned club." Phoenix shook his head, giving Micah a mock look of frustration before smiling. "In answer to your question, I think Kyle is the best bet."

"Agreed. And for what it's worth, I think he'll agree. Kyle and Kent have a unique perspective since Tobi is writing a book of her own. She used to work for a local magazine. It was actually her attempt to interview them that led to their first meeting." Micah shook his head before adding, "I'm sure you've heard the story, but I still laugh every time I think about her going toe-to-toe with Kyle West standing in the middle of a highway during a thunderstorm with lightening crashing all around them."

"I believe that is what's called a preview of coming attractions."

Micah leaned his head back and laughed, because Phoenix's description was dead on. Tobi West was without question one of the most spirited women Micah had ever met. She was also talented, loyal, and wickedly funny. But best of all, she'd been responsible for introducing him to Gracie, the wife he shared with Jax McDonald—and for *that* he would be forever grateful.

Chapter Seventeen

T AZ LEANED BACK against the bathroom counter waiting for Kodi to finish her shower. They'd let her sleep as late as possible this morning, but she was pushing their schedule too far at this point. He wasn't as anal about punctuality as Nate—whose blood pressure was probably nearing stroke range. Like any former soldier, he liked to be punctual. Taz was sure Kodi hadn't heard him enter the large bathroom, because she was still talking to herself in the large shower.

"I can't believe they aren't letting me wear my dress in the limo. It's not like I'm going to spill chocolate milk on it or anything. Geez. And where am I supposed to get dressed when we get there? On the sidewalk in front of the Morgan's house? Holy hand job, maybe I'll just show up in my birthday suit and see if anybody notices."

"They'd notice, I assure you." Taz spoke loud enough that she couldn't help but hear him. "We promised to explain everything when the time was right, but you're never going to find out if you don't get your sweet ass out of the shower and finish getting ready. You now have twelve minutes, sweet cheeks. Best get a move on. This isn't a party you want to show up to with your ass cheeks already crimson and burning with residual fire, which is exactly what will happen if Nate comes in here."

She appeared in the doorway of the shower, and he handed her a towel. Watching her lean forward to wrap her hair was another in a long list of ways she tested his control. Seeing her plump breasts sway made his cock sit up and take immediate notice. He stepped forward with a second towel and began brushing it lightly over her back, paying particular attention to the fleshy globes of her ass. Giving her a quick swat, he moved to the door.

"Ten minutes and then you will be leaving this apartment, ready or not. So, I suggest you don't waste any time. Landon has already taken your dress and shoes to the limo. We'll be waiting in the living room with the coat you'll wear downstairs." When she stood staring at him instead of moving, he leaned close, swatting her again, this one harder than the first. That was all it took to startle her into action. He smiled when the outline of his palm bloomed in pink on her ass. *That's going to be an interesting conversation starter when we get to the limo.*

Walking into the living room, Taz smiled when his brother tapped his watch—a clear gesture of impatience. "I can't believe you still wear a watch."

"How the hell else am I supposed to know what time it is? Pull my phone out of my pocket and activate it whenever I want to check the time?"

"That *is* what most people do, Nate." Holding up his hand to stay the argument he knew was coming, Taz laughed. "I know, I know. You aren't most people. And wearing a watch saves you at least five minutes each day which adds up to eighteen hundred and twenty-five minutes a year."

"Fucking A. That's over thirty hours. I can think of a lot more pleasurable ways to spend that much time, especially now." The gleam in Nate's eyes made it abundantly clear how his brother planned to use all those extra minutes. "Yes, indeed. Some very interesting options have recently come to my attention."

"And speaking of Kodi, she has exactly three minutes to make an appearance. After that, she's all yours. But let me warn you she's already gotten two swats, one of which I'm sure will still be a lovely shade of pink when she finally makes an appearance." He saw Nate grin as he moved to the sofa to retrieve the trench coat they'd left draped over the back. They'd also gotten her a lower pair of heels to wear in case they felt like dancing.

He'd learned a long time ago how much those cowboys liked wrapping their women in their arms and leading them around the dance floor. Grinning, he thought back on the times he'd watched them make a woman come apart in their arms just by whispering in their ears without missing a God damned step.

Taz knew Kodi was expecting a regular limousine. He could hardly wait to see the look on her face when she realized how spacious the interior of the Hummer was—and how they'd planned to utilize the open area.

Hearing Nate's soft laughter, Taz turned just in time to see Kodi skid to a stop beside them. "I didn't get to dry my hair, so it's going to curl and be crazy-assed wavy." Damn, he loved the little pout of her lips.

"We told you to leave it natural for a reason, baby. And I like what you've done with the front." *I hope you can re-do that in the limo before we get there, because I can assure you we're going to mess it up.* "Is that your make-up bag? Did you bring a brush?"

"Yes and yes. Geez, I'm not a third grader, you know. I can actually follow instructions."

Nate growled. "Is that so? Well, then. Turn around and

bend over the back of the sofa, Ayasha. I'm going to show you what happens to submissives who sass their Doms." Taz saw her breath catch, but she leaned over the sofa's back, bracing her hands on the seat cushion. "Spread your legs, pet. You'll get an extra swat because I had to remind you."

Pulling the jeweled plug from his pocket, Nate handed it to Taz. "Get this ready. I think we'll put it in before we go downstairs. Maybe we'll tuck the back of her coat under the belt and make a detour through the club. I'm sure our sassy sub would love to show off her new jewelry." Taz heard another hitch in her breathing, the soft intake of air signaling arousal with a side of apprehension. *Perfect.*

After six quick swats, she was soaking wet. Hell, they wouldn't even have to use the packet of lube in his pocket. Taz only needed to fuck her gently with the plug to make it slick with her sweet cream. Her ass cheeks were hot to the touch and a lovely shade of scarlet, but she hadn't made a sound during her punishment. Nate had used his fingers to stretch her pretty ass, and Taz slid the plug into place without much resistance. They'd chosen a small plug because she didn't have any experience with anal play. Taz was willing to bet Nate would grab the next larger plug when he returned to their room to wash his hands.

By the time Nate walked back into the living room, Taz had gotten Kodi into her coat and tucked the back up so her well-paddled ass was beautifully framed to draw attention to her throbbing backside. Sitting wasn't going to be pleasant, but he had a feeling walking through the club was going to be worse than the spanking. There weren't any club members downstairs at this time of day, but the cleaning crew would be around. And they weren't likely to miss the show she was about to give them.

Standing in the elevator, Taz saw her cast furtive glances at Nate, who hadn't missed her nervousness. "Do you have something to say, pet?"

"Yes, Sir. I wanted to say I'm sorry. I didn't mean to start our day off on the wrong foot."

"Apology accepted, but you are still going to walk through the club. Let it serve as an additional lesson, because I assure you, next time you'll get that spanking in front of the entire club." Taz bit back his laughter when he saw her fidget and press her legs together as she tried to hide the moisture he was sure coated her swollen nether lips.

When they stepped out the back door, Nate pulled Kodi to a stop. Landon moved from the back of the limo and smiled. Taz would bet he'd already gotten a call from the bartender inside the club. Nate turned Kodi so her bare ass was on full display for the passengers inside the limo before instructing her to spread her legs. This time her response was slightly delayed, but Taz knew it wasn't disobedience. No, this delay was because her brain was fogged with arousal.

Nate reached forward, and Taz watched his fingers slide through the wet folds. He made several passes before she swayed on her feet. When Nate pulled his fingers back, they were wet with her cream. He licked them clean as Kodi's eyes widened, the pupils dilating beautifully. "I do believe our woman enjoys being displayed more than we first believed, brother. I think this is something we're definitely going to have fun exploring." Nodding to the vehicle, he added, "She drops the coat at the door. Let's go."

KODI WAS CERTAIN her legs were going to fold out from under her. She'd only gotten halfway through the club's main room when the plug in her ass started vibrating. She stumbled; Nate and Taz had each grabbed an arm to steady her, but they hadn't slowed their pace. Watching Landon step out of the biggest vehicle she'd ever seen brought her up short. *This is the limo they were talking about? Holy fucking hellions, I can only imagine what they've got planned. It's huge.*

When she was finally reached the limo's door, she was shaking. It wasn't fear or the crisp temperature. It was arousal and anticipation. Landon looked down at her and smiled. "Sweetie, it looks like you've already gotten a head start. I'm looking forward to hearing what sort of mischief you've gotten into so early this morning."

"Hand Master Landon your coat, baby. He'll put it with your other clothing." Kodi knew Landon Nixon was a Master at the club, but this was the first time she'd interacted with him as a Dominant. Her only contact with him was as a co-worker...one whose teasing made her shift fun night after night. Taking a deep breath, she tried to focus her attention on the task, because there wasn't any doubt in her mind this was a test.

Her fingers were trembling so much Kodi was having trouble with the buttons. In her peripheral vision, she saw Taz give Landon a quick nod, and immediately, his fingers moved hers aside. "Let me help you, sweetness. There's no reason for you to stand out here with the cool breeze blowing over you pretty pink ass any longer than necessary. And I'm anxious to get back inside before Karl and

Tally start without me."

Kodi knew Landon was the other couple's third, but doubted the true nature of their relationship was common knowledge outside of the club. As a United States' Senator, Karl Tyson's reputation required a certain level of decorum. Having his kink made public would shatter the bright political future everyone saw was on the horizon for Montana's rising Washington star. She'd been curious about the dynamics of their triad, but had never been brave enough to ask questions.

Her coat opened and slid down her arms, the chill dancing over her skin tightening her nipples to rigid points. "Those are a lovely shade of pink, and much as I would enjoy looking my fill here in the sunlight, we need to get you somewhere a lot warmer." Stepping to the side, he cupped her elbow and moved her inside. She knew her bare ass was on display as she stepped inside and wondered which one of the men had moaned.

Tally looked at her with concerned eyes. "Oh damn, girl. How'd they find out? Well, fuckle sticks, nothing stays a secret around here." It took Kodi several seconds to hear anything over the thundering of her heart pounding in her ears. She heard the door close behind her and felt the tinge of pain when her tender backside settled on the blanket covered seat. The limo was in motion, but Kodi barely registered the shifting as the driver maneuvered the large vehicle out of the parking area behind the club.

Tally's stricken expression was filled with apology when she saw the horrified look on Kodi's face. Her pretty blue eyes were shining with unshed tears of sympathy. Kodi saw her mouth the words "I'm sorry" but wasn't sure if they'd been spoken aloud because she couldn't hear anything over the rapid beat of her heart. Black dots danced in her vision, and she shot a quick glance to the door handle, contemplating an escape before they were moving fast enough to cause her much harm.

"Don't even think about it, baby." Taz's voice was laced with steel despite the endearment, and Kodi felt herself sway as the dots dancing in her vision began to merge into large masses of darkness.

Nate picked her up and, in one fluid motion, settled her on his lap. She felt his fingers grip her chin, but that was the last thing she remembered before he sealed his lips over hers and blew air into her lungs. The sudden infusion of oxygen cleared her vision, and his concerned face slowly came into view. She pulled in a deep breath followed by another before realizing she was now reclining in his arms. "Breathing is not optional, Ayasha. Though I've done breath-play on occasion, it isn't something I particularly enjoy."

Kodi didn't respond...What could she possibly say? Her cheeks heated with embarrassment. When she tried to look away, his fingers held her still, forcing her to look into his eyes. "Don't you dare look away from me. Talk. Right fucking now." She gasped as his wool coat rasped against her abused bottom, sending sparks of need through her body despite her precarious perch.

"Perhaps Tally would like to explain. She seems to be privy to information she's failed to disclose to her Dom as well." Kodi heard the frustration in Karl Tyson's voice, but she made no attempt to shift her attention from Nate.

"God, Kodi, I'm so sorry. I saw your pink tush and assumed you'd told them about Brinn and they were just annoyed because you hadn't said anything sooner." Kodi could hear the anguish in Tally's voice. The sweet doctor had once told her one of the biggest downsides of being a doctor was her lack of free time and a social life. She'd lamented her lack of female friends, and Kodi had understood because writing seemed to isolate her, as well.

Kodi took a deep breath and tried to hold back her sigh. *Damn it to flaming donuts, how do I manage to get myself in so many pickles without even trying? It's really an amazing skill if you think about it. Might as well spill it since it's too late to jump out now. Asphalt and naked...not a good combination. And add in the cold? No, thanks.*

Taz's snort of laughter made her stiffen in Nate's arms. He turned her chin and smiled. "Yes, baby, you are in a pickle for sure. Now out with it. What happened with Brinn?"

It didn't take Kodi and Tally long to recount the incident in the bathroom. And despite Kodi's protests that it hadn't been a big deal, she could see the fury in Taz and Nate's eyes. Landon was also fuming while Karl's frustration seemed directed at his petite wife. "Tally, we've been over this." When she started to protest, his hand went up in a gesture clearly indicating she'd better remain silent. "There's no HIPPA shield for you to hide behind this time, so spare yourself the added swats. And since I'm too incensed to do it safely myself, you'll drape yourself over Master Landon's lap right now and submit to whatever he feels is appropriate."

As Tally moved into position, Nate turned Kodi so her back was pressed against his chest. "Spread your legs. Put them on the outsides of my knees and wrap your feet around the back of my calves. You'll remain open to Master Landon's and Master Karl's view and watch Tally take her punishment for keeping your secret. Remember, you asked her to remain silent, so you're partially responsible for the paddling she's going to get."

Nate's words weren't spoken harshly, but the effect was devastating. Kodi had never been the cause of anyone else's pain, and the thought felt like a kick to the gut. Watching Landon smooth his hand over the curves of Tally's ass while accepting the flexible ruler Karl placed in his other hand was both frightening and wildly erotic. Knowing Karl trusted his friend to administer Tally's punishment spoke volumes about the depth and scope of their relationship.

The first question about the men's sexuality filtered through her mind a split second before Taz leaned close to whisper in her ear. "No, baby, they are both as straight as my brother and I are. We don't judge others for their preferences, but men just don't do it for any of us. They are both solely focused on Tally, just as Nate and I are focused on you." As unnerved as she was that Taz had heard the question in her head, she found herself grateful for his answer. Realizing this was the first time his empathic gift had played out to her benefit, she turned enough to give him a grateful smile.

You're welcome, baby. Before she could focus on what she'd heard, the loud slap of the ruler striking Tally's tender ass filled the limo, drawing Kodi's attention back to the scene playing out only a few feet in front of her. Tally gasped in pain, but the soft moan that followed let Kodi know Landon was holding back.

Kodi had seen Master Landon administer punishments in the club with a variety of implements and never envied the submissive on the receiving end of his expertise. Tally wasn't going to sit comfortably for a few hours, but this punishment wasn't as severe as Kodi had feared it might be.

"You can breathe now, Ayasha. Master Landon isn't

going to push her too far. He knows Tally isn't a masochist. She doesn't enjoy pain for pain's sake, and he'd never betray the trust of either of his friends by taking her beyond her limits."

Karl must have heard Nate's reassurance, because he shifted his attention to her. Kodi was always surprised at the intensity she saw in his eyes. A deep river ran beneath his cool exterior. "This is an issue we've addressed before, Kodi. My lovely wife often has trouble drawing a line between her responsibilities as a physician and the rules she needs to follow as a sexual submissive. Fortunately, Landon is well-versed in ways to remind her, since he does so regularly when I'm in DC."

She'd often wondered if there were any boundaries drawn between the three when Master Karl was away from home, and now she was even more curious about how their unique relationship worked. Hopefully, her friendship with Tally survived this test, and she'd get a chance to hear more about the arrangement.

Karl's eyes moved over her, his perceptive look taking in every inch before sliding slowly back up with laser sharpness. "I'm not sure watching this is as much of a punishment as your Masters thought it would be, little sub. Your pussy is flooding with arousal, your eyes are dilated, and even from here, I can hear your soft panting breaths." She felt Nate's arms tighten around her as his fingers slid effortlessly through her slick folds.

Landon's eyes lifted from where his hand now caressed Tally's abused flesh. His gaze focused between Kodi's legs. "Make her come." *Damn him.* He knew exactly how embarrassing it was going to be for her, the rat bastard.

"Careful, baby. You're already in enough trouble." Letting out a frustrated sigh, Kodi held her response to Taz's comment to herself.

I take back what I said earlier about the possibility of a good side to this mind reading thing.

Chapter Eighteen

B RINN HID ON the hill behind the club and watched Nate and Taz lead Kodi out of the backdoor. Evidently, little Miss Perfect had managed to piss the two Dom's off because her ass was fire engine red. She recognized Landon Nixon's Hummer limo and only had a minute to wonder if he was accompanying them. As soon as the man she'd once dated stepped from the back of the limo, she knew Karl and Tally Tyson were inside.

Landon had dropped Brinn like a hot rock when he'd begun acting as the Senator and doctor's third. As angry as she'd been, Brinn had appreciated the fact he'd been brutally honest rather than stringing her along. She'd hoped their relationship would work out. Not because their kinks were particularly compatible—they weren't— but the Nixons were loaded. Second and third generation wealth, which in Montana was tantamount to *old money*. In her opinion, Landon didn't appreciate the perks of his family's money nearly as much as he should.

She'd been born on the wrong side of the tracks. Her dad's singular claim to fame was ridding himself of his wife and infant daughter at the first opportunity. Brinn's mother had taken little interest in the daughter she blamed for losing her meal ticket. She'd preferred the never-ending parade of men sharing her bed to paying attention to the young girl she'd brought into the world. For her part, Brinn kept her nose clean and her grades up, because she'd known college was going to be her escape.

God knew her mother couldn't fund her education, so Brinn diligently applied for every scholarship available and worked two jobs to pay for her way through college. It had been a long five years, but she'd finally walked away with a Master's Degree in Engineering. graduated. Unfortunately, she'd quickly discovered graduating with honors didn't necessarily mean honorably employed. Once things with Landon Nixon fell through, she'd re-set her sights on the Ledek brothers. Since their kink wasn't as harsh as their friend's, it would be easier to fake submission during scenes. It had taken her a while to find out the extent of their personal wealth, but she'd been pleasantly surprised when she'd finally managed to hack into the club's server.

Using her binoculars to scan the area as the Ledeks and Landon moved Kodi inside the Hummer, a glint of sunlight higher up the hill caught Brinn's attention. Turning, she gasped when she saw a man approximately thirty yards from her. He was also watching the club, but he was using a high-power scope mounted on a wicked looking black rifle. She wasn't well versed in guns, but the thing looked enormous. When he began moving slowly, skimming over his surroundings as she'd done, Brinn dropped to the ground. Flattening her body as much as possible, she prayed the thick shrubbery would conceal her from his view.

She heard the Hummer's souped-up engine roar off as the driver accelerated out of the driveway. Brinn assumed the group was on their way to Morgan's party, but since she couldn't see which way they'd turned, she couldn't be sure. She'd heard the club scuttlebutt about the party, but she hadn't been invited. Cold quickly seeped through her clothing, making her shiver. Waiting was terrifying, her imagination running completely amok. She'd never seen the man before and hoped she never saw him again.

The question burning in the back of her mind was who the man had been watching. In the end, it didn't really matter, but she was still curious. As near as Brinn could tell, the Hummer held a U.S. Senator, a well-liked physician, a wealthy local hot shot entrepreneur, two former SEALs, and a homeless waitress. Since her least favorite among them was also the least likely target, she wouldn't wait. She'd give them a heads-up as soon as she could. *Who am I kidding? I couldn't ignore a threat to anyone, even Kodi. I may not like her, but I'd still help her out...probably.*

NATE WAS FURIOUS they were just now hearing about Brinn's comments, but he had to admit, in some ways, he understood Kodi's reluctance to involve them. She was obviously used to fending for herself with what was evidently only intermittent help from her older brother. Aside from working in a kink club, she didn't have any previous experience as a sexual submissive. He doubted she fully understood how important it was to them to know she was safe—and how broad their definitions of *safe* and *protection* were.

It appeared Karl and Landon were holding Tally accountable since she'd been the one to interact with Brinn. She'd been in the lifestyle long enough to know she should have shared the information, especially since she'd walked right past him as she'd left the locker room. But Nate also appreciated her loyalty to Kodi. One of the things he'd learned over the years he'd been a Dom was the way submissives usually stuck together like glue. It made perfect sense, after all. Doms worked together to keeps subs in line. He doubted either of the women had many friends and understood why Tally would want to honor Kodi's request.

Pulling her back against his chest, Nate whispered over her shoulder. "Very soon, my brother and I will earn your trust, Ayasha. You'll feel confident enough to bring this sort of thing to us." She shifted on his lap, and he bit back a groan when the plug in her ass pressed against his erection. He knew the moment she felt his rigid length pushing against her sweet cheeks because she froze. "Yes, pet, that's all for you. And I can feel the need pouring off you in waves. We'll always give you exactly what your body is craving, but you may not always agree with our timeline."

Taz shifted around the corner of the seat so he could watch Kodi's facial expressions. Nate saw fire burning in his brother's eyes. Someday, he hoped Taz would be able to provide him a running narrative of what their woman was thinking as his fingers slid lazily through the slick folds of Kodi's labia. "You're so wet, Ayasha. So very ready for what we are more than willing to give you." Using the tip of his finger to circle her clit, Nate felt her hips tilt forward into his touch.

Whispering against her ear, Nate asked, "Did you see how Tally lifted her ass to meet each stroke? Her body no longer processed the pain; it's all pleasure at this point. She is floating in sub-space, but they'll bring her back down before taking her together." Kodi's head fell back against Nate's shoulders, and he knew she was getting dangerously close to coming from the bombardment of her sense. Being displayed intimately, their touch, and his words were setting him up perfectly to send her over quickly.

Landon's commanding voice telling him to make her come told Nate the other man was close to losing his own battle with control. Watching him finger fuck Kodi to orgasm was buying Landon a few minutes to pull himself back from the edge. Nodding, Nate gave him a wolfish grin. "My pleasure."

The first plunge of his fingers inside her sheath made the most deliciously wet sound. Nate heard Taz curse under his breath. "Fuck, that's hot." His brother lowered himself in front of Kodi in a move so quick Nate doubted she'd even noticed. Taz's training in the various martial arts was reflected in every move he made. Despite the fact he was over six and a half feet tall, Taz moved as stealthily as a jungle cat. Nate moved his hand aside a split second before Taz's mouth descended between Kodi's spread legs. Her entire body jerked as Taz used his tongue to fuck her with long, sure strokes.

Nate pinched her nipples as he spoke against her ear. "Come for us, Ayasha. Let yourself go. We'll always be there to catch you." Her response was immediate. A shrill wail filled the Hummer, and Kodi's back arched in a show of strength he hadn't anticipated. Worried he would hurt her if he forced her back against his chest, Nate just held her steady while Taz wrapped his arms around her calves, preventing her continued slide off his lap.

Kodi shuddered in his arms as the last tremors of her release pulsed through her lax muscles. Taz had moved once again, pressing his mouth against hers as he pulled her from Nate's arms into his own. Nate was grateful for the shift, because his cock was ready to explode just from having her pressed against him. Sucking in several deep breaths, he wondered when Taz had managed to shed his clothes. Looking around, he noted the other men were naked as well. *Christ, where have I been?*

Don't know, brother, but this party is going to be over far too soon. If you want to play, you'd better get with it. Taz didn't need to tell him twice. Nate was out of his clothing before Taz finished lowering Kodi onto his cock. He'd turned her so she was on her hands and knees on the Hummer's carpeted floor. Her luscious lips were swollen from Taz's kiss and her eyes were still glazed from the orgasm they'd just given her. Nate stroked himself until the first beads of pearly pre-cum appeared at his tip. Moving closer, he smiled when Kodi unconsciously licked her lips in anticipation.

"I'm going to fuck your sweet mouth while your other Master takes his pleasure from your pussy. Don't come until one of us gives your permission, or you'll find sitting very unpleasant for a few days, pet." Nate saw Taz's eyes roll up and knew she'd clamped down like a vice on his brother's cock. *God dammit, Nate, she's already pulsing around me.*

"Baby, you're going to have to rein yourself in, or you're going to be over my knee getting another spanking your tender ass doesn't need right now."

Kodi pulled in several gasping breaths before finally pushing the words "Yes, Sir" past her pouty lips. Taz nodded, and Nate slid his aching cock between her lips.

Looking to the side, he smiled when he saw Karl lounging back on the seat as he shoved Tally down on his rigid length. Her hands were bound tightly against in her chest in a hastily tied harness. Both breasts were fully exposed, and Tally's Master was feasting on them as Landon drizzled a generous amount of lube between her flaming red ass cheeks. "I'm going to fuck this hot little ass, Tally. When I push inside, you're going to be so full of our cocks you'll lose your mind. We're going to give Kodi a little preview of coming attractions. Let her see the soul-shattering pleasure that's in her future."

Taz leaned down and bit her shoulder hard enough to make her shudder. "You feel so good, baby. I swear your tight little pussy is pulling me deeper with every breath you take. And from the look on Nate's face, I'd say he's found his own little piece of heaven."

Her tongue slid along the sensitive crease at the base of his cockhead and Nate sucked in a deep breath. "I want you to come with us. When you feel us marking you with our seed, let go and enjoy the ride."

Kodi's mouth tightened around him as he pushed to the back of her throat. When she swallowed, he wavered so close to the edge Nate worried he was going to come before Taz was ready to take her over again. He was ready to pull back when he heard Taz's voice in his head. *I'm going and taking her with me.* Those seven words were all it took to send fire bursting from his balls and sending his seed streaming down Kodi's throat in hot pulses. She swallowed frantically while her own orgasm thundered through her. Taz's shout was followed by Kodi's scream around Nate's cock. He backed off, letting her pull in shuddering gulps of air. Nate wrapped one of the club's soft subbie blankets around Kodi's trembling shoulders and helped settle her on Taz's lap. Pulling bottles of water from the small fridge, he opened Kodi's before handing it to Taz.

Leaning back, Nate watched the scene taking place at the other end of the limo. His attention drifted between the heat generated between his three friends and the tender aftercare his brother was lavishing on the woman who'd just stolen the last pieces of his heart. Any final reservations he'd been holding on to about her being *the one* for them evaporated into a fine mist. She hadn't hesitated during their ménage scene; her responses to Nate and his brother were equal in every way.

One of the issues Nate and Taz always faced with a sub they'd shared was the way they responded to each man differently. It was a simple truth that women tended to respond to one of them more than the other. It was also something that would never work in a permanent relationship. They'd talked extensively with their friends involved in polyamorous relationships; both the men and women all cited this as the single most important issue, second only to a commitment to open and honest communication.

Relaxing back into the seat, Nate watched as Karl pushed himself into his wife's wet pussy in alternating thrusts as Landon stroked into her ass. Their pace was slowly driving the whimpering sub insane, but Nate had to bite back a grin at the pained looks on the men's faces. They might be pushing Tally's boundaries, but she was testing their control in equal measure. As the trio's tempo increased, so did Kodi's interest. Taz's soft words sent a flush over her cheeks, and Nate almost laughed out loud since he could well imagine how graphic his brother's narration was.

Damn straight it's graphic. Don't want her wondering all evening what we have planned. After all, this is a play party.

Chapter Nineteen

B RINN WALKED INTO the club's main room and scanned the area hoping she'd be able to figure out which one of the Dungeon Monitors Nate and Taz had left in charge. She'd tried to call Landon earlier, but all her calls had gone to voice mail. Obviously, the pig-licker had been serious when he'd told her he would no longer accept her calls. She didn't have Nate or Taz's private contact information. Their personal cell numbers were a closely guarded secret by the few people she knew actually had them. Hell, she could probably score the President's number before one of the Ledek's inner circle would give up theirs.

Before she gotten back to her apartment, Brinn made the mistake of answering her phone. Being called back into the small engineering firm where she worked was unusual on Saturdays. Since she was the most junior consultant on the project, she'd gotten the call. It had taken her the rest of the day to re-do the drawing and complete the scans. It was still early by club standards, but she couldn't shake her concern about what she'd seen earlier.

What Brinn didn't know was how she could explain why she'd been watching the club. That wasn't going to be easy, nor was it a point that would be left out of the discussion. There'd been several times during the day when she'd considered remaining silent. But she'd always gotten a sinking feeling, one that seemed too much like a glimpse of how she'd feel if something happened to any of the people involved. Dammit, her conscience was playing havoc with her plans to make the Ledek brothers see how perfect she was for them.

Sliding onto a bar stool, Brinn waited for Randy to notice her. Landon's backup bartender was a sub to one of the club's more popular Dommes. Mistress Ann wasn't known for letting him out of her sight, so Brinn was surprised to see him tending bar. Landon had obviously struck a deal with the woman highly regarded in local circles for her legal prowess. Brinn had heard horror stories from people who'd had to face her in court. Before Randy made his way to her, a man Brinn had never seen before slid onto the stool next to hers.

Brinn looked up into the darkest eyes she'd even seen and gasped at the intensity of his gaze. The corners of his lips lifted ever so slightly, as if he was well accustomed to the effect he had on women. Brinn fought the urge to drop her gaze, and his soft chuckle made her wonder if the struggle was obvious. "Darlin', you don't know me, so I won't demand you lower your eyes, but I'm betting there are a lot of Doms in this club who aren't as accommodating."

"Are you new? I haven't seen you here before." The tremor in her voice betrayed her nerves, but she kept her eyes focused on his.

"I stopped by to visit with a couple of old friends, but it seems I've missed them. Thankfully, I was on a list of potential guests, so I was able to come in and have a drink." His eyes moved over her conservative clothing, and once again, his brow quirked in question. "You don't seem dressed for an evening in a kink club, despite the obvious fact you're a submissive." He paused for a few seconds then grinned. "Though I'm guessing you are only submissive to a very few Doms. You're far too strong-willed to submit to a Dom who fails to prove himself worthy of the gift."

Whoever he was, he'd seen in seconds what most Doms at Mountain Mastery had yet to understand. Brinn couldn't submit to a Dom who failed to prove himself. If he was willing to settle for less than total surrender, she wasn't interested. Most of the Doms she'd played with had either failed miserably or they were much too aggressive, which was equally unappealing. Unable to find her voice, Brinn simply nodded. The small frown lines between his brows reminded her of mistake, and she quickly added her verbal assent.

"If you aren't here to play, what brings you into a kink club this early in the evening?" His inquiry didn't offend her, because he seemed to be genuinely interested in nothing more than conversation.

"I need to contact Master Nate and Master Taz." When he didn't respond, Brinn shifted in her seat. Damn, she hated it when Doms used silence to get information. It always made her chatter like a damned magpie. "I saw something strange this morning behind the club, and I think they should know about it."

"Strange? Define strange, little bird." She wasn't sure if being called a little bird was an endearment or some Freudian bull shit about her singing like a bird.

Mentally shrugging, Brinn looked around to make sure no one was close enough to overhear her before returning her attention to the man sitting beside her. "There was a man on the hill behind the club this morning with a rifle."

Before she could say any more, he stood and pulled her

to her feet. "I think we need to take this discussion some-place more private." When she tried to jerk her arm from his grip, he shook his head. "We aren't leaving this room, little bird. But I don't want to miss anything you're going to say, and there are too many distractions surrounding the bar." She finally nodded and let him lead her to one of the more secluded sitting areas. Brinn was unnerved when she realized he knew exactly where he was going. It made her wonder how long he'd been in the club before she ar-rived…and who he'd been there to meet.

KOI HAD A sinking feeling the little sub he was leading across the room was about to confirm his worst fear. The one man who was supposed to stand between Koi and the enemy, who'd sworn to always put his safety first, had become the enemy. And since handlers were typically retired agents—someone who had been in the field—they understood, better than anyone else could, the critical role they played in a field agent's success or failure. They also knew their agent's weakest points. Cases of them being *turned* were rare, but not unheard of.

"What's your name, little bird?"

"Brinn." He saw her eyes dart from side to side. *Smart girl, make sure you know exactly where all the escape routes are. I'd paddle your ass if you belonged to me for not putting up a fight and letting a stranger pull you away from the view of everyone else in the room.*

"It's nice to meet you, Brinn. My name is Koi, and I assure you the club's owners would give you permission to talk to me. We were all Navy SEALs and worked together a few times. I'm here because I had safety concerns related to…one of their club members. So, I'd appreciate you sharing what you saw this morning that caused you to make a special trip to the club to warn them." He watched her carefully, surprised at the assessing look she was giving him. Her eyes chocolate colored eyes shone with intelligence as she weighed his words.

"When is the last time you talked to Master Nate or Master Chaz?"

Good girl, make sure you know who you're dealing with before giving them what you obviously consider important information. He wasn't offended she'd just tested him. Koi would allay her fears a simply as possible.

"I haven't spoken to either Nathanial or *Tashunka* personally for a couple of years." He gave her a quick nod, when she grinned at his correction. "But we have communicated by email several times over the past year and a half." And wasn't that a point his little sister was going to be thrilled to learn? "I'm here because Kyle and Kent West from the Prairie Winds Club in Texas are also in Montana. I wanted to address my concerns here before meeting with them on Monday. I'm early, so no one was expecting me." He could see she was still trying to decide whether or not she should trust him.

"I've heard club members mention the Prairie Winds Club, but I…well, damn. It's a given I'm going to probably make the wrong call here." He watched her chew on her thumbnail, wanting to smile at the nervous *tell* that revealed so much. He was confident he'd won the battle when she took a deep breath and squared her shoulders. "Okay. Here's the deal."

Koi listened for several minutes while Brinn recounted in surprising detail what she'd seen. She answered all his questions with clear, concise responses and without any hint of deception. And damned if she hadn't described his handler perfectly.

She waited patiently while he typed and sent several messages. It wasn't until he returned his attention to her and asked why she'd been on the hill watching the club that he saw her close down. She wouldn't meet his gaze, and he was sure anything she told him from this point forward was only going to be half true, if that.

He finally grew tired of watching her look everywhere but at him. Gently gripping her chin, he held her still. "Don't doubt for minute I'll paddle your ass if you lie to me, little bird. I've been a Dom a long time, and I'll know—even if it's a lie by omission. You have three options. One, you tell me the truth. Two, you lie and accept the punishment you'll have earned. Or three, use your safe word and then answer to Nate and Taz when they return. So, what's it going to be?"

"Easy to see why you are friends with the Ledeks. You're probably friends with Brandt and Ryan Morgan, too. Geez."

Koi bit the insides of his cheeks to keep from laughing out loud, because she was right. They'd all worked together, and their shared interest in the BDSM lifestyle had bonded them as friends, even though they hadn't seen each other in a long time.

"Which of the men are you interested in? And what or who is standing in your way?" Koi knew he'd nailed it when her eyes widened in surprise before going glassy with unshed tears. He wasn't surprised that he was right, but he was shocked when she launched herself into his arms and started babbling about some guy named Landon rejecting her, the Ledeks not giving her the time of day, and how hurt she'd been by their interest in Kodi, That revelation didn't surprise him, because he'd suspected Kodi's story about how much she enjoyed her job had been a cover. It had been obvious she had more than monetary reasons for wanting to return to Montana.

What did surprise him was Brinn's confession about a confrontation with another submissive in the locker room when she'd been talking disrespectfully about his little sister. The only thing that kept him from walking away from her was his suspicion her snark was born of frustration rather than any true disdain for the woman she saw as competition. Koi could remember anyone who actually disliked Kodi. She'd always been one of those annoying people that didn't seem to have any real faults—something he'd often teased her about.

When Brinn was finally finished spilling the story, he didn't try to hold back his smile. Shaking his head, he stood up and set her on her feet. After drying her tears with his handkerchief, he asked, "Have you eaten?" His question seemed to surprise her, but she recovered quickly and shook her head. "Let's go. I'm hungry, and you're familiar with the area. We'll get something to eat and chat. If you're uncomfortable riding with me, I'll follow you. I'm not asking for anything other than your company at dinner, and I'll be happy to bring you back here so you can be sure I didn't follow you home." When she blinked at him in confusion, he laughed and took her hand. "Brinn, I have a sister about your age. I'm helping you stay safe, just as I've taught her to keep herself safe."

Taking her hand in his, Koi led her to the door. He was worried about the man she'd seen behind the club, but there wasn't anything to do about it just now. If his suspicions were right, the man was after Koi, not Kodi. His handler had baited the trap with his questions about his only sibling, knowing Koi would make a bee-line to check on her. What he hadn't counted on was being spotted by a snoopy sub.

CAILA LOOKED AROUND the room and grinned. All four of her sisters-in-law were chattering among themselves, and she couldn't help but remember the last time they'd all been together in this room. Three of her four future sisters-in-law had been pregnant, as in really, really pregnant. She'd had her own pregnancy scare a few months earlier, but it had turned out to be a false alarm. Caila still shuddered at the thought. It wasn't that she didn't want children, because she did. But she also wanted to wait and enjoy a little bit of time alone with Kip before they started a family.

"You know what frosts my ass?" Coral's voice sounded above the rest, and Caila turned her attention to the woman who'd captured the heart of the oldest Morgan brother. "The three of you have already gotten your pre-pregnancy bodies back. How is that possibly fair?"

"What did she say? I swear if I have to hear her whine about this again I'm going to take a flogger to her myself." Even when she was pretending to be annoyed with her best friend, Josie's beautiful voice couldn't be masked. Caila was still in awe that the woman the rest of the world knew as world-famous pop singer Josephine Alta had been one of her bridesmaids. And now they were members of the same family.

"I'm not scared of you, Josie. Colt wouldn't ever let

you anywhere near the controlling end of a flogger. He's too smart to make that mistake." Coral dodged a hairbrush the songstress sent sailing across the room as laughter rang out around them. The two women had been friends since they were kids, and now that they were married to brothers, their bond was closer than ever.

Joelle Morgan leaned against the bed and grinned. "Damn, I love this family. Growing up as an only child, I always longed for sisters. This is exactly what I knew I was missing."

Coral looked up and started shaking her head. "Oh, really? You had visions of five sisters sitting around in skimpy ass clothing waiting for their Masters to tell them it was time for the kinky party games to begin?"

Caila giggled when the renowned scientist stuck out her tongue at Coral.

But it was Aspen who gave Joelle a friendly nudge with her elbow. "Come on. Let's get your hair braided. The guys will be here any minute, and we don't want you being scalped by the turbo-fuck-master machine." The five of them had given all the equipment in the play room colorful names, much to the dismay of their Doms. Aspen tied off the braid with an elastic band just as a heavy knock sounded on the door.

Coral's voice once again filled the room. "Come on, sisters-mine. It's show time."

Yeah, yeah. I have a feeling I'm going to be showing people a lot of myself tonight.

Chapter Twenty

NATE LEANED BACK in his chair, his steepled fingers pressed against his chin as he listened to Kyle West explain how they'd tracked down the elusive author of the hottest book he'd ever read. Phoenix and Micah filled in details Nate hadn't been particularly interested in until a comment Phoenix made had him sitting up to take notice. "Did you just say the club's server was hacked?"

Phoenix looked at him like he'd grown a second head. "Out of everything you were just told, that's the piece you're pissed about?"

"Hell yes. We can use the other information to our advantage—and we will. I'd been worried about how we could explain the fact we were unwitting heroes in a porn book."

"But that doesn't seem like it's going to be an issue now." Taz's smile was positively sinister, and Nate could hardly wait to find out what his brother was planning.

"What was the hacker after? Membership files? Medical records?" Nate's mind was spinning just thinking about the damage control they were going to have to do.

"Hell no! I have that stuff locked up better than Fort Knox." Phoenix had designed their computer system, and Nate breathed a huge sigh of relief knowing their most sensitive information was still secure. "No, whoever this was wanted something a lot more personal. The trail leads right to your financial portfolio and stops."

Nate must have looked as stunned as he felt, because he heard Kent West snort with laughter. "Talk about your Kodak moment. I would have sworn I'd never live long enough to see the unflappable Nate Ledek speechless. Damn, Phoenix, you've done what terrorists all over the world couldn't do."

"Many tried, and many died." Ryan Morgan's mocking tone made Nate want to swat the good doctor upside the head. Ry had been one of the best SEAL medics Nate had ever worked with. Nate had been thrilled to learn he'd gone back and finished his medical training. If he was half the doctor Nate figured he was, he'd draw patients from far and near to Pine Creek's rapidly expanding medical center.

"Smart ass." Returning his attention to Phoenix, he finally asked the obvious question. "Any idea who it was?" The shameless smile on the computer guru's face made Nate shake his head. "Okay, let me rephrase my question. Who was it?"

"The device is registered to Brinn Peters." A red haze of fury instantly colored Nate's vision. Phoenix held up his hand telling Nate there was more. "Keep in mind, she went to one file and backed out. My best guess is she was checking out your net worth."

"There's a fucking surprise." Landon's words dripped with his disdain for the woman who had just landed herself in another big pile of trouble.

"I'm not excusing what she did, but I want you to understand she didn't make any attempt to see anything else. I wasn't aware you were saving your personal files outside of the club's umbrella of security coverage." Phoenix gave him a look that let him know he thought Nate had been unnecessarily careless. "I've moved everything into the...oh hell, never mind, it won't affect how you access your files, so forget it. But the next time you set up something on your computer you don't want someone to see, text me, and I'll move it over for you."

Nate looked over at Taz, who shrugged. "Don't look at me. I use my laptop to play Minecraft and watch stupid shit on YouTube." The other men in the room chuckled, but Nate knew his brother wasn't kidding. If Taz had his way, they'd still be using paper checks and a ledger for their bookkeeping.

Micah Drake leaned over and pointed to something on the paper in front of Phoenix, earning a nod of agreement. Nate liked and respected Micah and trusted that anything he considered an issue needed to be addressed. Raising a brow in question, Nate looked at Micah and asked, "What have we missed?"

The Prairie Winds Club computer and security expert gave Nate a small smile before speaking. "I just wanted to say your lady's book is kicking ass. The bank account she told you about in Denver is where her royalties are being paid, and they are rolling in. I suspect that's why the bank is stalling on transferring the funds. They're earning a lot of interest on her money."

"No doubt about it. If your local banker can get that money transferred, she can trade in that junker she's driving." Phoenix grinned. "Caila will be happy to know she's been bumped out of the top spot for most unsafe vehicle." He laughed when his younger brother wadded up a sheet of paper he'd been holding and lobbed it across the room. Phoenix caught it easily, slam-dunking it into a nearby trash container. "That was the last piece of the puzzle, by the way."

Nate heard Taz ask "What do you mean?", giving voice to his own question.

"Her SUV is registered to Koi Meadows-Green, which by the way is the surname on both siblings' birth certificates. And did either of you two guys stop to think about what the name Keme meant?"

Holy fucking hell. How did we miss that?

Phoenix chuckled. "Yeah, that's what I figured."

Before he could finish, Sage Morgan cleared his throat. "Spill it, Mensa-boy. Not all of us are fucking brainiacs with photographic mind trap memories."

Shrugging off his older brother's sarcasm, Phoenix explained, "Keme is Algonquin for 'secret' or 'thunder.' I'm assuming her use of it in this context relates more to the *secret* connotation."

Sage rolled his eyes at his brother's deliberately over-inflated explanation. Nice to know he wasn't the only one with a younger brother who could be a pain in the ass.

Kyle West stood and directed his attention at Nate and Taz. "I've got to check on Kodi, so I'm going to step out and chat with her for a moment. I think we're the source of the inquiries that set off her brother's alerts, I still want to make sure everything is okay with our resident erotic author."

Nate felt himself bristle, but Taz's words drifted into his mind. *He is honoring a promise he made to Koi's brother. And you know Kyle always keeps his promises.*

Sensing Nate's opposition, Kyle's expression softened as he added, "Koi has always been intensely protective of his sister. From what I remember, their parents were less than thrilled when she came along and they were more than happy to leave her care to her ten-year-old brother. He'll only relinquish that role to a man, or men, he's sure are in it for the long haul."

The underlying message wasn't lost on Nate. Nodding his understanding, Nate watched Kyle walk from the room, his stride intent and filled with purpose.

"Don't worry. I'm going along to make sure he doesn't scare her. He's anxious to start the party. When business stalls pleasure, it fucks with his usually bright and charming personality."

For the first time since they'd been pulled into Sage's office for this sit-rep, Nate felt himself smile. As Kent followed his brother out, Nate sent up a silent prayer to the heavens asking for the wisdom to handle the coming confrontation with Kodi with patience and wisdom.

"You know, I'm damned impressed with our woman. That book is fucking hot and well written to boot. If she wrote it as a fantasy about the two of us, we've been given a peek into her deepest, darkest desires. Hell, most Doms would kill for this kind of insight"

A peek? Hell, it's a detailed road map. "True. And I for one do not intend to ignore perfectly good intel." Nate couldn't hold back his laughter. He hadn't realized how much he missed their silent connection until it had been restored.

"OH, SHIT. I'VE seen that look before." The pretty blonde's whispered words made the woman next to her giggle.

"I'm sure you have, Tobi. That's your Master's *I'm going to get to the bottom of this* look."

"And it usually involves my bottom."

Kodi had just been introduced to Tobi and Gracie a few

minutes ago, but she already liked them. They'd chatted about the shops at Mountain Mastery, and Kodi was fascinated when she learned about the updates the two women were planning. Their ideas were fresh and innovative, and Kodi was sure the changes would be well received by the club's members.

"Kodi, a word please?" Startled from her thoughts, Kodi realized the man Tobi and Gracie had been talking about was standing beside her. Looking up, she was shocked by the intensity of his gaze and almost overcome by the urge to run.

"Brother, you really need to work on your people skills."

Kodi blinked in surprise as another man moved to stand beside the one who'd just spoken to her. *Holy shit, they look exactly alike.* Kodi felt a blush warm her cheeks when she realized she hadn't responded.

The second man grinned. "We get that look a lot, darlin'. I'm Kent West, and this is my ugly brother, Kyle." He nodded to the side where the other man stood scowling at him. "We've heard from your brother and would like to talk to you about it if you have a minute."

Kodi was on her feet before he'd even finished speaking. She didn't know these men, but if they'd talked to Koi, she didn't want to miss the chance to hear what they had to say. "Is he okay?" She'd tried to hold back her rising panic, but it was easy to hear in her voice.

"He's fine, sweetie." The man who'd just introduced himself as Kent answered as he held out his hand to her. He smiled when she placed her hand in his, accepting his help maneuvering around the living room's furniture. Flashing a triumphant smile at his brother, Kent gloated, "See? You talk sweet and the ladies are much more cooperative. You treat them like soldiers and they launch directly into fight or flight mode, and then you have to chase them down. This is much easier."

Kodi wasn't sure, but she could have sworn she heard the other man snarl behind them.

Stepping into a long room filled with feminine furnishings and décor, Kodi found herself focused on the wall of windows facing the mountains. Everything about the room drew her in, from the soft yellow and blue colors of the pillows to the pictures of small girls decorating the walls. This was the private space of a wife and mother who needed time alone, but who would always surround herself with reminders of what was important. The large picture at the end of the long room caught her attention.

Kodi found herself standing in front of what appeared to be a wedding portrait...but the bride was surrounded by five men. She recognized the one standing directly behind the bride as Sage Morgan, he'd greeted them when they'd first arrived. She'd seen a couple of the others at the club, but the other two were strangers. Their affection for the woman standing inside their semi-circle made Kodi long for that kind of support.

"It's a great picture, isn't it? And I can tell you it shows how all five Morgan brothers feel about Sage's wife, Coral. She was the first to marry into their family, and she still holds a special place in all their hearts. You'll meet Coral and the other Morgan wives in a few minutes."

Kodi turned and smiled up at Kent. He'd stepped up beside her to look at the picture she'd been admiring. "Come on. Let's talk so we can get back to the others. I'm anxious to play with the little trouble magnet you were sitting across from in the living room."

Kodi let him lead her back to where his brother stood

waiting patiently. They spent the next few minutes recounting the messages they'd gotten from Koi and his concerns about her safety. They inquired about where she was staying and seemed relieved to learn she was living in the Ledek's secure apartment. Kyle was all business. His questions were direct, and there was no doubt he was studying her closely for any sign of deception. His abruptness didn't bother her now that she recognized the behavior for what it was—his years as a SEAL team leader had definitely left their mark on him.

She watched as Kyle seemed to relax, and when she saw him smile for the first time, she was startled by how much it changed his entire appearance. Neither of them missed her quick inhalation of surprise. "See, Kyle, this is what I've been preaching to you forever. You're such a hard ass people are actually shocked when you finally lighten up."

"But why would I give up seeing the surprise in their expressions? I live for that moment when subs realize I'm human." The sarcasm in Kyle's tone matched the teasing in Kent's, and Kodi couldn't hold back her laughter.

She'd barely stepped over the threshold before Nate and Taz surrounded her. "Come with us, Ayasha. We want to hear about your conversation with Kent and Kyle before we join the party." They led her to a small sun-drenched patio. Even though the small space was outside, it was sheltered and still warm despite the fading sunlight.

"Are you alright, baby?" Taz's question surprised her. Kodi had expected them to quiz her about what the West brothers had said to her.

"Yes, I'm fine. They were both very polite, though Kyle was a little intimidating at first. I appreciate that they were following up on my brother's request...at least he hasn't completely forgotten about me." She hadn't intended to say the last part aloud, but her brain evidently forgot to turn off the sound.

Taz pulled her into a crushing hug and kissed the top of her head. "Baby, he hasn't forgotten about you. Missions are messy sometimes, and often communication is possible, but too dangerous. Your brother felt safe communicating with the Kyle and Kent because he knows their phones and servers are secured."

Kodi mulled over his reassuring words and agreed it was certainly something her brother would consider. The problem was she'd made so many attempts to contact him. Had she compromised his safety or her own with her insistent messages and requests for help?

Jarring her out of her introspection, Nate turned her so she faced him. "Now, Ayasha. We have something else we'd like to mention before we rejoin the others."

"I'd advise you to think very carefully about your answers, baby. And keep in mind we were just in a meeting with two of the best hackers in the country." Taz's words might have sounded light hearted, but she'd heard the steel laced warning in them. Letting her gaze flicker between them, Kodi felt her heart accelerate as her over-active imagination kicked into high gear. What had she done now?

I swear to all things holy I could get into trouble sitting all alone in church.

TAZ STOOD BEHIND Kodi, pulling her back against his chest and enjoying the feel of her softness contrasting with his strength. He'd never relished his ability to protect a woman more than he did with Kodi. There was something about her that brought his inner Tarzan roaring to the surface stronger than it ever had before. He wrapped his arm around her, pressing against the bottom swell of her breasts, lifting them and letting the fabric of her dress outline her peaked nipples.

She was frantically trying to remember what she'd done wrong. He listened to her fragmented thoughts, pleased she didn't consider the book she'd written to be a problem. They assumed from the publication date it had been written while she'd been away from the club. Knowing she'd been thinking about them gave him a ridiculous sense of satisfaction. Damn, if only his gift was as simple as plugging directly into someone's thoughts. He'd learned drawing conclusions when the information wasn't complete was a recipe for disaster.

Nate was using silence to unsettle her. It would make her reaction to his question more difficult to mask. Her heart was racing. Hell, it was beating so hard he could feel it thumping wildly against his arm. Once her respiration kicked up, his brother would continue.

The shuddering breath Kodi took was followed by an almost heartbreaking wave of resignation. *What the hell? She thinks we've changed our minds—that we don't want to participate in the party and you're trying to figure out a way to break the news gently.*

Nate met Taz's gaze over her shoulder, trying to gauge whether or not he'd heard him correctly. Nate's gift wasn't as strong, and he'd never been able to receive information as easily.

Taz gave him a quick nod and watched as his regret was reflected in his brother's eyes. "Kodi, I want you to look at me." Taz felt a tear splash against his arm and had to fight the urge to turn her around and assure her nothing between them was going to change. Using his fingers to tilt her face up, Nate leaned down, kissed the tear tracks, and shook his head. "We aren't walking away from you, Ayasha. I'm not sure where you got that idea, but you can put it right out of your mind."

A cautious sense of relief swept through her, and some of the tension moved out of her muscles...at least, she'd relaxed a bit before Nate spoke again. "Have you ever heard of a book called *Sealed Twice* written by a very talented author by the name of Keme Meadows?"

For a split second, Kodi went completely limp in his arms. Thank Goddess he'd already been holding her securely or she'd have collapsed at their feet. Before Taz could pick her up, she recovered and started struggling to get out of his hold.

He held her tight and gave her ass a sharp swat with his free hand. "Baby, stop fighting me. You're going to hurt yourself, and that's going to spoil the rest of the evening for all three of us." She went completely still as understanding dawned. He was pleased she'd figured out what he'd been trying to convey; her answer wasn't going to change their feelings for her.

The deep breath she took was filled with resignation, but not hopelessness. Taz was counting it as a win. "Yes, Sir. I've read the book, and I'm familiar with the au-thor...as I'm sure you're already aware." The last part had barely been a whisper, but neither Taz nor Nate had missed it.

"Ayasha, did you think we'd be angry?"

Oh, indeed she had. She'd evidently been living in fear of discovery since she'd returned to Montana. Suddenly, the courage it had taken her to come back took on a whole new meaning. She'd risked a lot to come back to Mountain Mastery. Hell, she hadn't even known if she could get her job back since their policy was to not rehire anyone leaving without giving proper notice.

"Yes. I'm sorry. It wasn't meant to be disrespectful. I...well, I was lonely and bored. My brother was spending hours and hours in all kinds of physical therapy, and I was stuck in waiting rooms, twiddling my thumbs. Then the stories he'd told me over the years started rolling around in my head, and the next thing I knew I'd spun it all together." She finally took a breath, and Taz grinned at Nate. How the hell had she spit all that out without pausing for air?

"Nobody was more surprised than I was when a publisher took it or when it was so popular. I'm anxious for my brother to fix the little problem I'm having with the publisher skimming my royalties, but you don't want to hear about that mess."

"What makes you think so, Ayasha? I thought Taz and I had been very clear about what we expect from you." Nate's voice was eerily quiet, and Kodi didn't miss the change.

"Oh, well, since...well, since this all happened before..." She waved her hand between them, but didn't continue.

"Ah, you have so much to learn, baby. No problem is too big or too small to bring to us. Even if all we do is act as your sounding board, I think you'll find it useful. But in this case, we have connections who will be more than happy to help." Taz had spoken close to her ear, letting the warmth of his breath waft over the sensitive spot before pressing a kiss against her smooth skin.

"Let's move to the playroom. I'm anxious to give our little author a preview of how worthwhile it will be to put herself in our hands. Hopefully, she'll begin to understand how important she is."

Taz was still shaking his head as they walked back into the Morgan's enormous home. Why she'd thought they'd be angry was a mystery to him. Maybe one of the other subs at the party could impart a few words of wisdom. He learned a long time ago a woman's mind was a wonderfully complex thing and often only understood by another woman. Taz wasn't afraid to ask for assistance if it would help him understand her better. Anything that strengthened the bond between them was worth pursuing. And speaking of binding—the significance of what they'd planned for this evening had just been ramped up exponentially.

Chapter Twenty-One

B RINN WAS RELIEVED to see her friend Keri sitting at the reception desk. Before she and Koi reached the front door of the club, she placed her hand on his forearm, stopping his progress. "Hang on. I want to check something...just to be on the safe side." He raised a brow in question, but nodded as she stepped up to the desk. "Keri, I know you can't tell me what's in this gentleman's file. But please look at it and tell me if you think it's safe for me to go to dinner with him."

She heard him chuckle behind her, but he stepped forward and handed his driver's license to Keri. "Well done, Brinn." Directing his attention to Keri, he added, "Just a reminder, Keri, you aren't at liberty to divulge *anything* in my file. You are only being asked to assess the information and state your opinion. Do you feel Brinn will be safe in my care for dinner?" Brinn heard the warning in his voice and wondered what Keri was going to see that he didn't want her to share.

Keri was already busy typing, but nodded her understanding. Brinn watched as her friend seemed to be skimming the information on the screen. Keri's job as a legal aid for a prominent local attorney had given her plenty of experience looking over material and drawing conclusions quickly. Brinn also knew her friend was one of the most honest people she'd ever met. When she saw Keri's eyes widen and then a small grin spread over her face, Brinn breathed a sigh of relief.

Turning back to them, Keri handed Koi's license to him before turning to her. "You'll be in good hands, Brinn. Enjoy your dinner."

In good hands? What an odd thing to say. Shrugging off her confusion over the weird phrasing, Brinn thanked Keri and let Koi help her with her coat. Waving good bye to her friend, Brinn took Koi's offered arm and walked out of the club.

KOI COULDN'T REMEMBER the last time he'd been so amused watching an exchange between two women. He'd bet his interest in hell the woman manning the front desk had burst out laughing the minute she'd been sure they were out of earshot. His reminder about confidentiality had troubled her at first, but he'd seen her pupils dilate while reading and knew exactly what she'd seen. The little brunette had just thrown her friend to the Big Bad Wolf. Without even asking, Koi was convinced the woman Brinn called Keri was the one she'd mentioned being in the locker room with her when she'd been rude to Kodi.

He wasn't a fool. He understood Brinn far better than she thought he did. She'd sized up his cock and his clothing with an equally critical eye. He'd wager she'd ordinarily gathered the details of a man's financial status long before agreeing to have dinner with him. He wasn't judging her, but he wasn't fooled by her, either. What he wanted was information from someone who had their ear to the ground in the club. By the end of dinner, he'd have learned all there was to know about Mountain Mastery. He'd also find out if there were any new members who were strangers to her.

Koi didn't know whether she'd decided to ride with him or drive herself. He suspected she was waiting to see what he was driving before making her decision. Seeing her eyes widen when she spotted the black Mercedes-AMG GT he'd borrowed from a friend in Billings confirmed his suspicions. No mystery why the Ledeks hadn't taken the bait this woman was casting.

It was no surprise when Brinn directed him to what was very likely the most expensive eating establishment in the area. Koi laughed to himself at her undisguised effort to test him. He'd been a Special Forces operative and "company" agent far too long to miss her subtle inquiries about his economic and social position. From questions about his job—*not tell you anything about that, sweet cheeks, not one single thing*—to her comments about how expensive the car was—*Yes, it is, but it doesn't belong to me. I'd never drive anything this pretentious*—he missed nothing.

After his parents died, Koi sold their considerable real estate holdings and all but their most personal possessions. Using the cash proceeds to pay for Kodi's education had ensured she'd be able to finish college without working herself to the bone. Purchasing a condo for her in a secured building hadn't been cheap, but it had been as much for his own peace of mind as it was for her safety. Koi had been certain he'd wouldn't have been able to fully focus on a mission if he was worrying about his sister. And distraction was the number one way to get yourself and your teammates killed.

Koi wasn't interested in running his dad's tech business—he probably wouldn't ever be interested in a desk job, no matter how much it paid. Invoking the surrogacy option of his trust fund, he'd let the Board of Directors chose his dad's successor and walked away. He'd split the majority stock with Kodi, adding it to the substantial trust funds their parents had already established for them.

By the time Koi returned Brinn to her car outside the club, he felt oddly drained by their verbal sparring. Ordinarily, the person he was interrogating wasn't interviewing him for a position as their next-ex. But he'd gotten most of the information he'd wanted and learned one thing he hadn't enjoyed hearing. Listening to Brinn sneer about Nate and Taz's new *fuck toy* living out of her car had almost sent him into orbit. He'd known his sister was short on money because some bitch in the bank in Denver was holding her it hostage—but living in her damned car? Koi planned to move all their holdings out of that financial institution at his first opportunity.

He had a hotel booked closer to the Morgan's ranch in anticipation of his meeting with Kent and Kyle, so after saying an awkward goodbye to Brinn, he headed north. The drive wasn't a particularly long one, and he doubted there would be a lot of traffic this late in the evening. Koi used the time to think back over the past year. He'd been so wrapped up in his job he'd failed to realize how much Kodi had needed him. Shaking his head at his selfishness, he was anxious to see for himself she was no worse for wear.

Driving down the desolate stretch of road didn't do anything to lift his spirits. Koi was so distracted by the black haze of guilt he didn't see the large truck barreling down on him until seconds before impact. Through the glare of headlights, Jack Cleeves snarling smile of satisfaction appeared in his rearview mirror a split second before the Mercedes lurched forward and began fishtailing wildly out of control. His handler, the man he'd trusted with his life, slammed into the small sports car again, this time from the side, launching it over a steep embankment. Over the din of crushing metal and shattering glass, all Koi could hear was his inner voice screaming that he'd known better than to let his guard down. The first rule for every mission was to be prepared for every contingency and never become complacent. He'd failed Kodi, and now he'd failed himself.

Chapter Twenty-Two

N ATE LOOPED THE first length of rope around Kodi's torso and began tying the chest harness. It wasn't a complicated pattern, but it would leave her breasts exposed and exquisitely sensitive. The bindings would force blood to pool in the tissues, making them throb with each beat of her heart. "Slow down your breathing, Ayasha, or you're going to pass out. Breathe as normally as you can. Panting or shallow breaths will allow the ties to be too tight, something we certainly want to avoid. I want to see how the rope marks your beautiful skin, but I don't want to injure you." He continued to work as he spoke, hoping the slow cadence of his voice would calm their anxious submissive.

Taz took his cue and stepped into Kodi's line of sight. Running his hand over the surface of the rope coil he held, Taz smiled. "No, baby. Don't hold your breath or the harness will be too loose. And, as odd as that may sound, that's every bit as dangerous as too tight."

Nate smiled at the airy sound of Kodi's voice when she acknowledged his brother's instructions. She was already slipping into the mist of subspace. Her mind was slowing down as she put herself in their hands. The burden of trust felt more significant with Kodi...more profound, and Nate knew it was because this was the woman they'd been waiting for.

Stepping in front of her, Nate was pleased to see her beautiful dark eyes half-lidded, the haze of lust clouding their usual sharp awareness. Leaning down, he used the tip of his tongue to trace circles around her exposed nipples before blowing puffs of air over them. Watching them draw into rigid peaks made his cock throb in response. Taz was already threading the first loops between her legs as Nate attached the nipple clamp. Kodi's entire body tensed, and the small bite of pain pulled her back from the edge she'd been rocketing toward.

"Breathe through the pain, Ayasha. In a few seconds, it will turn into a delicious burn and add nothing but pleasure as we finish highlighting this beautiful pussy. We're going to use the hoist to lift you up so everyone in the playroom sees how beautiful you are. I'm going to lick every inch as Taz fucks your pretty ass with a plug. We've got to prepare you for what's to come. When we're both inside you, pet, you're going to feel so full you won't know where your body ends and ours begin. The heat of our combined releases shooting as deep as we can get inside will feel like we've set you on fire."

Nate couldn't wait to push himself deep into her tight virgin ass while Taz claimed her sweet, pink pussy. The bonding of their first true ménage would be filled with romantic seduction, not an audience. That moment would be far too significant to share with anyone else. Tonight, Nate and Taz planned send her into the oblivion of ecstasy before sliding into her hot mouth and perfect pussy. The spiritual aspects of the other union deserved reverence and reflection. *Candlelight and soft music—and chocolate syrup.* Nate almost snorted his laughter at his brother's irreverent intrusion into his thoughts. *Well, someone needs to get your focus back on task.*

Taz attached the cables that would lift Kodi into the air as Nate quietly explained the process and assured her one of them would be right beside her. "One of us will keep our hands on you, pet. We'll never leave you when you are bound. There are safety shears in our pockets as well—you are safe with us...always." He'd wanted to ease her closer to awareness before the lift put any strain on the bindings; preventing panic was easier than calming it. Once she'd been bound a few times, Kodi would know what to expect, but the first few times could be very unnerving.

Taz held the remote control for the Morgan's elaborate hydraulic lift system in one hand. The system was sophisticated and almost silent, making Nate miss the clanking of chains on their old cog lift. There was an odd feeling of connection with the past associated with those sounds that seemed perfected suited for their club's warehouse vibe. Nate sensed the moment she began to panic and moved quickly to hold her face pressed between his large hands. The move forced her to center her attention on him rather than the sensation of floating without any way to control her own movement. He'd heard subs describe the experience as everything from a feeling of total freedom to terrifying knowing they had no way to brace themselves if they fell.

"Look at me, Ayasha. There is nothing in this world or the next that could make me leave your side. Submission is about trust, and we want you to trust us to keep you safe—*always*. There won't be a time when we won't catch you. And very soon you'll trust us enough to bare all your hopes and fears to us as well, because you'll understand—clear to the depths of your soul—we won't ever let you down." As the lift shifted her into position, Nate accepted the stool

Taz sent rolling his way and settled between her legs.

"I'll bet this soft rope feels rough against your sensitive clit, doesn't it, pet? Do you know why your Master positioned two strands on either side of this sensitive little bundle of nerves?" Her response was little more than a mewing sound, but he didn't mind. Knowing she'd gone back to the place where all she needed to do was let go was fine as far as Nate was concerned. "It teases with the sweetest possible touch. When we bind you, then make you walk around the club, you'll understand. After a few steps, you'll swear you're being tortured with pleasure. If you'll trust us to guide you, we'll take you to unimaginable heights." Flicking his tongue over the swollen nub then humming in approval when she stiffened, Nate was surprised when her entire body went rigid. Hell, her reaction had been so strong she'd set herself in motion.

Nate knew Taz wouldn't let her move more than was safe so he didn't make any effort to stop the gentle rocking. Each time she moved close, he used the tip of his tongue to tease her. "You're going to have to learn to hold still if you don't want to move away from what pleases you, baby. You'll learn not moving is a skill we'll soon require, and you'll probably find yourself being denied an orgasm or two before you master it."

"She's spun up pretty tight, brother. Send her over so our friends can hear how beautifully she calls out our names when she comes." Taz was a firm believer in the power of suggestion, and Nate had just insured Kodi would shout their names at the top of her lungs when she came. Wrapping his arms around her calves and pulling her close, Nate lapped up the cream coating her labia and then plunged his tongue deep into her sheath. Fucking her with quick, hard strokes, it took less than ten seconds to make her come.

She screamed, the sound of their names chanted in a benediction resonating to the depths of Nate's soul. Feeling her vaginal walls clamp tightly around his tongue was the most erotic thing he'd ever experienced. For several seconds, Nate had been so lost in the sensation of Kodi coming against his mouth he'd tuned out everything around him. *When was the last time that happened?* After all his years in the military, he couldn't remember ever falling so deep into Dom-space he'd shut out everything but the submissive he was topping. Experiencing her pleasure had gone beyond the physical. Nate wasn't even sure he had the words to describe the feeling. But he wasn't going to waste time now trying to figure it out. He needed to be inside her—*Now!*

Nate and Taz were naked in record time, and after a slight adjustment of the hoist, Nate watched Taz slide his cock between the folds of Kodi's sex. She moaned in response, and the sound was so filled with desire and anticipation Nate fought the urge to slam his cock between her pouting lips. "Oh, baby, you are burning me alive. The heat is searing over the head of my cock, and I feel your longing to be filled—I feel it in every cell in my body, baby. Your cream is molten, and your pretty cunt looks like an open rose. Relax and let me in, baby."

Kodi took as deep a breath as she could, but the bindings quickly reminded her of her submission, and Nate could see her entire body relax. *Fuck me, she is perfect.* Bound for their pleasure, she hadn't fought against the restraints. Even the rope harness couldn't hide the way her body slackened as she surrendered to them again. Watching it had stolen his breath and flayed his soul wide open.

Taz was making slow progress inching into Kodi's tight

sex. The look on his face said it all; the feeling was both heaven and hell. The delicious experience was equal parts pleasure and soul searing pain as he fought to control the urge to plunge as deep as he could in one thrust. *Holding back is the hardest thing I've ever done. Distract her or I'm never going to be able to last.* Nate nodded. He certainly didn't need to be told twice to push himself between her sweet lips.

"Open for me, Ayasha. I'm going to fuck your pretty mouth." He painted her lips with the pre-cum at his tip and smiled when she opened for him. "Feeling your hot mouth surrounding me makes me understand why men have given up everything for chance to be with the woman they love. Feeling my cock slide over your tongue and touch the back of your throat lights my entire body on fire, pet." He was astonished at how far he was able to push her. *Hell, doesn't she doesn't have a gag reflex?*

Fuck you, Nate. You're not helping my control.

Nate was so lost in the exquisite feeling of his cock sliding in and out of Kodi's hot mouth, he pushed Taz's words aside. Now that Taz was fully seated, they could begin alternating their thrusts. Taking a small step back, Nate put enough space between them to let Kodi swing between them. Taz thrust, pushing her forward, her mouth wide open. Nate felt the tip of his cock slide into her throat. Leaning his head back, Nate groaned as liquid heat surrounded him.

"The next time he plunges into you, Ayasha, I want you to swallow." He knew it would take her a few seconds to process the command, and by then, he'd be exactly where he needed to be. Moving his hands to the clamps on her nipples, he nodded to Taz. Everything happened so quickly, Nate could barely keep up, and he'd known what was on tap.

Taz had shifted his position so his thrust pushed the hard edge of his corona against her G-spot. At the same time, Nate released the nipple clamps, letting blood surge back into the sensitive tips of her breasts. The harness had forced blood to pool in her breasts, intensifying the effect, and Kodi's response was lightning fast. She screamed around his cock and instinctively swallowed when he hit the back of her throat.

Fire burst from his testicles, burning its way through his entire body before finally shooting in hot spurts down Kodi's throat. Brilliant white bursts of light exploded behind his eyelids, and Nate locked his knees and sent up a silent prayer he'd stay on his feet. Searing pleasure unlike anything he'd ever experienced decimated his control, and wave after wave of pure ecstasy washed over him. Nate heard Taz shout Kodi's name and knew he'd followed them into bliss.

In the back of his mind, Nate registered the sound of phones ringing because it wasn't a sound usually heard in kink clubs or play rooms. Pulling in deep gulping breaths, he hoped the infusion of oxygen into his system would kick his orgasm numbed brain back into gear. He kept one hand on Kodi, sliding his fingers through the sweat soaked hair at her nape as he used the hoist's remote to slowly return her to an upright position.

Taz staggered to a small nearby table to retrieve a warm, moist towel. He gently wiped away his seed from between Kodi's legs before blotting away the moisture with a dry cloth. Nate noted her legs trembling from the extended isometric rigor of two back to back orgasms. He'd let Taz hold her while he used his safety shears to slice through the harness. Ropes were easy to replace, and Kodi needed to be cuddled to minimize the effect of sub-drop. The sudden adrenaline crash could forever taint her memory of this experience if it wasn't properly managed.

Nate's scissors were so sharp they practically slid through the ropes, and in seconds, they fell into a puddle of hemp around Kodi's feet. Wrapping her in a soft subbie blanket, Nate turned her face to his. "You've stolen my heart, Ayasha. Let Taz cuddle you for a few minutes; I think you could both use it. I'll take care of things here and join you." She stood mutely blinking as if that was going to somehow clear her mind. Nate loved that look—the glaze of confusion in a woman's eyes when they're so sexually sated their bodies and ability to think are still a bit out of sync.

He realized the rest of the room was buzzing with activity, but there were none of the usual noises associated with a playroom. These sounds were of people talking in hushed tones on phones and others scrambling to retrieve clothing they'd discarded in sexually fueled haste. Nate pulled on his jeans, but hadn't bothered with his shirt before turning to find Brandt Morgan standing a few feet away. Kyle was behind them, pressing a kiss against Tobi's forehead before turning her into Kent's arms.

Tally was already dressed, all traces of the submissive woman who'd ridden in the limo earlier completely erased. Dr. Tally Tyson was back in residence as she barked instructions into her phone. Kissing both Karl and Landon quickly, she gave Ryan an impatient wave. The two of them followed Aspen Morgan, who was already sprinting up the stairs.

Returning his attention to Brandt and Kyle, he saw their emotions completely masked by the face only another SEAL would recognize. It was the face of leaders who knew things were officially FUBAR. In a SEALs world, fucked up beyond all recognition often meant people died. For a few harrowing seconds, Nate found himself completely lost in a flashback so strong he struggled to stay on his feet. Something was wrong...something was *terribly wrong.*

Kent West's voice reached through the fog and pulled Nate back from the dark memory of the fateful night when three young men under his command died needlessly. The one time the enemy had known they were coming. Nate had sworn one day he would find out who sold them out, and he or she would pay with their life.

"Not now, Nate. We need to talk to you. Listen to what Brandt has to say. Then we'll figure out the logistics. But Kodi needs to be your first priority."

Kodi? What the fuck? She's safely curled in Taz's arms. What could this have to do with the woman who just melted a good number of my brain cells?

Chapter Twenty-Three

BRANDT QUICKLY OUTLINED what little information he'd been given about Koi Green's accident. The owner of the car had given officers Kyle West's name. One of the deputies who'd helped pull Koi out of the wrecked Mercedes remembered hearing his boss refer to Kyle as a friend, so he'd called Brandt immediately. Nate knew Taz was listening, because he could hear him speaking softly to Kodi. He was trying to bring her around as quickly as possible, anticipating the moment Nate was forced to break the bad news. *Fuck!*

"I assume he's still alive since Tally and Ryan ran out of here like their tails were on fire."

Kyle nodded and waved his hand to where Sage stood talking on the phone. "Sage has Aspen flying them down the mountain in their helicopter. It won't save them a lot of time, but as you know, sometimes it only takes a minute to make a huge difference."

Sage ended his call and stepped into their circle. Brandt looked at his older brother and said, "If you'll organize things on this end, Kyle and I are going to head out. I want to investigate the crash site and interview the woman who witnessed the accident. Evidently, she'd gone to dinner with Koi and was curious where he was headed after taking her back to her car at the club."

"Our club?"

"Seems so. Brinn Peters is our witness."

"Fuck." Nate's growled words had Brandt raising a brow in question. "Never mind, I'm just frustrated with her at the moment. It's a long story, but suffice to say we'll be having a chat about what she had to say about Kodi in the ladies' locker room a couple of days ago. We also need to address the hacking issue. But all that aside, how the hell did she hook up with Koi Green?"

"No clue, but that's one of several questions I'm going to ask her." Turning to Kyle, he said, "Let's go. I've got people standing out along the highway in the fucking dark, and nothing good is going to come of that. But I didn't want them to move the car until I could see it." This time it was Nate's turn to give the other man a questioning look. Brandt sighed, but finally answered. "Look, I don't have all the details yet, but it sounds like this wasn't really an accident. Brinn's account has red pickup hitting the car twice."

Nate was shocked. "I may be frustrated with Brinn, but I hope your people are making sure she's safe." Brandt nodded. "Please keep us posted. We'll be at the hospital with Kodi." Before he'd finished speaking, Brant and Kyle were jogging toward the stairs.

Nate took a deep breath, trying to bring the last few minutes into focus. Sage's hand settled on his shoulder. "I wish I could help you, but the truth is I don't think there is an easy way to break this to Kodi. But I do know the longer you put it off, the worse it's going to be. Landon has already brought the limo around, and Coral and Caila are upstairs putting together something for Kodi to wear."

Hell, he hadn't even thought about finding Kodi something warm or appropriate to wear to the hospital.

Evidently, he didn't have as good a handle on the shelter and protect aspect of being Dom as he'd thought.

"Don't be so hard on yourself. It's easy to forget details like clothes when you're worried about hurting someone you care about."

Sage's words sent a lump straight to his throat. The two of them had been friends since the club opened. Sage had even offered his input on several aspects of the expansion they were planning. But this was the first time their friendship felt *personal*. Aside from Taz and Landon, Nate didn't have any friends. He had a lot of people he was *friendly with*...but business associates weren't the same thing. It felt damned good to expand his inner circle.

"Thanks. I'll go talk to her, and we'll be upstairs in a few minutes." Sage nodded then rounded up the others, moving them upstairs to give the three of them a little privacy. He worried Kodi was going to need a few minutes alone to pull herself together.

TAZ'S HEART CLENCHED when he saw Nate turn and start toward them. Kodi was still sitting in his lap, but the water and chocolate Gracie brought her earlier had gone a long way to bring her around. He'd heard a lot of what Nate had been told, but as anxious as he was to find out how Kodi's brother was, he dreaded telling her the bad news. Pulling her in for quick hug, he turned her so she was facing where Nate settled at the other end of the sofa.

Giving her ass a quick pat, he nodded to his brother. "Your other Master needs to talk to you, baby." Her eyes were still foggy, but they were slowly clearing. Taz hoped she would be able to fully process what Nate was going to tell her. He'd known subs who took several hours to come back to themselves after an intense scene.

Nate took her hands in his and gave her a regretful smile. "Ayasha, there's been an accident south of town. A *bad* accident. That's why Tally and Ryan left so quickly. The man in the car was seriously hurt, and they're being flown down to the local hospital in the Morgan's small helicopter." Taz watched Kodi blink a few times, trying to make sense of Nate's words. He could hear the echoes of confusion in her mind. She didn't understand why Nate was telling her about a car crash.

"Brandt and Kyle have gone to the scene to investigate. It appears as though another vehicle caused the car to plunge over the embankment."

Kodi stiffened in his arms. "Why are you telling me this?" Her voice was filled with trepidation, and Taz could feel her anxiety growing.

"Pet, it's your brother. He was on his way to Pine Creek when the car he was driving…" Nate didn't get to finish his sentence before Kodi scrambled off Taz's lap. She darted toward the stairs clutching the blanket around her when she realized her clothes were behind her. When she turned, Taz was shocked at the wide-eyed look of pure terror in her dark eyes.

"I have to go. I need clothes. Can someone please take me to the hospital? I'm the only one who can sign for him. Is he going to be alright? Please help me! I need to find my clothes and shoes. I need shoes. What time is it? How long ago was he hurt? Oh, God, I have to go." Taz was already on his feet and moving to her, his brother right behind him. They surrounded her, holding her close for several seconds without saying a word—they simply held her, hoping to calm some of the frantic energy coursing through her. If they could replace some of her panic with calm resolve, she would be much more effective as an advocate for her beloved brother.

Taz pulled back and looked down at her. The heart-break and fear he saw felt like a punch to the gut. Nate stepped around her and leaned down, kissing her forehead. "Your friends are rounding up clothes for you. Landon has the limo warming up, and we'll be on the road in a few minutes. But first, I want your head in the right place. You won't be any use to your brother if you blow into the hospital like a tornado. He deserves better, and you are capable of so much more."

A single tear rolled down her cheek as she nodded. "You're right. I'm sorry. I always get like this when he's hurt. Koi is just so damned important to me I panic when I think about losing him. This is why I left without saying goodbye the last time."

Taz understood now. She'd panicked and hadn't had anyone to hold her long enough for her to let her brain retake control.

As soldiers, they'd been trained to never let their emotions rule them during battle. Logic and reasoning saved lives; emotions got people killed. But Kodi wasn't a soldier. She was young woman who'd lost her parents too young and loved her only brother with her whole heart. Taz hoped like hell Koi Green appreciated what an amazing woman his sister was.

Nate and Taz dressed quickly and made their way upstairs. Coral and Caila were waiting and whisked Kodi off with promises of being back in ten minutes or less. Kip leaned a hip against the kitchen's large bar and shook his head. "You just as well get a cup of coffee. Coral's clock doesn't work like everybody else's."

Sage's snort of laughter drew Taz's attention to where he stood near the sink. "It's even worse now that we have children. She got a lot of spankings for it before I finally decided it was something completely out of her control. My lovely wife tends to people, they are what's important, not time. Once I figured that out, my whole outlook changed."

"And she started being able to sit at dinner again." Colt grinned and nudged his brother. "Listen, Josie and I will stay here and help Mom and Dad with all the kiddos. They all love her, and I get to play bad-cop." He waggled his eyebrows, and his brothers rolled their eyes.

Joelle stepped forward and gave her brother-in-law a quick hug. "You're the best. I'd like to go along. We have a lot of specialty drugs at the lab the hospital might otherwise have to order in. I could save them a lot of time if they needed something."

A flurry of movement caught his eye as Kodi raced into the room. "I'm ready. Let's go." He saw Nate glance at his watch as his eyes widened in surprise. "I know, I know. I'm a minute late, but Coral and Caila kept fussing."

"We weren't finished fussing, either, but she took off like a jack rabbit." Coral's voice sounded from around the corner.

"She's quick, I'll say that. Kept squeaking about being late and being raised by a brother with *a thing* for punctuality."

Taz smiled to himself. Damn, Coral was adorable. It was easy to see why Sage's brothers were so fond of her.

Kip pulled Caila into his arms and gave her backside a quick swat. "Get our coat, wench. We're leaving, too. My truck is behind the house."

Taz helped Kodi into her jacket, and within minutes, they were on their way. He and Nate sat on either side of her, close enough their thighs bracketed hers. The connection was intentional. They wanted the message to be clear: They would be beside her all the way. As they pulled into town, Nate took her hand. "Remember when I told you we would always catch you, Ayasha?" When she nodded, Nate smiled and continued. "I meant that in the broadest sense possible. We'll have your back and support you in any way that doesn't cause you harm. But we will also step in if we think you are putting yourself at risk."

"And, baby, exhaustion counts. I can feel the fatigue already pushing at you, so while you and Nate check on your brother, I'm going to find you something to eat."

"Something healthy. No more chocolate until after she's had some real rest."

She surprised him with a hesitant grin. "So...that means I get chocolate for breakfast? I think I can live with that."

Taz burst out laughing as Nate growled at her. "Minx."

Chapter Twenty-Four

NATE LOOKED ACROSS the room where Kodi lay curled up sleeping on one of the long sofas in the hospitals waiting room. She'd spent the past two days pacing the floor, only sitting down when they insisted and sleeping in a chair for ten minutes at a time. He knew the only reason she was fast asleep now was because Ryan had slipped something in her drink. Nate doubted Ry would ever admit it. But when he'd come in a few hours ago to give them an update, he'd taken one look at her and frowned.

After giving them the best news they'd had since first arriving at the hospital, he'd glared in Kodi's direction. As pleased as she'd been to hear Koi was finally responding to treatment and things were looking up, she'd been too exhausted to do much more than smile. Ryan had walked out, only to return a few minutes later with a small glass of juice. "Drink this, Kodi." When she started to argue, he held up his hand. "I don't want to hear it. You drink the juice and get some nutrients into your system or I'm going to admit you."

She scowled at him, but took a tentative sip. "You can't just admit me because you want to."

"I can. And I will. You'd be surprised what I can do to a submissive who is misbehaving. You think I haven't heard your Masters telling you to rest? I'd be willing to bet the only reason you haven't had a sound paddling is because they don't want to make a scene in the waiting room." He took a quick step forward, crowding into her personal space. "Don't forget, sweetness, I am a Dom. And I will find them a place to take you in hand, I promise you. So, drink the juice like a good girl, and when you see your brother in a few hours, he will probably be awake enough to realize you are there. I'm trying to make sure he isn't the only one awake."

Kodi's eyes showed her surprise, and as much as he suspected she wanted to defy the doctor's order, she wasn't going to take the chance. She downed the juice in a few gulps and handed the glass back to him. Ryan gave her a quick nod of approval before turning to leave. On his way out, Nate had seen his self-satisfied smirk and understood instantly what he'd done. There was still a lot of SEAL medic in Ryan Morgan, and they were well known for knocking your ass out if you weren't cooperating with their treatment.

Taz had known what Ryan was up to, also, and struggled to contain his laughter when Kodi called him "bossy boots" after the door closed behind him. "Joelle should have gotten that Nobel Peace Prize for dealing with him, instead of her discovery."

"Come on, baby. Sit with me. I'm pooped, and I want to feel you up when no one is looking."

She gapped at Taz and shook her head. "You are incorrigible. But I'm going to give you points for creativity. That's the best story either of you has come up with to trick me into sitting down." She stopped to yawn then waved her hand to the sofa. "Let's sit over there. I really do want to cuddle. I needed that juice, but don't you dare tell Ryan I said so." Those were the last words she'd said before falling into a blissful sleep several hours ago.

Brandt stepped into the room and smiled at her sleeping form. "Let me guess. Ryan brought her some juice?" When Nate and Taz both snorted with laughter, he shook his head and grinned. "It was an educated guess. He's done the same thing to Joelle when she is so immersed in a project she can't make her mind shut down to rest. The last time she drank it knowing full well what he'd done, but she was so desperate for sleep she didn't care. Thank God, we were both off and could watch after Donnie. It's humbling to realize it takes two former SEALs to keep up with one baby."

Brandt and Ryan shared Joelle—the two men had made it clear from the beginning it made no difference which one of them was little Donnie's biological father. The baby was named after Ryan's dad, who also happened to be Brandt's uncle. Nate had only seen him a couple of times, but his dark hair and violet eyes made him the spitting image of Ryan. Nate laughed at Brandt's confession. He'd heard from the other Morgan brothers how worried they'd been about Brandt when he'd first returned home from the SEALs. Like Nate, his last mission had gone to hell in a heartbeat, and he'd struggled with survivor's guilt for months before Joelle entered his life. All the Morgan's credited the brilliant red head with bringing back the brother and son they loved.

Brandt shook his head. "Damned if he isn't already showing signs of being a Morgan through and through. The minute he learned to turn over, he was pulling himself all over in his crib. At this rate, he's going to either be the smartest kid who ever lived or an escape artist. Personally, I think it could go either way." Nate burst out laughing, because with a mother who'd already won a Nobel Prize for her discovery of a drug that cures cancer and an uncle whose I.Q. was so high it was almost impossible to measure, it was little wonder Donnie was advanced.

"Listen, as much as I enjoy bragging about my son, that's not why I'm here. Remember me telling you the paramedics said the only thing Koi said was 'handler'? I think we all know how much the CIA likes to recruit SEALs, and it seemed to fit with his use of the word *handler*. Of course, I hit several brick walls trying to find out whether or not he was working for the agency, so I asked for Phoenix's help. Koi Green is a NOC, a non-official Cover, one of those the agency denies any knowledge of. And his handler has been under investigation for months and out of the office for over a week."

Kyle and Kent West stepped into their small circle and motioned them down the hall. When they into a small office, he leaned back against the desk, crossing his arms and his ankles. "Don't worry about Kodi—we sent Tobi in to watch over her."

"The words *don't worry* and *Tobi* don't belong in the same sentence, Kyle. Hell, you've probably jinxed us." Kent's easygoing smile helped Nate relax. This was one of the things he missed the most about the teams. The sense of camaraderie.

"Shit. Okay, forget what I said. Anyway, I would have told you this sooner if I'd known you were asking questions. Koi was indeed a NOC; he was also getting out. He'd contacted us a while back asking about our team, and we extended him an open-ended offer. Recently—actually, very recently—he had reason to believe something wasn't right in the agency, but he didn't know how far up it went."

"And he didn't really care. He just wanted out. As soon

as he's talked to Kodi, we're flying him to Texas to a private hospital close to the club. After that, he'll move into one of our cabins and do all his re-habilitation on-site."

People assumed Kyle was the more dominant twin, but in Nate's experience, they were equals in every way. It was only their ways of approaching a problem that made them different.

Looking between Nate and Taz, Kyle smiled. "What Koi wants you two to do is keep Kodi here in Montana. Koi believes—and we agree—she's already been used as bait. He thinks the threat will follow him to Texas and she'll be safe with the two of you." Nate wasn't sure what surprised him more, the fact Koi had just entrusted them with his sister or how much he'd been communicating with the Wests when he'd appeared to be sleeping every time they'd been in to see him.

Taz crossed his arms over his chest and glared. "What the fuck? He talked to you guys, but won't even open his eyes for his sister? She's going crazy worrying about him." Nate sighed. He should have known his brother would be thinking along the same line.

Kyle shrugged, "For what it's worth, I agree with you—and I've told him so. But he has assured us he knows what he's doing. He believes the sun rises and sets in Kodi, so I'm trusting he's doing what's best for her. He has promised to talk to her later today. And then we'll move him out of here during the middle of the night. We have team members flying in as we speak."

Nate ran his hands through his hair in frustration. "And we're supposed to convince Kodi to stay here? That is exactly what we want, but I'm not taking the heat on this. It's not fair to Kodi to be misled. Her brother needs to level with her."

"Yes, I agree. He certainly does. And he can start by explaining to her why he's been playing possum for the past twenty-four hours." Kodi's voice was calm, but he heard the underlying note of pain. "If he thinks I didn't know he was pretending to be asleep, he needs to get out of the CIA because he's no good at lying."

Nate turned and looked at her in shock. Hell, he hadn't even heard the door open. She looked at him and shrugged. "I might have picked up some of Koi's ninja skills over the years." When he laughed and shook his head, she shrugged.

She looked over at Brandt and gave him a mocking smile. "You can tell Ryan he needs to use different sleepy time meds next time. I could taste whatever he put in the juice. Also, he needs to do his research. All my medical records make note of the fact my body metabolizes those drugs very quickly."

This time it was Brandt's turn to laugh. "Damn, Kodi, you're going to fit in perfectly with our wives. They are going to love this story. You tell your brother his buddy in Billings isn't a happy camper about his fancy assed car. He says Koi owes him a couple rounds in the ring. Sounds like they've had a friendly rivalry going for a long time."

"I'll be sure to add that to the list of things I'm going to tell him. Damn, I'm so mad I could just spit." They all tried to contain their laughter, because it was obvious she was genuinely perturbed.

Tobi, who'd positioned herself between Kent and Kyle, gave Kodi a thumbs-up. "I totally understand, sister. And I promise to torture him every chance I get. I'll recruit the other subs, too. He'll think you're the best thing since sliced bread by the time we're through."

Kyle frowned at her. "You'll do no such thing. You'll

behave and encourage the others to do the same. It's called leading by example." Tobi gave him a saccharin sweet smile that didn't fool anyone. As soon as her husbands refocused their attention on Kodi, the little trouble maker gave her new friend a double thumbs-up.

Note to self...keep Kodi and Tobi apart as much as possible.

Chapter Twenty-Five

Six Weeks Later

KODI DANCED AROUND the enormous living room, her short shorts and skin tight tank doing little to hide her curves, and she shimmied and shook in celebration. She'd finished the last book in the trilogy and sent in off to be formatted ahead of her self-imposed deadline. At first, she'd struggled to maintain any semblance of concentration when she knew her brother was in Texas recovering from the injuries he'd sustained. But she'd eventually found a routine that worked for her. *Yep, after a couple of sessions on the St. Andrew's cross, it cleared right up.*

Shrugging off her harpy inner voice, she cranked the music up a notch or two every time she danced by the stereo system. There was nothing like rockin' out to the Nitty Gritty Dirt Band, and *Fishin' in the Dark* was just too catchy to sit through. Her brother had always teased her about her preference for the older country tunes, but she consistently reminded him it really was his fault. It was the music he and his friends listened to when she was younger, and since she'd idolized her brother, it seemed natural to like his music, as well. She'd told him once she'd been imprinted. He had laughed at her and told her not to take freshman psych too seriously.

Now that she thought about it, this wasn't her playlist.

"Holy crap." She was momentarily stunned by the realization she and the Ledek brothers liked the same music. It wasn't the type of music they usually played in the club, so she'd never considered they might be classic county fans. Dammit, they just got more perfect every day. How was she ever going to be able to leave them?

On their way back from Pine Creek, they'd made her promise to stay while she got all her financial troubles squared away. With their help, it had only taken a couple of weeks to free up her money. But then they'd persuaded her to stay until she'd finished the book she'd been working on. Once they'd discovered it was a three-part series, they'd amended their request. But she couldn't see them asking her to stay any longer...and she worried she might have worn out her welcome.

Staring out the large window, Kodi tried to tamp down her anxiety. It wasn't that she didn't have the money to get her own place, because she did. But just thinking about not sleeping between Nate and Taz made her stomach twist into a tight knot.

She was lost in her thoughts; she didn't notice the tracks switch. When the Bellamy Brothers started singing *If I Said You Had a Beautiful Body Would You Hold It Against Me?*, she swayed to the music, lost in the lyrics and her worries about being forced to leave the home she'd come to love. Her mood was slipping close to melancholy when strong arms wrapped around her, pulling her back against a rock hard chest.

Taz. She knew her Masters by their touch. Nate's was usually more sensual while Taz's was stronger, more forceful. In the beginning, she'd been surprised, because as an employee, Nate had been the one she feared the most. "That's because he has that business hard ass thing down to a fine science, baby. I save all my hard ass points for my sub, and I really like to cash them in when she's naked."

He turned her in his arms, pressing her close, and began dancing around the room in a slow two-step that felt more like foreplay than dancing. Maybe it was his years of training, that highly developed sense of awareness of one's own body athletes develop, knowing exactly how to move his body through space to maximize the effort. Or maybe it was simply what it seemed, a prelude to sex set to music.

"My brother and I came upstairs to check on you, baby." She went from relaxed to tense in a heartbeat. "And we were treated to one of the best floor shows I've ever had the pleasure of watching." *Oh fuck-a-doodle, just kill me now.* The rumble of his soft laughter vibrated through the solid muscles of his chest. "I'd swat your ass for that, but you didn't actually say it aloud." *Note to self…remember who you are dealing with…always.*

"Seeing you dance—completely lost in joy and carefree—it's something Nate and I both want to see again and again. I'm not sure you understand what a difference you've made in our lives. Or how long we'd been waiting for you. And having you in our home these past few weeks has been perfect. But it's time for things to change."

Kodi felt like someone had sucked all the air out of the room. Looking frantically around the room for Nate, she felt lost when didn't see him. "He's gone back downstairs to check on a few things. There's something we need to resolve later tonight."

Looking up at him, Kodi felt another pang of anxiety. Were they planning to cut her lose tonight? Would she be able to stay in Montana if they did? It would break her heart to see them with someone else. Her head was spinning, and she stepped back out of his embrace.

"Sorry, I'm not feeling well."

She ran as quickly as she could out of the room. Locking herself in the bathroom, she felt the first waves of heartbreak wash over her. Sliding to the floor, Kodi let silent tears fall, forcing her mind to go completely blank. There was no reason to let him know how much she was hurting.

TAZ STOOD OUTSIDE the bathroom door, puzzled by Kodi's behavior. Mulling it over, he wondered if they shouldn't cancel tonight's ceremony. Maybe she wasn't as ready as they'd believed. Had she changed her mind about staying with them? If she was really ill, he didn't want to leave her alone, but he'd heard the distinctive snick of the door being locked and knew she wouldn't welcome his intrusion.

Moving back into the living room, he sent a quick text to Nate asking him to bring Tally upstairs. Maybe Kodi would talk to her. Now that he thought about it, Kodi had seemed to be walking on eggshells around them for the past week or so. She'd told them she was close to finishing her project, so they'd tried to give her as much space as possible. But the more they'd stepped back, the stranger her behavior had gotten. His phone chimed softly, Nate's message telling him they were on their way.

He'd been so caught up in the beauty of watching her dancing uninhibited around the room he hadn't been reading her. And once he'd taken her in his arms, he'd been so focused on setting the mood for what they had planned he hadn't been able to hear anything but his own heart beating in anticipation of seeing her naked and kneeling on a bed of rose petals. Fuck it, if he'd been paying attention, he might have a better idea what had happened.

Nate led Tally and Karl into the room, concern darkening his expression. "What they hell happened? She was dancing like a forest nymph a few minutes ago, and now she's ill?"

Tally turned and placed her hand on Nate's chest. "Let me check on her. Women are complicated creatures, Nate."

Nate pulled her hand to his lips and pressed a soft kiss against the back. "Thank you. I don't mean to seem ungrateful, because I'm not." Leading her down the hall, Nate pointed to the door and then stepped back into the hall where Taz stood.

"I don't know. We were dancing, and I was talking to her about how long we'd been waiting for her. And how great it's been to have her here, but that it was time for things to change"

"Change? You told her it was time for things to change? For fuck's sake, Taz. She probably thinks we're dumping her."

Karl laid a hand on each of their shoulders and motioned down the hall with a quick tilt of his head. "Gentlemen, I think we could all use a drink."

Leave it to the good Senator to intercede at the right moment. His ability to negotiate compromise between opposing parties was one of the reasons he was one of the most popular politicians in Washington. Following him back to the living room, Taz made his way to the bar and poured their best whiskey into three highball glasses. Karl smiled as he lifted his glass. "I'm honored. You're sharing your best with me."

Tipping his head back toward the hall, Taz smiled. "It

seems appropriate, since you are *sharing* your best with us, as well." Karl nodded, and they all downed their drinks quickly. Letting the warmth seep into his system, Taz once again let his mind drift over their conversation. And this time, he could see where Nate was coming from.

Fuck, I should have spent more time with Mom and less time with Dad at the dojo.

TALLY KNOCKED GENTLY on the door and spoke softly against the rich textured wood. "Kodi, it's me, Tally. Let me in please." She heard the door lock release and opened it to find Kodi leaning against the marble counter, tear tracks staining her flushed cheeks. "Taz tells me you aren't feeling well. But I suspect this is more about heartache than any real physical illness."

Kodi didn't answer, her expression carefully masked.

"Are you scared? Do you think tonight is going to be overwhelming?" Tally wasn't sure how much she could say about what she knew the two club owners had planned. She didn't want to spoil their surprise, but then again, there might not be any surprise if she didn't figure out what was going on.

Kodi didn't respond. She just blinked several times as tears continued to stream unchecked down her cheeks.

"Are you really sick, Kodi? Or is it you fear of the unknown? Because I can assure you, what they have planned is nothing to fear." For the first time, she saw a glimmer of response, so she continued. "I can't tell you any-thing...well, not much, because I'd rather be able to sit down next week. But I *can* tell you they've put a lot of time and effort into making sure everything is perfect. They plan to make it a night you will all three remember forever."

A fresh stream of tears appeared, and Kodi's expression went blank once again. *Shit! What did I say?* Before she could speak again, the door banged open with a resounding crack, and she turned to see Nate Ledek filling the doorway.

"Tally, I appreciate your time. But I'll take it from here. If you'd head back downstairs and double check everything, I'd appreciate it. We'll be down soon. I know we'd planned to do this later, but I'm shifting the timeline up."

Tally nodded her understanding before turning to give Kodi a quick hug. "I'll see you downstairs in a few minutes." Stepping from the room, Tally hoped like hell Nate knew what he was doing, because she'd never seen Kodi look so forlorn. She didn't have any idea why Kodi seemed to have changed her mind about Nate and Taz, but she hoped he could turn her heart around because they all seemed perfect for one another. And the truth was, she envied the fact they could live openly in a polyamorous relationship while she had to hide her love and affection for Landon. Pushing aside the wave of sadness she was certain would follow that line of thinking, Tally let Karl lead her to the elevator.

Snuggling into his embrace, she felt his hard shaft pressing against her. He groaned, and she heard Taz chuckle behind them. "Fuck it." Karl surprised her by slapping his hand against the elevator's emergency stop, halting the car's movement between floors. "Enjoy the show, Taz." His words were practically growled as he lifted Tally and pushed her bare back against the wall. The micro-mini halter dress she wore offered no protection from the cool steel or her Dom's hard thrust.

Holy crap-a-roni, when did he open his leathers? Tally loved the burn that always followed the first hard push between tissues swollen with desire. When she gasped, he bit down on the top of her shoulder. He hadn't broken the skin, but she knew the mark would remind her of his possession long after he left for Washington tomorrow.

"There's the sound I love to hear. Give me what's mine, love." His strokes were hard and fast, the ridge surrounding the hot head of his cock pressing against her G-spot with increasing speed until she couldn't hold back any longer.

Her scream bounced off the walls of the small space. His muscles stiffened beneath her hands as his cock swelled just before his hot seed splashed against her cervix. The sensation launched her into another orgasm stronger than the first.

Over her own heavy breathing, Tally heard Taz groan "Fuck that was hot" just before he let out a heavy sigh. Peeking around her Dom's shoulder, she watched Taz stoke himself to completion, catching his release in a handkerchief. He wasn't embarrassed that she'd watched, and it gave her a warm sense of satisfaction to have such a huge affect him. Damn, if she and Karl could turn on a man who owned a sex club, they had to be doing something right.

Once they'd all set their clothing to rights, Taz leaned over and kissed her cheek. "Watching you is always a privilege, little sub." Turning to Karl, he smiled. "Thanks for the hottest scene I've watched in a long time. And I needed the distraction more than I can tell you, but we better re-start the elevator before somebody calls the damned fire department." Using his palm to re-engage the biometric control, he set the small elevator car in motion.

Tally squirmed when she felt the evidence of her Dom's possession slide in rivulets down the inside of her thighs. The dirty dog knew exactly why she was wiggling around, too. "Leave it. I'm going to parade you around the club and flaunt the fact I just fucked you in the elevator. Seeing my cum mark your thighs will be as close to beating my chest in victory as I can get without some asshole calling me Tarzan for the next several months."

Taz snorted a laugh as they stepped out into the club.

"Come, Tally. I want to tease Landon. I'm going to bend you over behind the bar so he can see my seed glisten on your legs. What do you say we make it interesting and place a little wager on how long until he's buried balls deep in your pussy? I'm guessing under two minutes." She felt herself stumble; she was so surprised by his words. "If it's under two, you'll get ten swats with the implement of my choice later tonight. For every half-minute thereafter, I'll deduct one slap against your pretty ass." God in heaven, she was almost ready to come again before he led her behind the bar. This was going to be the first time they'd played out in the open at the club and she could hardly wait.

Landon turned and smiled when they stepped behind the bar, but his expression went quickly from a warm welcome to blazing hot lust as he let his gaze skim over her. Tally knew what he was seeing. Her checks would still be flushed from the orgasm Karl had given her, and there wasn't a Dom at the club who couldn't recognize the well-fucked look of a sub who'd just come.

She watched Landon's eyes dilate as his mouth set in a firm line when his gaze lowered to the dampness between her legs. "Turn around and bend over, Tally. Spread those wet thighs nice and wide. Show Master Landon what he missed. You have a new rule to obey, my luscious little sub. No panties in elevators—ever. Elevators are made for fucking, and I will always want instant access."

Tally heard the shuffle of feet and clothing a second before Landon's soft curse. "Fucking hell" sounded above the noise in the club. Before she'd taken her next breath, he filled her with his hot length, and Tally's entire body quivered as her orgasm blindsided her. The pulsing of her vagina around him made Landon groan. "You're milking my cock, sweetness. Squeezing every bit of resistance I have right out of me. Hang on. I'm coming with you." Several hard thrusts later, she felt his release heating her from the inside out.

Tally's knees started to shake, but Landon's arm banded tightly around her waist before they gave out. Karl helped her stand, and Tally was pleased to see his wide smile. "Well, it's nice to know I'm not the only one who loses their control with you, love. Come on. We'll give Master Landon a couple of minutes to recover while I get you properly cleaned up and cuddled before the festivities." She was grateful when he picked her up, because she wasn't sure her legs would hold her.

Landon caught them before they'd made their way out from behind the bar, giving her a passionate kiss. "Rest up, sweet girl, because I'm not finished with you tonight."

"She's got five swats coming, plus whatever you add for good measure. After the Ledek's claim Kodi, we'll give the club a little show of our own." Tally felt a wave pulse through her sex and wondered how she was going to be able to deal with Karl being gone for the next three weeks.

Chapter Twenty-Six

KODI LOOKED AT Nate and took an involuntary step back. Holy hell, he looked pissed. A crease formed between his brows as he frowned at her movement. "Stop. Strip and bend over the counter. Legs spread and ass high. I want to see how wet you are." She was momentarily stunned by the command. "Right fucking now, Ayasha. My patience is dangerously thin. You and my brother have not been communicating, and I'm going to remedy that." Kodi slid her shorts and thong down before stepping out of them, and he shook his head.

"What are the rules about panties, pet? That's going to cost you ten. Now lose the shirt and bend over." Dammit, she hadn't expected them back upstairs until after she'd showered. Peeling her skin-tight tank over her head, Kodi felt her nipples tighten under his gaze. "We'll take care of your punishment first, while I ask you some questions. Remember, you do not permission to come."

She lay over the dark marble counter and gasped when her peaked nipples met the cool surface. "Legs apart, Ayasha. I want your pussy too feel each stroke. You'll get five with my hand and five with this." He pulled her wooden handled hairbrush from the drawer and set in on the counter where she'd be forced to look at it. The first five swats rained down on her ass so fast she barely had time to gasp before it was done.

Nate slid his fingers through the folds of her sex, and she wanted to moan in frustration. It was too much and not enough all at the same time. "You're very wet already. How are you ever going to make it through the next five, pet?" He rotated his fingers, pressing gently against her G-spot, and Kodi sucked in a quick gasp as she tried to hold off the orgasm that was already dangerously close. "How many times have we told you we aren't going to let you go, Ayasha?"

What? He wants to chat? Now?

She'd been lost in thought and didn't realize he'd picked up the brush until it landed with a wicked smack against the center of her ass. Her ass burned like it had been set on fire. Even her pussy felt the heat. "I asked you a question, little sub."

Question?

Four more swats with the brush followed, but none were as hard as the first. "How many times, Kodi?"

"I don't know, Sir. Too many to count." Kodi wasn't sure where the answer had come from, because the response seemed to have by-passed her brain to fly directly out her mouth.

"That's right. Now tell me how you and your other Master managed to miscommunicate this a few minutes ago, because I am damned confused." Before she could respond, he pulled her up to face him. The light of love in his eyes melted all her doubts into a puddle that seemed to evaporate into steam under his heated gaze. "There isn't a chance in hell we're letting you go, pet. You belong to us, and we're going to enjoy sharing that news with our friends."

She felt tears burn the backs of her eyes, but he shook

his head. "No tears. I'm going to the kitchen. You have twenty minutes to shower, primp, and dress. You'll wear the new dress you'll find hanging in the closet and nothing else. If you aren't in the kitchen in twenty, you'll be making an appearance in the club's main room in whatever you're wearing when I come to get you." She nodded, but felt like her feet were glued to the floor. "Ayasha, you are going to have to *move*." His words were spoken softly and despite the fact they were filled with amusement, still couldn't seem to move.

Tilting his head to the side, he smiled. "Pet, do you need to come so badly your sharp mind isn't able to swim through all those wonderful neurotransmitters screaming for orgasm?"

What? I don't know what you said, but I'll agree to anything if it means I can come.

NATE FELL MORE in love with Kodi with each passing minute. Watching her look up at him, trembling with need, unable to move because her body was craving the release only he could grant, was enough to humble any Dom. There was no way she'd ever be ready in twenty minutes if he brought her to completion. But she wasn't going to even be able to move if he didn't finish what he'd started. He was still learning how amazingly responsive she was.

Wrapping his large hands around her waist, he felt her body trembling beneath his palms and shook his head. "You were doing a damned good job of hiding all that quaking, Ayasha." Her eyes widened, but she didn't say anything. "Hold on to the edge of the counter, pet. You can come when you're ready." Without waiting for her to answer, he knelt in front of her and sealed his mouth over her sex. Flicking his tongue over her clit, he knew why she hadn't been able to move. The small bundle of nerves was already fully exposed and throbbing with need. Any movement would have sent her over, but she'd held off because she hadn't had permission to come.

Within seconds, she screamed his name, and her sweet cream coat his tongue. He pulled back when she sagged forward. Any more stimulation and she'd be too spent to be trusted alone in the shower. Setting her on her feet, Nate leaned down and slanted his mouth over hers. He wanted her to taste herself on his lips. Pulling back, he kissed the tip of her nose before moving her into the shower. "Your time starts now, Ayasha. Better not waste any more of it. Dry your hair enough you aren't chilled. I'll braid it for you when you come into the kitchen. Any questions?"

"No, Sir. Well, actually... yes. How did you know?"

He didn't even try to hold back his smile, "Pet, it's my *job* to *know*. One of the great things about poly-relationships is having two men focused on providing everything you need. When one of us misses a cue, the other one is there to pick it up." He waited until he saw the light of understanding in her eyes before nodding and stepping back. He tapped his watch and laughed to himself when she scrambled into action.

NATE CHECKED THE time and smiled when Kodi stepped

into the kitchen with thirty seconds to spare. Fucking hell, she looked like a walking wet dream in the short dress they'd gotten for her to wear tonight. The sheer material was deep sapphire to match the stones in the collar they'd commissioned for her. Diamonds and sapphires set in an intricate rose gold design including a small padlock with two keys he and Taz would wear on chains around their necks. The soft fabric of her dress ended an inch below the bottom curve of her ass and was lightweight enough to give teasing glimpses of her naked flesh with every move she made. He could see her nipples through the translucent fabric, and he wondered what she'd say if he suggested piercing them.

He braided her hair quickly and led her from the apartment before he gave in to temptation and spread her out on the kitchen table and fucked her until neither of them could stagger into the elevator. They rode in silence down to the main floor. When the elevator doors opened, he stepped in front of her, blocking her view of the room. "Kodi, do you trust me? Do you trust Master Taz?"

"Yes, Sir." He was pleased with her lack of hesitation and gave her a quick kiss.

"Remember that. Everything that happens tonight is for you. *Everything*. Don't forget that, Ayasha. Let's go." Shackling her small wrist with his hand, he led her into the room.

It looked like every member of the club had shown up. He wasn't surprised. Word would have spread quickly once the first notices were sent out. All the members seemed excited to see Mountain Mastery's owners finally collar a sub of their own, but they didn't know there was also a diamond ring in his pocket.

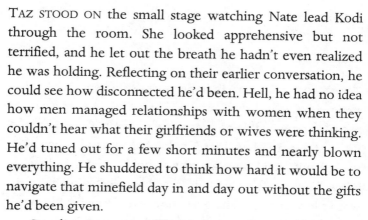

Taz stood on the small stage watching Nate lead Kodi through the room. She looked apprehensive but not terrified, and he let out the breath he hadn't even realized he was holding. Reflecting on their earlier conversation, he could see how disconnected he'd been. Hell, he had no idea how men managed relationships with women when they couldn't hear what their girlfriends or wives were thinking. He'd tuned out for a few short minutes and nearly blown everything. He shuddered to think how hard it would be to navigate that minefield day in and day out without the gifts he'd been given.

Standing in a room filled with people in high states of arousal ordinarily had a predictable effect on him, but tonight, that was all secondary to one woman. Nate was leading Kodi to the bar where he would leave her in Landon's care before making his way to the stage. Landon Nixon would play his part perfectly. He'd paint the picture in Kodi's imagination so vividly she'd believe the tale spun just for her.

In Taz's opinion, Landon might be a little too good at role play for it to be a coincidence. Someday, he was going to break through the other man's defenses and find out about his mysterious business trips. Most of the people Taz knew didn't return from legitimate business meetings with deep tissue bruises.

Kodi was doing remarkably well considering how distraught she'd been earlier. Whatever Nate had done had obviously worked well. *Will I ever outgrow needing my brother's help?*

He'd no sooner ask himself the question than he heard Nate's answer echo through his mind. *I certainly hope not. That, little brother, is my superpower.*

KODI HADN'T TRIED to hide her surprise when Master Nate stepped aside and she saw the room. She'd never seen the room so crowded. Was every single member here tonight? Both of her Masters loved holding her hand when they walked with her, but Nate wasn't holding her hand gently in his. The significance of his large hand shackling her wrist wasn't lost on her. Whatever they had planned had started the moment she'd stepped from the elevator. There was an electric buzz of excitement in the room. It was so intense the fine hairs on the back of neck were standing on end.

By the time they reached the bar, Kodi felt like she'd been wired into the power surrounding them. Her heart was pounding against her chest, and she felt almost lightheaded her breathing was so shallow. Landon Nixon was standing in front of the bar, his arms crossed over his chest, highlighting the fact his shirt was unbuttoned almost to his waist. This was Landon the Master, not the affable bartender who'd been her friend and coworker.

Nate turned to her and gave her a smile so quick she almost missed it. When he spoke, his voice was deep and the words loud enough for everyone nearby to hear. Kodi was mesmerized by his shift from the introspective, passionate man she'd fallen in love with to Master and performer. The easy way she accepted the fact she'd fallen in love with Nate...and Taz stunned her. For a few seconds, she couldn't breathe, and it had nothing to do with what was happening around her.

"Ayasha, I'm leaving you in Master Landon's care. You are to obey him as you would Master Taz or myself. Do you understand?"

Nate's booming voice brought her back to the moment. It took her a second for his words to settle in her mind, but she finally nodded and spoke the words she knew he wanted to hear. "Yes, Master." His nostrils flared, and his eyes were instantly molten. He'd been pleased by her use of the more honorific term, and it gave her an odd sense of satisfaction to know how much those simple words meant to him.

When he leaned forward to kiss her cheek, she whispered, "I love you, Master," and heard him suck in a quick breath. For several heartbeats, he didn't move. His lips were suspended just above the surface of her skin, and she could practically feel his internal battle. When he finally kissed her flushed cheek, she was certain something important had just transpired between them. After he'd turned and walked away, Kodi realized it was the first time she'd said those words to him.

Landon didn't give her any time to worry about their exchange. Stepping forward, he forced her to focus on him. She'd never seen him look so formidable and wondered briefly if this was the Dom other subs saw when they played with him.

"I do believe I'll enjoy these few moments of having you in my care, sweetness."

She blinked in surprise at his softly spoken words. On the outside, Landon looked every inch the intimidating sexual Dominant she'd heard he could be. But the sparkle in his eyes eased her anxiety. It was a relief to know her that her friend was inside.

"Yes, Sir." At her response, he gave her a quick wink. Her confidence returned as the tension drained away. Whatever they'd planned for her, she was confident it wasn't going to be more than she could handle. An odd sense of inner peace settle over her, and with a deep cleansing breath, Kodi straightened her shoulders. She was ready for whatever was to come.

"Strip." Like Nate, Landon's voice boomed through the room. Kodi had worked at the club long enough to recognize the command of a Master when she heard it.

Okay. Maybe she wasn't as ready as she'd thought.

Chapter Twenty-Seven

KODI'S HANDS WERE trembling as she drew the dress over her head. *Hell, why did they even let me wear it if I was going to have to give it up so soon?* Even as she asked herself the question, she knew the answer. This was about feeling vulnerable. Being forced to surrender her clothing in front of a group of people was an act of submission. She either trusted her Masters, and by extension Master Landon, or she didn't. It was a test, and she wasn't going to fail.

Placing the dress in his outstretched hand, she took a deep breath when he gave her a small nod of approval. "I've been charged with delivering you to the men who have chosen you as their own. And I intend to make sure you are a prize no man could resist. Hold still." It was the only warning she had before his mouth descended on her breast.

Fuckadilly Circus.

The heat and strength of the suction brought her up onto her toes. The movement was met with a ferrous growl, and she froze. Her entire body was shaking, and every cell seemed to vibrate in time with the lashes of his tongue over the sensitive flesh. Kodi felt him shift, but hadn't been able to pull herself back from the pleasure until she felt Landon's fingers slide the nipple clamp around the aching tip of her right breast. Instinctively, she started to raise her hands, only to find them held tight at her sides.

Looking first one way and then the other, Kodi was surprised to see Kip and Phoenix Morgan flanking her. Both men gave her a small smile before Kip leaned down and spoke quietly against her ear. "We're going to make sure you don't get into trouble by moving, sweetheart. I'd say by the look of your pretty ass, you've already had enough for one night."

She should probably be embarrassed by his words, but she'd heard the affection in his voice and whispered her thanks.

"Our pleasure, darlin'. Your men have been planning this for a long time, and we're happy to help them catch the woman of their dreams."

Kodi felt tears burn the backs of her eyes at Kip's sweet words, but she didn't have time to fall into the emotion of the moment. Landon's hot mouth covered her left nipple. At the same time, the first clamp was tightening, and Kodi opened her eyes to see Karl Tyson's dark eyes focused on her. Holy hell, was she some sort of community service project or what?

Landon froze, and she saw Karl's lips twitch.

Shit, shit, shit! Please tell me I didn't say that aloud.

A sharp swat landed on her ass, and Phoenix's voice whispered in her ear. "Stay quiet, little one. You were not given permission to speak." After a second of hesitation, he added, "Your Masters will have our heads if we laugh. Be good, and we'll get you where you need to be in no time."

She felt a measure of her fear drain away. Knowing they weren't angry with her was a huge relief. Kodi pulled in a deep breath and focused on letting her apprehension go with her exhalation.

"That's perfect, little one. Let us take you were you need to go. We promise you'll be glad you put yourself in our capable hands." She appreciated Phoenix's words of encouragement. He'd stopped the wave of uncertainty that had snuck up on her. Her breasts were throbbing, but she knew the pain would soon cross the line into pleasure if she would just surrender to it. "Spread your legs, sweetie. Master Landon has more jewelry for you."

In the back of her mind, Kodi was relieved that the only man touching her sexually was the one who wasn't married. She appreciated the fact her Masters hadn't put her in a difficult position with their wives. She didn't want embarrassment or jealousy to come between the women she now considered her friends. Kodi's knees folded out from under her when Master Landon's mouth covered the top of her sex. He sucked her clit between his teeth and bit down gently, making her gasp as her entire body began shaking. She was grateful for Kip and Phoenix's support, because she'd been unprepared for her powerful response to Landon's ministrations.

As quickly as it had come, the heat was gone, and she felt a small ring slide over her clit. *Oh, holy hand bells and sea shells. They're going to play me like a song.* Her Masters had only used the ring a couple of times, but she remembered vividly how it held her most sensitive bundle of nerves captive and exposed. Even the smallest brush of air would feel like the gentle lick of a lover's tongue. Walking would be torture, and she'd be teetering on the edge of orgasm by the time she'd taken a dozen steps.

Kodi's barely registered the cool metal chain sliding over her heated skin. She was too lost in the sensations battering her to focus enough to sort out what it meant. Warm lips covered hers, and she tasted herself. Forcing her eyes open, she found Landon looking at her with a wild fire burning in his eyes. "You are so fucking perfect. I hope like hell my friends know how lucky they are." His words warmed her heart, and despite the fact her body was ready to vibrate out her skin, she managed a small smile.

"We have one more gift to give you, Kodi. Turn around and bend over." She sucked in a breath when she saw the jeweled butt plug he held in his hand. She frantically looked around her and wanted to cry with relief when she saw the small circle surrounding her. Tally, Tobi West, Gracie McDonald, and all five of the Morgan wives stood shoulder to shoulder—with their men behind them. They'd formed a barrier of friendship between her and a roomful of people who were little more than acquaintances. Each one of the women standing beside her had lent their support in one way or another during those first days after her brother's accident. They'd held her while she cried and cheered with her at each small step he'd made on the long road to recovery.

She might well have burst into tears of gratitude if she hadn't heard Tally whisper, "You got this, sister."

Kodi nodded, more thankful than she could say for their love and support. Turning, she bent at the waist and arched her back. She'd seen the position Doms referred to as *present* enough times to know what was expected. Phoenix and Kip held her as Landon slid the tip of the plug through the wet folds of her sex. It wasn't a large plug, and she was relieved when it slid easily into place. Straightening, she swayed as blood drained from her head. Tightening the tight ring of muscles surrounding her ass set off a butterfly vibration that made her gasp.

"The plug will vibrate when you clench the muscles around your pretty rosette, little one."

What? Oh, my merciful God. She was going to come before she ever got to her men. She might have forgotten about the damned plug if he hadn't mentioned its special attributes. There wasn't any chance she'd forget now. *Dang it!*

"You are such a delight, Kodi. Your Masters don't need their gifts to know what you're thinking if they'll just pay attention."

"Isn't that the truth? Every thought plays out beautifully over her sweet face. It's easy to see why the men in her life are so protective." Kyle West's words made her smile, because she knew he was speaking about her brother without mentioning his name. She appreciated the subtle reference since it seemed insanely inappropriate talk about her brother when she was naked, clamped, and plugged in the middle of a kink club.

The absurdity of her situation made a bubble of hysteria form in her throat. "Uh oh. I know that look. Better get a move on before she has any more time to think." Kent's voice pulled her attention to where he stood behind Tobi. "You're every Dom's dream, sweetness. Don't ever question what a precious gift you are. But I've seen that look on my sweet sub's face, the one that says I'm a heartbeat away from dissolving into a fit of tears or giggles because I've obviously lost my ever-lovin' mind."

She blinked back tears as she looked at Kent West, because he'd just thrown her a lifeline. How he'd know exactly how close she'd been to losing it, she wasn't sure. His words validated the emotional turmoil and, in turn, seemed to calm the storm.

"I swear he always does this...upstages me at every turn." When she let her gaze flick to Kyle, she sighed at the soft smile she curving his lips. For the first time, she saw a side of Kyle she suspected he shared with very few people. And the significance of that gift wasn't lost on her. Nodding her thanks, she took a steadying breath and returned her gaze to Landon.

He held a long piece of deep blue silk in his hands…a blindfold. The last test of trust before he took her to her Masters. Landon didn't say anything for several seconds, letting her thoughts catch up with her emotions. He must have finally seen whatever he'd been looking for, because he gave her a curt nod and slid the blindfold over her eyes. The blanket of darkness was a relief in many ways. She didn't need to worry about the looks on anyone's face or where she was being led. She only had to trust Landon to take her where she needed to go.

Every step was an exercise in control. Without the distraction of her sight, she became acutely aware of every pulse of need as her body responded to the clamps and plug. The room fell silent as she was paraded through the group she could feel parting to let Master Landon lead her through. Even without being able to see, Kodi knew they were taking a serpentine path to the main room's largest stage. Her skin was damp with sweat as she battled to keep from succumbing to the barrage of stimulation.

The chains dangling from the nipple clamps held small gems, giving them enough weight to tug gently on her flaming flesh with each step she took. She knew how they'd look, engorged with blood and swollen with need. The plug in her ass vibrated with her footfalls and anytime she thought about the damned thing. All it took to activate the vibration was a gentle tightening of her sphincter muscles, and the tighter she clenched, the more distracting the vibration became. And as disruptive as the small plug was to her clear thinking, it was the clamp around her clit that was making her shake with need.

Landon stopped her, and she felt him lean close. "I'll always treasure tonight, little one. You hold a special place in my heart, and I'm so glad I was chosen to participate in tonight's special ceremony."

Before she could respond, Kodi felt him step away. The loss left her cold, and she knew anyone watching would have seen the shiver move over her. But chill was fleeting because she was quickly surrounded by the warmth and masculine scents of her Masters. The relief she felt was almost overwhelming, and she wanted to wrap herself around them and never let go.

"Ayasha, you have made us so very proud. Your submission was beautiful to watch." Nate's words weren't spoken loud enough for the entire room to hear, but he hadn't tried to hide them, either.

"Baby, some clubs require submissives to be whipped before these ceremonies, as proof of their willingness to submit to their Masters. We didn't want anything that would cause you pain, because that's not what holds hearts together. Tonight has been about showing you how strong you are and how many people love and support you." Kodi hadn't realized they were walking up the steps leading to the stage until she felt something velvety soft beneath her bare feet. She only had to wonder briefly about what she was walking on before the sweet scent of roses filled her nostrils.

The blindfold slid smoothly away, and Kodi opened her eyes slowly, anticipating the harsh glare of the stage lights. But she needn't have worried, because the entire room was dark. The only light emanated from the circle of candles surrounding the stage. Rose petals covered the entire surface, and her heart almost burst from her chest when she thought about everything they'd done for her. "Kneel, Ayasha." Lowering herself gracefully before spreading her knees apart, Kodi enjoyed the way her skin slid smoothly over the velvety carpet.

Her gaze returned to the men standing in front of her. Her breath caught in her throat when she saw the long, slender jewelry box Taz held in his hand. "Baby, will you wear our collar? Submit to us in all ways related to your well-being, safety, and pleasure? We'll never ask for more than you can give, but I never want you to doubt we'll push your boundaries every single day."

The crashing wave of emotion kept her response from being more than a whispered, "Yes, Master." The diamond and sapphire collar was so beautiful she couldn't take her eyes from it. When she heard the soft snick of the lock, her heart skipped a beat. But watching the two men she loved slip matching chains over their heads and tuck the keys against their own hearts brought tears to her eyes.

Blinking back the blur of her tears, she was surprised when she was lifted quickly to her feet and their mouths descend upon her breasts. The clamps were released slowly, minimizing the pain and maximizing the pleasure. Within seconds, her entire body was screaming toward release, but just as she approached a point of no return, they stepped back. Panting, she swayed on her feet. Nate knelt in front of her. As Taz took his position behind her, a soft towel in his hands brushed against the backs of her thighs before she felt the small plug being pulled from her ass.

There was no time for embarrassment before Nate's tongue flicked in quick strokes over her sensitive clit. The primal scream felt like it had been ripped from her throat, and she heard Taz's command to come a micro-second before the world around her erupted in a kaleidoscope of brilliant swirling colors. Taz held her up while Nate's relentless assault continued until the last tremors eased, leaving her weak and quaking in his hold.

When Nate stood in front of her, her worries melted under the molten look in his eyes. The months of living in her car too afraid to sleep soundly, days of desperate horror while Koi was in the hospital, and the endless minutes worrying the ass hat who'd hurt him would return were erased. While she'd been relieved the man had been detained, she wouldn't be able to fully relax until he was permanently behind bars. But the biggest heartbreak had been her certainly Nate and Taz were going to cut her loose. Nate's gentle fingers brushed over her cheek, pulling her back to the moment. "Never, Ayasha. We're never letting you go."

He dropped to one knee, pulling a small velvet box from his pocket. "Kodi, we've waited for you for so long I can still scarcely believe we've finally found you. Every time I look at you, I find something new to love...another small glimpse of you I'd never seen before. I can't imagine not having you in our lives. We'd be honored if you would be our wife." He must have seen the question in her eyes, because he smiled. "As the oldest, I'll be the one the world sees as your husband. But don't doubt for a minute that Taz will be my equal in every way."

Kodi barely remembered saying yes before the entire room erupted in applause, whistles, and shouts of congratulations. Nate slid the most beautiful ring she'd ever seen on her finger, and Taz helped her into a rich blue silk robe. Even though friends and club members surrounded her, all she wanted to do was go back upstairs and make love to her men.

Looking around them, Kodi was overcome with a sense of wonder. She didn't think the night could get any better...until Tobi stepped in front of her carrying the largest bouquet of flowers she'd ever seen. Roses and tulips were mixed with wildflowers, and it was all tied together with an enormous bow. "These are from your brother. He wanted you to know he was thinking about you. And he wanted me to make sure you how very proud he is of you."

Once again, she was wrong.

The night had just gone from amazing to perfect.

The End

Books by Avery Gale

The ShadowDance Club
Katarina's Return – Book One
Jenna's Submission – Book Two
Rissa's Recovery – Book Three
Trace & Tori – Book Four
Reborn as Bree – Book Five
Red Clouds Dancing – Book Six
Perfect Picture – Book Seven

Club Isola
Capturing Callie – Book One
Healing Holly – Book Two
Claiming Abby – Book Three

Masters of the Prairie Winds Club
Out of the Storm
Saving Grace
Jen's Journey
Bound Treasure
Punishing for Pleasure
Accidental Trifecta
Missionary Position

The Wolf Pack Series
Mated – Book One
Fated Magic – Book Two
Tempted by Darkness – Book Three

The Knights of the Boardroom
Book One
Book Two
Book Three

The Morgan Brothers of Montana
Coral Hearts – Book One
Dancing with Deception – Book Two
Caged Songbird – Book Three
Game On – Book Four
Well Bred – Book Five

Mountain Mastery
Well Written

I would love to hear from you!

Website:
www.averygalebooks.com/index.html

Facebook:
facebook.com/avery.gale.3

Twitter:
@avery_gale